NOBODY'S VICTIMS

Leslie Fish

apocalypsewriters.com

Nobody's Victims
Fish, Leslie

Published by The Writers of the Apocalypse
117 N Carbon Street, PMB 208
Marion, IL 62959

Find our books online at: http://woksprint.com

ISBN Print: 978-1-944322-35-9
Digital: 978-1-944322-36-6

Cover image: dollartreephoto.com
Cover assembly: K. J. Joyner

Nobody's Victims

Contents

The Ninth Tenant

"The rent's very cheap," said Mr. Dubcek, turning the key slowly with stiff arthritic fingers. "Such a bargain you won't find every day."

The lock worked smoothly, as always. He pushed the Number Four door open with a subtly dramatic flourish, long practiced.

As expected, the prospective tenant gasped in astonishment at the revealed view. She took several automatic steps into the enormous front room, gaping shamelessly at the high ceilings, the tall windows with their cut-glass top panels, the hardwood floors, the dark wood paneling, the lustrous space, the size. Yes, entranced. Definitely hooked.

"It's… incredible," she almost whispered. "Only $450 a month?!"

Dubcek smiled inwardly, waiting for the

next question. He had it down to a science by now: the rent announcement, the inevitable variations on a theme of 'why so cheap?', his unconvincing evasions, the insistent and growing curiosity, the final revelation, the widening eyes and the ill-hidden fearful excitement. The mystery always drew them, flame for the moths.

To her credit, Ms. Hart held her curiosity longer than most. She paced from room to room with that steady athletic walk of hers, looking, admiring, courteously silent while her mind calculated furiously and still came up with answers that didn't compute. How long before she asked?

The sixth tenant since the murder, stolid Mr. Holloway of the painfully-respectable bank, hadn't thought to ask until he'd been there a full month. He'd taken the longest to crack, too—a year and a half—but the finish had been truly spectacular. One week after his wife had fled back uptown Mr. Holloway had filled the bathtub, placed his neatly folded bathrobe on the stool beside it, settled himself carefully in the water—and slashed both wrists clean to the bone.

Precisely how he'd managed the second wrist had provided an intriguing secondary mystery to the other tenants of the building, until the coroner's report publicly concluded

that Holloway had held the knife in his teeth–
and it had been slow, sloppy work.

It had taken eight days for the deceased's worried family and associates to call the police, and by then the scene in the bathroom was too grotesque for even the seasoned police sergeant to describe in much detail. The apartment had stood empty for the rest of the summer, but the spectacle had sated the other residents more than enough for the extensive time involved. It was a truly great Haunting.

Perhaps Ms. Hart would do even better.

Dubcek smiled openly, studying her as she inspected the apartment. One of these Liberated businesswomen, no doubt: all efficiency and no-nonsense on the surface, pent-up imagination and wells of amenable hysteria well hidden below. It would be interesting to see how she reacted; the apartment hadn't dealt with any of that breed before–although the fourth tenant, Ms. Koker, had come close.

Then again, perhaps that wasn't quite true. Ms. Koker had been one of those Artistic types, recently divorced, trying to Find Herself through painting, basically nervous and high-strung. Her paintings had become truly amazing in her five-month term of tenure, right up to the day she ran screaming out the front door in the middle of the sunny afternoon. Her refusal to go back inside for any reason had given the neighbors a fine charitable excuse to carry out all her belongings for her—and to judge the paintings first-hand for themselves. One of the more evocative had quietly disappeared in the confusion, to end up tastefully framed on Miss Pierce's parlor wall.

That had been a satisfactory Haunting for all concerned. Ms. Koker had escaped alive, and with a story that she could no doubt dine out on for the rest of her life. Her account of the Haunting, related at great and hysterical length over Mrs. Donatello's kitchen table and sympathetic cups of tea down in #1-B, had provided entertainment for the neighbors far longer than Koker's stay in #4. It had also provided Mr. Glimke—alias Eric Prince, apartment #2-A—with material for a supernatural thriller that had sold nicely in paperback. He'd even gotten a nibble from a TV-movie producer, though that hadn't panned out and Glimke was still grumbling about it.

Of course, to give Glimke his due, he was the one who had insisted—even rallied the other tenants into a committee to petition the landlord—that #4 must absolutely not be rented, ever again, to any family with children. Everybody in the building had followed his lead on that one. The sad case of the little Wallinsky boy, who hanged himself in the coat-closet after his family had lived in #4 for barely six months, had been a little too much for everyone–even the cynical old Gallondri brothers in #2-B.

The Wallinskys–how could such thick-skinned parents have bred such a fragile, sensitive child, anyway?–had been the first tenants after the big Bradley murder. Eight subsequent Hauntings could only make the horror more intense, whatever form it chose to take. One could feel it lurking in the walls, even now. Dubcek glanced back automatically, making certain the front door was wide open, as he followed the Hart woman through the apartment. He'd never risk coming in here alone.

Ah, she was going to the front windows. Would she notice the scar on the sill where old Mr. Johnson had caught his foot during his panicked dive into the yard below?

"Beautiful windows," Ms. Hart commented, looking fondly out the nearest of them, apparently not noticing the scar. "And so many!"

"The apartment does cover the entire top floor," Dubcek reminded her. "Very private. Very quiet."

"Lovely big kitchen, too."

Ah, but she only glanced that way, seeing nothing unusual about the stove. Well, there was nothing really to see at the moment; the oven door was closed, with no ghostly body sprawled before it. No doubt that would come later.

Ms. Hart proceeded down the corridor, pausing to examine the bathroom. Dubcek caught himself holding his breath as she studied the ill-fated bathtub, but she gave no sign of seeing anything odd. He grimaced, remembering the trouble he'd had cleaning that thing after the Haunting of Holloway; he'd had to flush the drain repeatedly with muriatic acid. For $450 a month on a jinxed apartment, the landlord wasn't about to spend money on a new bathtub.

Oh there: Ms. Hart was going into the bed-room! Dubcek hurried quietly after her, won-dering what would happen when she saw The Stain. That was the undeniable giveaway. All these years and coats of paint later, the Bradley Bloodstain was still there on the wall, ominous and ineradicable, the watermark of the supernatural.

The only problem with The Stain was that it was low down in the corner, by the baseboard, where Suzanne Bradley had fallen and blindly clawed at the wall in the last seconds of her life. Even with no furniture in the way, a quick glance might miss it. Maybe Ms. Hart wouldn't see The Stain.

But no: she was staring directly at it,

bronze eyebrows pulled together. Any second now...

"Mr. Dubcek," she asked, "Did anybody ever die in this room?"

Oh, perfect!

"What? Oh no, no..." he fumbled artfully. "Nobody was ever killed in here. I don't know how these rumors get started. This is a fine place, really. Very nice, Ma'am. Very nice place."

Ms. Hart raised an eyebrow at him, gaining a brief but startling resemblance to *Star Trek's* Mr. Spock. "Is that why the rent's so low?" she asked sweetly.

"No, no, certainly not." Dubcek looked away, carefully fidgeting with his keys. "It's just... Hmmm, this is, uhm, a very quiet old neighborhood. Mostly old folks here, you know. Old buildings. Dull. No stores nearby, no busses, not very convenient. No young folks, no big parties, no entertainments or anything like that. Boring place, that's what it is. I guess that's why. Wouldn't know, myself. Landlord sets the rent. He lives out of town, but you might phone and ask him." He guessed that she wouldn't.

Even if she did phone and ask, Better Neighborhoods Realty Inc. was very close-mouthed on the subject of apartment #4. No, she'd have to get the details from the other tenants, and he knew how they'd answer. Priming the pump, old Miss Pierce had once called it.

Trust Miss Pierce to do it right, too. She'd had plenty of practice, reading mysteries and thrillers for years. Of course she had auto-graphed copies of all Mr. Glimke's books. Those two were such tight cronies that Dubcek sometimes wondered why they didn't just move in together and save on the rent. At other times he suspected that after sixty years of ruthless propriety, Miss Pierce got more pleasure from safeguarding her long-withered maidenhood than she could have obtained now by losing it. Her other passion, naturally, was apartment #4. Dubcek guessed that at the moment she was standing on her dining room table, one ear plastered to a water tumbler pressed against the ceiling, listening breath-lessly for the slightest sound from upstairs. Well, she'd get the details soon enough.

"Mhm," Ms. Hart was purring, chin lifted decisively. She turned around, actually smiling. "Never mind that; I'll take it. An apartment like this for a rent like that– I don't care if it's housed a dozen murderers and a whole cult of Satanists. How much down?"

Dubcek gave her his well-practiced star-tled/guilty look. They always said something along this line. "First month's rent, last month's rent, plus $200 damage deposit," he rattled off, chuckling inside.

Ms. Hart reached into her purse. "I'll give you $100 in cash right now, and I'll be back with the rest in an hour. Can you have the lease ready by then?"

"Sure." Dubcek wondered why she didn't have a checking account; all these young modern types did. The last tenant of #4 to pay in cash had been Robbie Jackson, the fifth, a moderate-volume drug dealer who was always prepared to decamp fast. True to form, he'd taken Mr. Johnson's way out–straight out the front window–one night during his third month of tenure, supposedly after sampling his own wares. Ms. Hart didn't look the type; there was probably some minor, irrelevant explanation. Maybe she just didn't trust banks. "Sure," he repeated. "My receipt book's downstairs."

On the way down the long stairway, he saw Miss Pierce peeping out through her barely-opened door, watching them go. He tossed her a polite smile and a conspirator's wink, and saw her smile back in sweet, malicious delight.

At 6PM precisely, everyone except bedridden old Mr. Brown in #3-B was in the accustomed place at Miss Pierce's lace-covered dining room table. As usual, everyone except the

Gallondri brothers drank the mint tea, and everyone except Mrs. Brown took at least a token glass of sherry. Everyone, without exception, nibbled the excellent macaroons. Miss Pierce was a meticulous hostess, and provided only the best.

Nobody really paid attention to the Monopoly game on the table, or was expected to.

"She came back with the money," Dubcek recounted. "All of it in cash, no less, in just over an hour. Handed it right over, signed the lease, and said she'd move in tomorrow. She's quick, anyway."

"Efficient." Glimke made notes on his perennial spiral-bound pad. "One of these new businesswoman types, all right. But then, why didn't she have a checking account? Did she say what she did for a living?"

"Not to me. There: give me $200."

"You should have asked. Ah, advance three steps…"

"I tried. She said something about natural food and herbal supplies."

"There're plenty of those stores downtown," Mrs. Brown quavered, reaching a slow hand toward a token on Atlantic Avenue. "Maybe she works at one of them. I want to mortgage this hotel."

"Some kind of New Age artsy type, probably," sneered George Gallondri. "That kind doesn't trust banks. Even from the window, I could see her big silver earrings."

"Rich artsy-mystic type," Bruno Gallondri amended. "That fancy pantsuit of hers must've cost her plenty. Card here."

"So, practical and businesslike on the surface, but sensitive and mystical underneath, hmm?" Glimke made notes. "Secretive and other-worldly at heart. Yes, interesting."

"I wonder if she's a slovenly housekeeper," Miss Pierce smirked, glancing around her fussily well-kept parlor. "I wonder how long it will take her to notice The Stain spreading."

"I give her a week, maybe two," Mrs. Donatello laughed, her folds of fat shaking. Pass Go: give me $200. And I'll bet she hears the little Wallinsky boy's crying, first. That's how Koker got it."

"No, even a ghost can tell she's not the tender-hearted sort," Miss Pierce sniffed, counting her pile of play-money. "*I* say she'll hear the Mad Lover first, lurching around with his dripping butcher-knife, looking for Suzanne Bradley." She gave a delighted little shiver. The Deranged Boyfriend was her favorite among the ghosts. "After all," she added, inevitably, "He *was* the first!"

"Then maybe he'll be the first one she sees, too," said Bruno Gallondri, rattling the dice, "Swinging by his neck from the chandelier."

"No," pronounced Mrs. Brown, "The Bathtub Full of Blood–and Holloway floating in it."

"Surfacing," Glimke corrected, scribbling more notes. "First the hands, hanging loose from his cut wrists. Then his bloated face. Then the rest of him... But I don't think she'll stay and watch that long."

"Maybe she'll see old Mrs. Gomez, with her head still in the oven," Dubcek considered. "She was number three, wasn't she? Ah, Mrs. Holloway was the only tenant who saw that one; that's what made her give up and run."

"When do you think Ms. Hart will run?" Glimke started a new page. "Or do you think she'll... stay?"

"She'll stay," smirked George Gallondri. "You know these Liberated types: too stubborn for their own good."

"And too greedy to give up that nice, cheap rent," his brother added. "She'll stay until she drops."

Glimke frowned. He'd already started shaping a plot with a good Love Interest, and it properly had to end with the heroine/victim throwing her pride to the winds and herself– sobbing abandonedly, of course–into her True Love's arms. Still, he could always work it the other way: Proud Hart holds out and Dies Gruesomely For It. A modern morality play. "How do you think she'll do it?" he asked.

"Too many sleeping pills," shrugged Mrs. Brown, who wasn't terribly imaginative. "I want to buy the waterworks."

"You're over-mortgaged," Miss Pierce cautioned. "*I* think she'll cut her throat with a kitchen-knife."

"It's been done," Dubcek reminded her. "Mr. Olson, remember?"

"Yes, he was number seven." Mrs. Donatello grinned at the dice. "Say, nobody's seen *his* ghost yet. Maybe she will."

"I think those Jesus People saw him," said George Gallondri, scratching his chin. "They saw everybody."

There was a moment's uncomfortable silence. The last tenants–Reverend and Mrs. Falmon and their half-dozen hard-praying friends–had caused considerable argument among the regulars. Nobody wanted to speak ill of religion, of course, but then again the Falmons and their friends had been really awful people: unbearably smug and utterly sure they could "exorcise the spirit of evil" from apartment #4 with their noisy and nonstop praying. The ghosts had driven them out in two months flat, which ended the problem, but the Jesus People were still something of a sore topic.

"Uhm, well," Bruno amended, "They saw just about everybody, to hear them tell it, though they didn't give many details. The more they prayed, the more the ghosts came out. Couldn't eat, sleep or turn their backs without something nasty happening. Couldn't take baths, either. Heh!"

"Couldn't take it, period." Mrs. Donatello laughed again, quaking like a plateful of molded pink jell-o. "And the things they said as they left... My, my! For such proper, God-fearing folk, they sure knew a lot of nasty words!"

"Miz Hart doesn't seem the religious type," commented Mrs. Brown. "Hmph. Does anybody want to buy a railroad?"

"I wonder just what type she is," Glimke pondered, nibbling his pen. "I mean, back-ground: education, personal quirks, love life... That sort of thing."

"College graduate, majored in Archeology." Mrs. Donatello smiled sweetly as she dropped her well-timed bomb. "Couldn't get work in it, though. She tried teaching, but had to quit. Some sort of scandal, I think. She said the faculty didn't like the way she taught, uh, 'details of third-millennium BCE goddess worship', whatever that means. My bet is, she had an affair with one of her students. Hee-hee!"

"That wouldn't be much of a scandal *these* days," Miss Pierce sniffed. She hated to be upstaged in her own parlor. "But how would *you* know all that about her?"

"Oh, I made a point of being in the hallway when she came to sign the lease," Mrs. Donatello preened, "And we struck up a little conversation."

"Not so little, knowing you," Dubcek snickered. "What else did she say?"

"Well…" Mrs. Donatello paused briefly for dramatic effect. "I invited her in for some tea, and she accepted, and we talked about tea for a bit. She knows quite a lot about herbal remedies, and home pickling, and homemade perfumes and incenses, and that sort of thing. Oh yes, she also knows how to hand-weave, and sew, and knit, and make pottery and jewelry. She made those silver earrings herself, you know. Those big hoops with the little crystal stars inside, they're supposed to represent 'Inanna, Queen of Heaven', or some such thing. She made that pendant, too: that abstract thing that looks sort of like a long-tailed butterfly or a two-sided tomahawk. Solid silver, all of it—except for the inlaid stones of course. And—"

"Another Artistic Type," Glimke pronounced, scribbling notes.

"But what did she *say*?" Miss Pierce insisted.

"Why, my dear…" Mrs. Donatello smiled wickedly. "She asked me right out: 'Who was murdered in that apartment?'"

There was shocked silence for all of five seconds, while Mrs. Donatello triumphantly plunked down a house on Park Place.

"And you *told* her?!" Mrs. Brown shrilled.

"Well, yes. Everything," Mrs. Donatello confessed.

"Everything?!" Glimke threw down his pen. "Bad art! You should have told her only about the Bradley Murder, and let her learn the rest by degrees!"

"Damn right," growled Bruno Gallondri. "She would've had to come around to each of us, the way it's always been."

"We'd have told her about the other tenants, one at a time," George Gallondri added.

"Each in turn," snapped Miss Pierce. "Plenty of stories for all of us."

"We've practically got it down by heart," Dubcek finished. "But you– You went and told it all at once!"

"Why, I couldn't help it!" Mrs. Donatello almost wailed, doing her best to cower in her chair, though there wasn't much room for that. "She kept asking and asking, wanting more details. I swear, I actually had trouble getting rid of her! You never saw anyone so eager to find out all about apartment #4."

The other regulars looked at each other.

"Another Koker, maybe?" Dubcek ventured.

"Maybe another Falmon," George Gallondri gloomed.

"Perhaps a trifle different," Miss Pierce considered. "More likely one of these New Age mystics, downright eager to see a real, live ghost."

"If so, she'll get more than she bargained for." Mrs. Brown laughed nastily.

"They'll eat her alive," Bruno Gallondri agreed.

"Or seduce her into joining them." Glimke smiled, eyes narrowing. "After a suitable period of growing madness, of course. Yes, she might be an interesting novelty after all." He picked up his pen and began making more notes.

Ms. Hart moved in the next day—or rather, her furnishings did. Furniture, boxes, crates, suitcases and all were brought up to the top floor and left in the long hall, almost blocking the way to the door. Nothing was brought into the apartment itself. Miss Pierce and Mr. Glimke were the first to notice the stalled train of items stringing down to the landing, and took care to ask the impassive movers about the odd arrangement.

The moving-men only shrugged and reported that the customer had particularly asked them to do it this way. They had no further information, and weren't interested in speculating on the customer's peculiar request. They unloaded the last boxes, left them in the hallway, and drove off.

Glimke lost no time reporting this odd development to the other tenants, while Miss Pierce took the opportunity to inspect the unguarded property. She was quivering with excitement by the time the other tenants filed up to her apartment to hear the latest news.

"I couldn't get into the trunks, of course," Miss Pierce reported as she handed out tea and macaroons, "But I did manage to look in some of the cardboard cartons, and my dears, they're all stuffed with books on the most *arcane* sort of things."

"Such as?" Dubcek mumbled around a mouthful of sherry.

"Herbalism, of course–I expected that–and anthropology and archeology too, but Classical studies? I swear, some of those books are written in Latin, and Greek, and the other languages I can't even guess. There's a whole set of hardcover books–it must be the complete version–of *The Golden Bough*. Enormous thing! And there's another, called *The White Goddess*, that looks terribly well-thumbed–"

"In... deed?" Glimke sat up a bit straighter, intrigued. He'd heard of those titles, somewhere, a long time ago.

"–And there was another box packed *full* of all sorts of metal… things: brass and copper, and I think I saw some silver–or at least silver-plate. All candlesticks, little bowls, cups, bells, little statuettes and things–simply a curio-collector's delight. The furniture is terribly elegant, very simple, classical, almost severe design. She has excellent taste in furnishings, that's for certain."

"So she's got money and taste." Dubcek shrugged. "But do you have any idea why she left all that valuable stuff lying out in the hallway?"

"I haven't a clue… unless perhaps she wants to paint the place first."

"Painting takes too long," George Gallondri opined. "She wouldn't leave her stuff lying out for that much time."

"Maybe she just wants to scrub the place down first," Mrs. Brown speculated. "That wouldn't take too long."

"Ooh, maybe she's seen The Stain growing!" Mrs. Donatello enthused, "Or noticed the smell in the bathroom, showing up already."

"Or she's just naturally fussy-clean," Bruno Gallondri suggested. "I'd like to know, though, just how she expects to drag all that furniture in by herself."

"Hope she doesn't expect me to help," Dubcek sniffed.

"I can't get a handle on this," Glimke muttered, chewing the end of his pen. "She's some sort of businesswoman, has money but no checking account… as if she wanted to avoid official notice. Mystic, scholarly, ex-teacher, downright eager to see the ghosts… but somehow she doesn't look like the high-strung, wafty, nervous type."

"Maybe she wants to study the ghosts," Mrs. Brown shrugged, reaching for another macaroon. "Maybe she's the dedicated scholar type."

"That wouldn't sell." Glimke frowned at his notes. "You don't want a super-competent type for a heroine, not in a thriller."

"We'll see how competent she is when the ghosts come to get her," snickered Bruno Gallondri, refilling his sherry glass. "They'll knock the smarts out of her."

"But how?" Glimke puzzled, scribbling another note. "How will they express…? Hmmm, just what is a ghost, anyway?"

"A Spirit of the Departed, of course," sniffed Miss Pierce, "Bound to earth by some great passion of love, duty or… terror."

"But what powers them? Where do they get the energy to show themselves, or make physical things happen?" Glimke tapped his pen against his teeth. "'Upon what meat doth this, our Caesar, feed'?"

Just then they heard the front door open-ing. They all froze, listening.

Sure enough, the footsteps were character-istically light and quick, and came steadily up the stairs, flight after flight.

"It's her," Dubcek whispered. "Wait, wait..."

They crouched immobile about the dining room table, silent as conspirators, listening. The light, firm footsteps passed the door and thudded up the hallway to the last flight of stairs.

Glimke dared to get up from the table and tiptoe out to the door to watch Ms. Hart's progress. He was back in a moment to report. "She was carrying a big suitcase, and she looked... hmm, I'd say purposeful–but smiling. Definitely smiling. An odd sort of smile..." He frowned, puzzled. "Of course, I only got a quick glimpse of her face, made sure she didn't see me. It could have meant nothing."

"We can leave the door open now," said Mrs. Brown.

The little company duly opened the door and peered out. There was nothing to be seen now, but they could all hear the thump of the suitcase hitting the floor, then the rattle of keys, the #4 apartment door opening, foot-steps clacking across the hardwood floor and a second thump of the suitcase.

"She's left the door open," Mrs. Donatello noted.

Then the footsteps returned, coming back down the stairs. The tenants hastily retreated back into Miss Pierce's apartment, set their ears to the door and their eyes to the crack between the edge and the jamb, jostling silently for position. The footsteps paused, then retreated slowly back up the stairs, accompanied by heavy scrapes and thumps.

Dubcek dared to open the door another six inches and peer out. "Hey," he whispered, almost awed, "She–she's wrestling that heavy butcher-block table up the stairs–all by herself! She must be… uh, remarkably strong."

"An amateur athlete?" Glimke marveled, reaching for his note-pad. "A would-be Olympic woman weight-lifter? Now *there's* a new angle."

"Why did she pick that one?" Mrs. Donatello wondered, wincing at the occasional thwacks of the table against the banisters and walls. "Out of all her furniture…"

They all heard the table being dragged into the center of the vast living room upstairs– and then nothing. They waited, increasingly impatient, as the minutes dragged past.

"We could try going upstairs," Bruno Gallondri suggested. "Her door hasn't shut, or we'd have heard."

"If she sees us," George added, "We can always say we heard the noise and were coming to help move her stuff in."

"Shhh," Miss Pierce whispered, eyes fixed on the ceiling. "I could swear I heard water… Oh, there. It's stopped."

Silence again. Dubcek began easing his way out the door to the hall, the Gallondri brothers close behind.

"Shh!" said Miss Pierce again, stretching her wattled neck to listen to the ceiling. "There's a soft… scraping sort of noise. It's going… all around the floor up there. What on earth is she doing?"

"Drawing a circle, in chalk," Glimke guessed. "New Age types do that to make a Meditation Space, or whatever."

Faintly, from upstairs, came the sweet chiming of a small bell.

The men by the door looked at each other. Miss Pierce grabbed a water-glass, clambered up on the table and shamelessly listened to the floor above. They all heard what happened next.

"*Incipiamus*!" rang the voice on the top floor, a much stronger voice than any of them had yet heard from Ms. Hart. "*Adeste fideles. Descedant omnes profani. Hic locus sanctus est!*"

"That's not a New Age thing," Glimke

gulped.

The words were followed by the sharp slamming of something hard and massive, striking the floor three times. Then came more chanting.

"What the hell is going on up there?" Dubcek asked at large, inching his way out toward the stairs.

"That was Latin," Bruno Gallondri remembered. "Is she trying to exorcise the place? Catholic ritual—"

"She can't," George reminded him. "Only a priest can do that."

"Wrong Latin," Glimke murmured, recalling his long-past school teaching days. The more he listened, the more he was certain; that wasn't the soft, sibilant tongue of the old church but the clanging, hard-syllabled, military-style Latin of Golden Age Rome. The implications were disturbing. "I... don't think she's a Catholic, George."

"She said she was a—a 'classical scholar'." Mrs. Donatello turned to Miss Pierce. "How far does that go? What does it get into?"

"I don't *know*," Miss Pierce quavered. "Just what was that scandal about, the one that cost her the teaching job?"

"Something about 'unbecoming conduct'..."

Then a faint breeze brought the smell drifting down the stairwell. The advance party, one at a time, paused to sniff and ponder.

"Incense!" The Gallondris recognized it together. "Not the kind they use in church… It's like flowers. … Or trees. … Or maybe…"

There was another chant, in yet another language, very long and singsong. Miss Pierce, drawing on her long-vanished schooldays, finally identified it. "Greek! Classical, ancient Attic Greek. She seems to be reciting names…"

"Ancient Greek gods?" Glimke asked. He was beginning to form an idea about Ms. Hart's odd little ceremony.

"No… goddesses." A strange look spread over Miss Pierce's face. "Some of them I've heard of, some I haven't. Artemis, Hera, Hecate I recognize–but who's Djana, or Eurynome?"

"I don't like this…" muttered Bruno Gallondri, edging toward the relative safety of the wall.

"What is she, a witch or something?" Mrs. Brown whispered.

Nobody answered.

Upstairs, footsteps padded away from the living room. They led into the dining room, followed by a burst of chanting and then the chiming of the bell.

"Not Greek anymore," said Miss Pierce. "I don't know what it is, but it sounds somewhat like Greek and somewhat like Hebrew. Very strange…"

"Glimke, you're the one who does history

research." Dubcek hurried back into the apartment to clutch urgently at the writer's arm. "Each language she's used so far has been older than the last. What's older than ancient Greek?"

"In the western world? I'm not sure… Mycenae, Egypt, Crete, Sumer, Catal Huyuk–they just discovered that one a few years ago, dates from at least 6000 BC. They had writing, but to the best of my knowledge nobody's cracked the language yet. There are inscriptions, but nobody knows how to read them." Glimke glanced nervously toward the ceiling. "How the hell could she learn the language when the archeologists haven't?"

"The other archeologists, you mean," whispered Mrs. Brown.

The footsteps upstairs thudded from room to room, pausing in each for the same chanting and chiming. The smell of incense grew thicker, overpowering.

"Getting damn hot," George Gallondri muttered, easing his way back from the door. His brother followed, tugging open his limp collar.

"More than hot," Mrs. Donatello panted. "Damn! Can't you feel it?"

The others paused, listening and sniffing in the semi-dark. Mrs. Brown noticed the change. "P-pressure," she gulped. "The air. Feels like a lead weight in here."

"Yes," said Glimke, eyes widening.

"What if...?" Dubcek let his question trail off.

The tenants looked at each other, dismay settling across their faces. Upstairs, Ms. Hart's footsteps came back into the living room and a new chant hammered through the thickening air: first in the unknown language, then in recognizable Greek, then Latin again. Everyone could hear the words: *"Te exorsciso."*

"Right, she's some kind of a witch," gulped George Gallondri. "A real one!"

"Can she do it?" Bruno turned to Glimke, almost pleading. "If she's into something older than the Church... Can she really exorcise apartment #4?"

"I don't know," whispered Glimke, wiping sweat off his forehead. The air felt like hot oil. "We know–nobody better–that ghosts are real. Maybe witchcraft is, too. Maybe they're all of a piece: ghosts, magic, psychic powers..."

"She can't do that!" Miss Pierce almost cried, skittering down from the table. "They're *our* ghosts! She can't take them away from us! Somebody, do something! We have to stop her! Somebody–"

The sound from upstairs interrupted the appeal. It was a heavy thumping, not foot-steps, more like an axe striking the floor. After that came shouted words that they could all understand.

"Come forth, into my circle, all you unclean spirits! Come forth, into my circle, all you ghosts, daemons, demigods, souls of the evil-minded! Come out from the walls, from the floors, from the ceilings. Come out from the storage spaces, from the hidden rooms, from the gaps in the walls, from all space between rooftree and foundation. Come forth from your hiding-places, mortal or immortal, and come into this circle. Come! Come now! As moves my will, so mote it be!"

The words echoed, echoed impossibly.

Sudden darkness squeezed down, dimming out the apartment and the hallway. The air closed in, hot and crushing. The room seemed to close up, like cloth in a rolling-press, forcing everyone out, forward, into the unseen hallway and toward the stairs. Miss Pierce screamed thinly, the sound stretching out to a wavering thread in the ringing distortion of space. Dubcek's voice could be heard groaning endlessly, like the settling of heavy timbers in the dark.

The tenants stumbled and crawled forward on the uncertain floor, feeling their way blindly, moving because they had no more choice in moving than does the juice burst from the grape in the winepress. Glimke felt the risers of the stairs under his hands and cried helplessly as he pawed his way upward through the dark. He knew where they were going.

Vision resumed ahead, at the end of the corridor: the bright rectangle of an open doorway. They stumbled through it, across polished hardwood boards, over the curved chalk line of a circle's edge. Beyond the chalk line the intolerable pressure stopped. The tenants tumbled and huddled together in the circle, rubbing their eyes and blinking at the sudden restoration of light. The sobs and whimpers cut off sharply as they saw, all at the same time, what had brought them here.

Beyond the circle stood the butcher's-block table set with candles, little bowls, a red-filled cup, a smoking incense-burner, a bell, a small bronze statuette of a woman with a flounced skirt and bare breasts and snakes coiled around her outstretched arms. No one could have mistaken the assemblage for anything but an altar.

Beyond the altar stood a very different Ms. Hart. She wore nothing but a flounced skirt, a crown of flowers, the strange butterfly pendant, and bronze snake-shaped bracelets that coiled up her arms. Her skin had been oiled, and gleamed in the candlelight like polished ivory. In her hands she held something that few of them had ever seen, even in a museum, but which somehow all of them could recognize. It was a two-bladed axe, the head made of dark chipped stone, the handle a single piece of age-darkened bone. The shape and spiral markings of the blades exactly matched those of the silver pendant.

"Not a butterfly," Glimke whispered inanely. "It's not a butterfly at all."

Ms. Hart stood looking down at them for a long moment, a slow and powerful smile spreading across her face. She held out the dull-glittering axe above their heads, and they could see that it was very, very old.

"The haunters!" she laughed. "The true haunters of apartment #4!"

The other tenants cowered on the floor, not daring to move or speak. Glimke managed to form a thought: ..."*upon what meat...*" *We fed them! We made it happen! All those Monopoly parties... gossiping, plotting... our own witches' Sabbath! ... But she understood, and did it better... and she's stronger...*

"Get up, you haunters," Hart commanded. "Go out and fetch in my belongings. As of now, this place is mine–and so are you."

As one, shuffling and snuffling, they got up to do their new mistress' bidding.

Script Change

Enter, pursued by a monster.

As usual. It's an old, old dream.

The Girl runs endlessly through the night-forest set, all lipsticked scream, hair flying fetchingly. High-heeled scamper in a curve-tight dress, painted eyes a-roll, cute tits a-bounce. Hopeless flight in moving mid-shot. Hopeless shrieks in stereo. Typical.

Standard Victim, grade A, no. 1,783,949, throwaway model.

Close enough behind lopes/lurches/shambles/slobbers The Monster, radiating his full portable supply of Menace. He's in fine form tonight. In fact, he's in several forms. Mask-change, shape-shift, he runs through all the Classics: Vampire, Wolfman, Frankenstein, Mummy, a Zombie or two, a couple versions each of Mr. Hyde and the Phantom of the

Opera. Next, the Nuke-Giants: oversized ants, grasshoppers, spiders mantids, squids, lobsters and lizards, a passing homage to the Colossal Man, and various ponderously-animated Japanese unpronounceables. Then the Sci-Fi flick crowd: the Thing, the Alien, the Fly, the Blob, the Plasma-Man, the Ape-Man, assorted robots and mutants and space-invaders from dozens of grade-Z late-night features. Finally he slides into the gore-sleaze roles: mad scientists, mad wax museum sculptors, half-mad devil-cult high priests, maybe-not-mad axe-murderers, somewhat-degenerate Chainsaw Massacre hack-artists, and several similar goons. He seems more at home in this league. Sign of the Times in a celluloid zodiac.

Girly runs fleet-foot, face black-and-white soot.

Threadbare nightmare. Worn film begins to tear.

Wear of endless repetition weakens the illusion, drains the shock-value of its thought-paralyzing impact. Scratchy, grainy, color leached out, soundtrack wobbling. Too many reprints, reruns, replays. It's been done to death.

So has The Girl, a million times over.

Repetition unto monotony. Horror turns predictable, then boring. You could get used to hanging if you could live long enough.

Listen, and I will tell you a Mystery: fear wears out.

Into the void sneaks an original thought. *Why the hell am I screaming like a fool? He can track me by the noise.*

The Girl shuts her mouth and settles down to some serious running.

The Monster, surprised and annoyed, bellows to shake the ground and runs through several of his scariest shapes. Leeches! Sea-monsters! Pus-creatures! Crawly crustaceans! Spiders and snakes!

None of them have the desired effect. The Girl doesn't even bother to look back.

Outraged, The Monster sprouts workable hop-toad legs and goes slobber-gibber after her in lurching leaps and bounds.

The Girl, scampering pickety-pickety on her teetery high-heeled shoesies, realizes that it's just about time for a heel to snap off, or catch on an opportune tree-root, or otherwise break her ankle.

Again, a thought. *Kick off the damn shoes! So what if I cut up my bare feet? Beats dying, doesn't it?*

She kicks off her shoes and runs on, gaining ground.

Distinctly peeved, The Monster mutters imprecations at the unseen director, drops his scare-displays and concentrates on speed. He wasn't expecting a hard workout, but damned if he'll give up.

Barefoot, striding strong, The Girl remembers—from forbidden days of pre-pubescent freedom—how to really run. Lean forward, breathe deep, knees up, stretch. Good, good…

But there's a catch. The sexy-tight skirt binds, shortening every step. Hobbling. Shackling.

Thinking, too, comes easier with practice. *Pull it up, or rip out a seam. Who cares how it looks? The point is survival.*

Without missing a step, she grabs the hem of the skirt and yanks it up, hard. Threads part with a satisfying rip. Seams tear open clean up to her waist. Cloth shackles in impotent rags. Her freed legs flash long, covering ground by the yard and more. Seditious surge of forbidden pride in the clean, fast strides.

The Monster tries cunning. He hoots, hollers, leers, whistles, sucky-kissies and makes loud-lewd comments at the sight of her flashing bare legs and hips. She ought to blush/clutch, divert to Modestly Covering Herself—and thereby slow down. It's always worked before.

The Girl only grits her teeth. By now she's thinking steadily. Practice makes perfect. *Let the creep look. Just don't let him catch. Eyes don't hurt you; hands do.*

Downright dismayed, The Monster tries bellowing specifics. Oboy, what he'll do when he catches her! Intricate-graphic, imaginative-obscene, mamma-jamma, woo-woo, slobber-slurp-slop. And angry promises to himself that he'll get her, he'll eventually get her and make her pay for the extra work she's costing him. It's in his contract, by God, and he's always gotten his payoff before.

He's long since forgotten to drape his shape in symbolic disguises. His real form, fatally, begins to show through.

The Girl, glancing back to judge distance, sees and begins to recognize. Truth almost bared. The Emperor Fear naked enough for a good guess.

Slavemaker, I know you!

Of course. The real leering-lurking shape in the real-world shadows. Terrorist-enforcer, keeping you-know-who obedient to the will of self-styled protectors; *do what I say, Girl, or I'll throw you to Him.* The stick to the co-conspirator's carrot; monstrous bargain behind the scenes. The Girl understands, at long last. Her grinding teeth strike a cold spark of bone-deep ex-victim's fury.

The Monster comes lurch/jump/reel, claws a-grope, too obvious, too clear in his intentions. He pulled it off better as a vague, shapeless, unnameable menace.

Too sharp, now. Too much knowing light. At

a reflective focal point, something heats enough to catch fire. The film shrivels to a hard knot of fury, resentment, revenge-lust. Sunlight kills vampires.

You too can die!

The Girl bares her teeth in a silent snarl. The Worm, turning at last…

Into what?

She bends low, hands to the ground, reaching, feeling, fumbling, searching. There! Perfect. A big heavy rock, just the right size for throwing.

Point, pivot, turn and aim. Smooth as a dancer's motion. Yes, dancing is legitimate: graceful decoration, hiding the real muscle/wind/coordination training. And somewhere, sometime, she learned how to throw. Whip up in a long, smooth arc. Let go at the top of the circle. Arm follow through. End with the hand pointing straight at the target. Done. Fine art. Very pretty. Good Girl.

The stone sails straight and true, hurtling across the dark open air. In the high-contrast shadow and moonlight, The Monster doesn't see it in time to duck. Besides, he wasn't expecting any such thing. He's not very imaginative on some points.

The rock hits him smack between the eyes.

Crunch. Sweet, solid, satisfactory sound of effective impact. On target. True.

The Monster, his unsuspecting skull neatly cracked, stops dead. His eyes roll upward in surprise. Almost gently, he falls over backward. Thud. Arms and feet rebound clumsily. No grace. Tsk.

The Girl stalks forward in the stark moonlight, torn skirt swinging in solemn cadence with her long-striding legs. She pauses to look down on her one-time pursuer, arms crossed, face calm, eyes cool and thoughtful. Sphinx. Were-lioness. She's the predator now.

I too can change my shape.

And she means to be certain that her former pursuer won't get up to pursue again.

Calmly she reaches down, feels about, and comes up with another rock. She kneels smoothly beside the downed Monster, takes the rock in both hands and coolly pounds his skull to moon-shadow-black jelly.

"Cut! Cut!" screams the unseen director, voice verging on hysteria. "This wasn't in the script!"

Fade to black.

By the dawn's early light the alarm clock goes off. It squalls and dances across the nightstand-top until a sleepy, skinny, adolescent hand falls on it and thumbs it to resentful silence. An audible yawn in a young female voice. Pillows creak. Sheets whisper. The Girl rolls over, slowly blinking unconsciousness out of her eyes, and remembers that she dreamed again, something important.

She sits up, remembering; it takes a long time to screen completely. Fourteen nights of retakes, re-edits, and last night the end was different–and it worked. She crouches there for several minutes, pondering the conclusion.

A voice from below, female-maternal, bays up the echoing stairwell. Summons for break-fast, with silent asides: don't be late for school, don't throw Mama's desperate schedule out of whack, don't make Papa angry. Cardinal sin.

"Coming." The Girl slides out of the warm nest of blankets, still thoughtful. She glances at the closet and decides to finally complain to the costuming department. For once she'll wear what she likes. Cotton socks and under-wear, soft-worn blue jeans, a sleeveless pullover that's easy to move in, old leather loafers that fit like loyal friends. Good for running in, at least. Also within the school dress codes, if not quite What We'd Prefer, Dear. She shrugs, brushes her short hair quickly, picks up her schoolbooks and goes on down the hall.

Just for the hell of it, she slides down the banisters.

In the breakfast alcove Mama sees her coming, and throws a fearful-tearful look like a cue. First scene's opening directions: don't make noise, don't make work for me, don't upstage me. Just take your chair and sit down.

At the table, behind his wall of newspaper, the immaculately dressed Director sits. He rumbles and mutters like a not-safely-extinct volcano. The Mountain of God. Mount Sinai, with sinus trouble.

The Girl understands, but she ignores Mama's cues. Normally she'd be inclined to mercy, but not today. She's nursing a complaint about her contract, but the old Prima Donna is satisfied with her own. No solidarity, no support there. So no favors, either. Sorry, scab.

Cool-eyed, The Girl marches to the table, slides easily into her chair, studies the fashionable breakfast-pap, shrugs, pours milk on it, eats.

Papa raises his head to review the newly arrived troops. Instant displeasure. Out of uniform! Insubordination! This requires Instant Discipline!

He explodes in his usual Masterly fashion. What do you mean coming to breakfast like that? You can't go to school dressed like that! It's a disgrace! Can't get away with it! You kids today! No sense of Family Values! No daughter of mine, etc.

Straight clichés. Quoting bad script. He must be preoccupied with More Important Things. Usually is.

It's within the dress codes, and comfortable, The Girl replies calmly, giving the logical and reasonable answer, knowing all too well that logic and reason are not the point, and never were. She's only testing, only making absolutely sure of something she already knows.

The Director, actually challenged by a mere ingénue, and underage, and his own get/property at that, erupts to the second degree of Outraged Authority tantrum. Shut your mouth! Can't talk back to me! Sassy! Kids today have no respect! Ought to be whipped! You do what I tell you, Girl! Etc.

The Girl replies with the ultimate insult; she ignores him. Goes on eating.

The Director does his best to turn his face red, windmill his arms, swell up like a bullfrog. Going through all his masks of power and terror and Divine Right of Kings.

The old Prima Donna whimpers around the periphery of the stage, ignored. Ineffective as the habitual screams of the Pursued Victim. She made her choice long ago.

The Girl made her choice last night.

The Director bellows on, howling and flailing his fat would-be threatening hands, wagging his usual badges of authority, angry of course but certain of his ultimate victory. It's part of his contract.

The Girl, unruffled, lifts her glass of milk and sips it. Her eyes narrow, calculating, watching.

He hasn't even noticed that she no longer cringes.

She idly hefts the loaded glass in her hand, considers its weight, and measures the throwing-distance to his skull.

Crone's Gambit

The single road up the mountain climbed back and forth in long meandering loops, giving the watchers at the pass more than enough time to see the army coming. Even if Ashrayan's vision hadn't warned her two nights before, the keen eyes of the Guard Maidens would have alerted the women with time to spare. No one entered High Valley unseen; the hardiest mountaineers couldn't scale the surrounding scarps, nor the stealthiest spies sneak through the solitary well-guarded pass. Few even tried anymore.

This army—easily a hundred mounted men and a hundred more on foot, all of them heavily armored—made no attempt at secrecy. Like a glittering centipede it crawled up the mountain road, setting a leisurely pace, on a clear day in full sunlight. The approach was meant to be seen, to impress if not to terror-ize.

The chief observer was not even impressed.

Was it all of thirty-two years ago that Bar-on Mog tried this same trick with three hun-dred men? Ashrayan thought, watching the ponderous display. *I remember how terrified I was, watching from cover in the woods. Then I noticed the sheer beauty of the new pennants snapping in the wind, the sun glittering from the polished armor–and suddenly I wondered why anyone would polish armor soon to be bloodstained. That was when I knew it for a show, a display like a rooster's. Men always pose and bluster when they don't really want to fight. Goddess, I grow old and cynical.*

A polite cough from behind her and an equally polite tug at her sleeve made Ashrayan turn. Myrweal, the Guard Commander, was shuffling irritably from foot to foot. Lurias, the young junior priestess, was rubbing her interlaced fingers together. Both so impatient, so young.

"Reverence, how soon?" Myrweal burst out. "Can you probe their commander yet? The Guard is in position; we could strike at any time."

So eager to blood your sword? Ashrayan

suppressed a smile. "Wait," was all she said. *Wolf-cub, learn a wider sense of tactics—and economy.* She gestured to Lurias.

The junior priestess took the offered hand, sat neatly beside Ashrayan on the bench, and obediently set her mind to the first level of Reach. Ashrayan felt her presence almost instantly and acknowledged it, adding a touch of approval for Lurias' skill. Lips moving silently in the habitual chant, Ashrayan pulled their linked minds to the second level and stretched them outward into the air.

Down and down in the brightness their linked minds probed. Lurias flinched a trifle at the first contact with the leading point-rider, her natural fastidiousness well controlled. With enough practice, Ashrayan knew, even that reaction would fade; the girl would enter the foulest of minds without a tremor. *Like the hardened soldier Myrweal yearns to be...* Ashrayan caught herself procrastinating, put the thought aside and searched for the information she needed.

It was quickly and easily done. The thought lay clear at the surface: *...No arrows yet. Hope his bloody Lordship was right...* Image of a face, a voice, a commanding personality.

Prince Tian. There. Their joined minds swept down the column of riders, found the face and mind that fit, and slid silently within.

Prince Tian, new Lord of Riverfort, rode in the first rank behind the point-men, as he thought proper. Like everyone else in the column, he was dressed in plain battle-armor. The only indication of his rank was the slight elaboration and crest-height of his helmet. He carried a sword, shield, lance, mace and dagger, a single water bag and a small pouch of travel-food, like the rest of his riders. He had brought no baggage-train and no camp followers. He had come for conquest and meant to supply his troops from the land he conquered. As the somewhat-disgraced fourth son of the king of Edris, he had been sent up to Riverfort to keep him busy and out of trouble. He intended to do more than that.

...Land hidden in the Mountain of Witches... Witches? Nonsense. The excuse men make for failure... Land of women. Never taken. Said to be rich. With such a conquest win glory, wealth, power to be reckoned with...

Ahsrayan pulled away, drawing Lurias with her. They'd seen enough. A fitting strategy emerged from memory: sure, profitable, with little or no risk. Myrweal wouldn't like it, but perhaps her cheated hopes of glorious battle could be compensated. Ashrayan pulled Lurias back up the levels to full waking. Time to report.

"I don't like it." Myrweal screwed up her face like a girl much younger than her nineteen years. "It's so... so underhanded!"

"All strategy is," Ashrayan replied.

"Why don't we just attack as soon as they're within bowshot? There's no cover on the road, and if they charged the pass we could rain down arrows and fire and boulders–"

Ashrayan raised her hand and pinned Myrweal with a quelling stare. "Seed," she said explicitly.

Myrweal closed her mouth and blushed crimson.

"Now deploy your troops as you think best, and send the messengers. Bid the people hurry; that army should reach the Apron in another two spans."

Myrweal bowed grudging obedience and departed.

"Aunt," Lurias announced the moment they were alone, "The priesthood assembles in the forecourt. You must speak to them."

"Yes." Ashrayan smiled inwardly. A year ago, or less, Lurias would have asked 'Will you speak to them?' She had more confidence now, and her Gift was formidable. The child was maturing well, and would be a fit successor. Ashrayan leaned her weight indulgently on the junior priestess' arm as they went down to the shrine's courtyard.

The eight waiting women in their varied ritual gowns resembled a standing rainbow in the sun. Ashrayan twitched at the irony, thinking of the storm to come. The others felt it too, for their faces were grim. One of them, predictably Binnell of the First-Fruits Shrine, was actually scowling. Ashrayan could feel the woman's angry thought: *Is this ugly business necessary?*

Yes, it is. Ashrayan settled on the central chair and bade the others sit. "The Prince Tian, unloved fourth son of the lowland king, approaches with 200 armed men," she began without preamble. "He is determined on conquest to improve his standing. He has no mage, priest, nor other Gifted adept in his train, and discounts the legends. I have select-ed the Strategy of Valtona. Are you all familiar with it?"

They were. A moment's rustling, a few som-ber looks, and they were quiet again. Only Binnell raised a hesitant hand. "Can they not be frightened off?" she asked.

"No. Too well-trained and well-disciplined."

"Is the... preliminary rite necessary?" Binnell almost squirmed.

Damn her squeamishness. Ashrayan merely turned to the senior priestess of the Queen Temple, Turaga the Records Keeper.

"It is," the older woman said. "The breeding-records show it is more than time for an outcross, and since the Men's Village was destroyed by the avalanche two years ago..." She paused to let each woman there remember. "Well, you know what our present birthrate is."

In the ensuing silence Ashrayan knew there would be no further argument.

"You'll want us all to support the Illusion, I suppose," Binnell grumbled, with a laughably transparent hope.

"Of course," Ashrayan smiled. "Once the trap is sprung we might spare one or two women from the supporting Web, but not more, and surely not for long."

There. Now any woman who wished to could join the main party, and any who preferred to stay aloof could do so. Ashrayan guessed that Binnell would exhaust herself maintaining the Web of Power to give herself a good excuse for staying: anything rather than deal with the despised lowland creatures. So, even prejudice could be put to good use.

"Let us take positions and begin now," said Ashrayan, rising. "The army will reach the Apron soon, and there is much to do."

She took Lurias' hand and led her out of the courtyard, feeling the others settle themselves for the long labor ahead. Many of the women worked quickly; Ashrayan could feel the silent hum of rising power follow her out into the open air like an invisible wave. Lurias' hand tightened in her own, and Ashrayan felt a moment's twinge of sympathy. The girl had served as focus for a Web of Power many times, but never for so long or vast an operation as this.

"You can endure it," Ashrayan murmured as they walked through the gate. "Hold to your purpose. It will be exhausting, but not painful."

Lurias nodded once, resolute. She would last.

The Apron was a triangular, almost-flat field lying before the entrance to the pass. Its lower edge fell away to stony slopes: its two upper sides were bounded by steep wooded ridges that converged in a grove of tall mountain pines. Only the inhabitants of High Valley knew just where, behind the trees, lay the fortified gateway and the pass beyond. The symbolism of the geography was not lost on its defenders.

Ashrayan could have walked the forest path blindfolded, but as always she studied it while she walked. Were the concealing bushes well grown? Did the overhanging briars look impassible? Had years of pacing feet worn the twisting path too deep, too wide, too visible? *Acceptable,* she concluded, noting minor details for the shrine's acolytes to handle once the coming battle was over.

They came to the edge of the little forest, to the last large tree, to the niche carved into the living wood and the image stored within. Lurias gently pulled the thing into the light. "The veils," she complained. "They need work. Some of the scales have fallen off."

"It will serve. Set it in place. Sometimes perfectionism is unnecessary." Ashrayan could remember when the image had been no more than a pole with a blank bone for a face, a single rag for a gown, and a mere hank of animal hair; the Illusion had done the rest. Nowadays the image sported an artfully painted clay-covered skull, eyes of inset mussel-shell, hair that was quite genuine and attached to a tanned scalp, and a full-length veiling robe of black homespun sewn with fish-scales. The parts were set on a slender pole, slightly longer than human height, with a crosspiece that suggested shoulders.

The skull and scalp had been involuntarily donated by the last spy to attempt running the pass.

Lurias took the image to its place in front of the trees, set the foot of the pole in its waiting socket, and fussed with the arrangement of hair and cloth. Watching, Ashrayan recalled that the Guard Maidens had wanted to use the spy's entire skeleton, even to cover it with clay and sculpt it to the form of a particularly voluptuous woman, on the theory that the image of an attractive nude would surely hold attention. She had argued them down by pointing out that an invader might want to test the image with a few arrows, and it was far more impressive to see an arrow strike its target and disappear than to see it strike and stay without doing damage. Besides, too realistic an image could encourage laziness, letting the priestesses trust more to the sculpture than to maintaining the Illusion. That way lay disaster, and there was no excuse for such laziness, not with as many Gifted priestesses as the valley had now.

"There. Will it serve, Aunt?" Lurias asked, inspecting her handiwork.

"Quite well. Tie the branches." Lurias took out two long cords and went to the tall bushes that stood to either side of the image, their overlapping branches obscuring it from the meadow's view. She tied the cords to the branches and studied the arrangement carefully. "They're ready, Aunt."

At the repetition of the title, Ashrayan smiled. Remarkable, how phrases evolved. 'Mother' was reserved for one's blood-mother or the Goddess, 'Sister' for one's social equals, military titles for the Guard, 'Lady' for the

Goddess alone. That left only 'Aunt' for one's non-related senior. *Not that I would mind being Lurias' true aunt, or even mother...*

But there was no time for such maundering; the sound of marching feet and hooves was growing on the road.

"Come. To places, and make ready." Ashrayan took one of the cords and walked to the end of its length away from the image, hearing Lurias pad off in the opposite direction. In the woods around her she could hear and sometimes see the valley women sneaking into position. One of them set an armload of wineskins nearby. Good: all ready. Ashrayan sat, made herself as comfortable as possible, took a few deep breaths and dropped down the levels of Reach.

Beyond her half-focused eyes the meadow grew bright, throat-catchingly beautiful, with a light that had nothing to do with the sun. She could see/feel the busy life of Nature growing, feeding, scurrying, scarcely mindful of the approaching weight of men, horses and cruel intent. And there was Lurias beside her, a few yards off, closer than her skin.

Link... So easy, like clasping hands. *Good, my girl. Now to the Web...* A deep sense of contact, power, expansion: eight familiar presences pouring out a wave-front of strength. And now it must be used. *Form the*

Illusion. Form and maintain.

Flicker of acknowledgment, tightening of focus, slight pulling away: then the surge of power, the almost-visible thickening of the air that centered on the waiting image. If she had looked, Ashrayan knew, she would have seen the form of wood, bone, clay, hair and cloth take the shape of a beautiful woman veiled in shimmering darkness, with hair like a raven's wing, face white as the moon, eyes like dark rainbows. Along with the visual impression came a subtle emotional current of wonder, mystery, and fascination. It was a splendid Illusion, fine art for all that it was ephemeral. Indeed, Lurias was very, very good.

Hold in check, Ashrayan warned. *Wait for my signal. Wait...*

Now for her own part. She Reached out, into the meadow ahead and the road below, seeking that one key mind. The point-man rode into the meadow, reined in where the road ended in wildflowers, and studied the ground before him. There was no one in the field, nor cover in it to hide more than a rabbit. The brush and trees beyond might conceal an ambush, but there was no hint of one. Warily, he deliberately rode within bowshot but well out of javelin-range. No arrow came, nor any sign of human presence, and the birds flittered and cheeped without interruption. If troops waited in those woods they were extraordinarily quiet, well disciplined, and well hidden. And where was the road? He could see no way through the wood, and dared not ride closer to hunt for one. Best to go back and report. He turned his horse, tapped it lightly with blunt-spurred heels, and cantered back down the road.

Prince Tian didn't realize he'd been daydreaming until the approaching point-rider caught his attention. "Well, what?" he snapped defensively.

The point-rider backed off a pace, threw a smart salute, reported quickly and concisely with an utterly neutral face.

Prince Tian calculated for a moment, then ordered the man into line and bade the trumpeter signal for armed advance. They could ride no more than two abreast on this narrow track, but they could draw steel and proceed at the ready. Tian surreptitiously scratched at a pesky itch under his armor, sweating with impatience. The road ended in an ungrazed, empty field? This had to be a trap, and he would be ready. He considered ordering an advance at the trot, perhaps rattling the ambushers into showing their hand too soon—but then the road stopped and the field spread before him.

It was empty, as he'd been told. Tian rode forward, almost to the trees, and then swept to one side. Best to make room, bring all his forces into the meadow, before dealing with the woods. He snapped quick orders to the trumpeter and rode in a tightening spiral until the last footman was in place. The trumpet pealed two quick, short bursts. The troops halted, turned in place, and faced their weapons toward the trees.

Nothing happened except that birds took flight, abandoning the field to the iron-draped men.

The soldiers waited, sweating in their sun-drenched armor, beginning to trade looks with each other. Another few minutes of this, Tian knew, and they'd begin to feel foolish for pointing their blades at harmless trees. Some action must be taken, and now. He stood in his stirrups and peered at the silent woods.

"Well?" he bellowed to the leafy green wall, "Do we have a welcome or not?"

For a few seconds there was no reply. Tian was about to order an advance on the woods when a motion to one side of the meadow caught everybody's eye.

Two bushes pulled apart as if thrust by un-seen hands. In the revealed space stood a woman: midnight-haired, snowy-faced, draped in glimmering shadows, eerie and beautiful as quiet dreams.

"Prince Tian!" she called, her voice like dark honey.

Startled, Tian dropped back to his saddle, upsetting his horse. He covered the slip by spurring the beast forward, shouldering riders out of his way, until he reached the ranks of his footmen. "I am Prince Tian, Lord of Riverfort, son of King Vernalt," he announced in his best parade voice. "Who are you, and how do you know me?"

"I am Ashrayan, Priestess of Our Lady, Keeper of the Gate. Your fame is known through all these lands, great prince."

Tian raised an eyebrow, surprised and pleased. So, these women didn't cut themselves off from news of the lowlands. That meant spies, or commerce. Useful. "What folk live here?" he proceeded, "And who rules them?"

"This is the Mountain of Women, and none rules here save our Lady."

"Your Lady?" Tian pressed. That could mean either a single baroness and her gossips, or a local goddess and her priestesses. If the former, he need persuade only one woman. If the latter, he might have to work his way through a whole gaggle of females. "Who is she?"

"Our Lady is the Great Mother of All Living, of whom I am the foremost priestess." Ashrayan smiled to herself; she was, in fact, sitting in the foremost position at the moment, so the statement wasn't entirely a lie.

Oho. Tian sat up straighter in the saddle, raising his head to catch the light at the best angle. The effective ruler of this mysterious mountain stood before him, unprotected, young and pretty. He could neatly break the resistance of the whole mountain-clan with a single well-placed arrow—or one artful seduction. The latter course would be more pleasant, and probably more profitable.

"She is the Mistress of Heaven," Ashrayan went on, "Source of Fruitfulness—and Queen of Love."

Oho! Tian grinned. This might be easier than he had thought. He could already hear the snickering in the ranks.

"It is She who guards our gate, and She has commanded us to let no man enter our lands—unless first he lies with our childless maidens for three full nights."

It took an instant for that to sink in. Then a great bellow of laughter went up from the troops, with Tian leading. Next came a hubbub of jokes about bridge-tolls and tariffs. Weapons lowered, almost forgotten.

"Oh, indeed," Tian chuckled, wiping his

eyes. "That's an entry-fee we'll gladly pay. Have you enough maidens to go around?" There might be trouble with the troops otherwise. And what of housing and supplies for three days?

"Surely we have more than enough." The priestess gave no visible signal, but the brush parted all around the clearing and women stepped into the meadow. For an instant the sunlight seemed to pulse brighter, dazzling the eye. Then it passed, and the men could see scores of young girls strolling out from under the trees. Some were tall, some short, some slender and some buxom, but all were dressed in soft light gowns and flower wreaths, and all were as lovely as spring. Some carried rolls of cloth and tent-poles in their arms, some bore wide bowls of food, some held great wineskins and trays of wine cups, and all were smiling, smiling eagerly.

If only one of them were carrying the crown of Edris, Tian thought, *This would be a vision of heaven.*

The girls reached the first line of footmen, made giggling introductions and traded glances of frank appraisal. The men resembled dogs straining at the leash. Tian guessed that he must give orders quickly, before discipline broke altogether. "Ground arms!" he bellowed above the sly murmur of voices. "Dismount and set up camp, then let the women come in. We'll lie here tonight."

Appreciative laughter followed his last comment. The men complied somewhat sloppily, but fast. Swords went back into sheaths, riders dismounted, spears were racked in narrow sheaves like glittering shocks of corn. The horses were led off to the lower end of the meadow to be picketed, and an impatient Sergeant Major marked out a ditch for the latrines.

The girls waited, with commendable discipline of their own, until the preparations were finished. Then they hurried, giggling merrily, into the impromptu camp and began setting up their tents. Others set down their bowls and cups and wineskins, or spread soft blankets on the ground, then obligingly turned to help the men remove their armor.

Within moments, the 200 best troops of Riverfort abandoned all thought of battle and discipline, and busied themselves with selecting girls. Some made their choices quickly, and hurried the girls into the tents. Others took more time, sitting or reclining on the grass to study the candidates over handfuls of cheese and fruit and cups of the thick red wine. A few inveterate gamblers let dice or coins make their choices for them. Some of the men sat back, smiled, pulled in their stomachs and waited for the girls to do the choosing.

Not so much a bivouac as a jolly picnic, Tian noted, strolling thoughtfully through the crowd. He saw that even the sentries were pacing their rounds with girls on their arms, and paying far more attention to their companions than to the surrounding terrain. It occurred to him that a clever enemy could have disarmed his forces no better and no faster. What if there were armed troops waiting in those woods? They might not dare to strike while their women were entangled with his men, but what about later? Perhaps a quick signal could send the women running away, leaving exhausted and unarmored men to deal with the attack. *Take precautions. Increase the number of sentries. As soon as those quick-rutters finish with their girls, get them back into armor and on duty...*

A sudden wave of calm and confidence swept him like a breeze from the peaks. What was there to worry about? This was the 'Mountain of Women', as both the priestess and local history had said; there were no men here. The enemies were only women, after all: fickle of course, treacherous perhaps, but no match for good trained fighting-men. There was no ambush in the woods; birds sang there, uninterrupted. Let it be. Choose a woman for himself and spend a very pleasant afternoon and evening, and another two days and nights beyond that, earning his passage into the valley.

He shook off the feeling with some effort. No, this was too easy. There had to be a trap here, somewhere. *Remember the tales. Other armies came this way, and never came back.*

But perhaps, the expansive mood suggested, they too had been welcomed in the same fashion—and had chosen to stay. Imagine a valley full of pretty women, eager for men, willing to serve a man's slightest wish in exchange for child-making. Paradise indeed! What man would refuse, or be so foolish as to leave, or let other men learn the secret?

Any man with ambition. Besides, if there are other men waiting in that valley, they'll not appreciate 200 more. Best make plans...

But that could wait. The women had offered three nights, and the intervening days, of well-fed stud service. There was plenty of time to plan the invasion.

No. Best begin now. Seek out the priest-ess... The bushes at the edge of the meadow had closed again, leaving no sign of the mysterious woman, but she had to be near. No commander would walk away from engaged troops, no matter precisely how they were engaged. Tian strode to the place where the priestess had stood.

A strong mind, and determined, Ashrayan noted, watching him approach. *He resists well, but this can be dealt with.* His intention was clear and simple; a little wit and patience would suffice. She Reached for Lurias.

Oh Aunt, must I? Lurias' revulsion was strong, breaking barriers of discipline. There were still some things that Lurias could not force herself to do.

I should insist, Ashrayan thought, then reconsidered. Her own mentor, these long years dead, had had the good sense not to press one's weaknesses too hard, too soon. All folk had their flaws; one shouldn't risk damaging a valuable trainee. *I'll do what I can, child. Pull the cord.*

Tian halted as the bushes parted before him and the woman reappeared. How strange: at so close a distance she seemed even more enigmatic, elusive. Aside from the dark hair and eyes, he could not have described her face except as pale and lovely.

"Yes, good Prince?" she purred. "What do you wish?"

Tian smiled, showing his excellent teeth. "You, Lady."

She demurred sweetly, giving the barest impression of a blush. "I thank you for the compliment, Milord, but my duties forbid me—"

Tian reached a quick hand to where her

wrist should have been—and caught nothing but an edge of gem-stiffened cloth. How had she moved so fast without his seeing it? He kept his grip on her robe, and she didn't try to pull away. "Lady, I must insist. We are both commanders here, and we have much to discuss."

Lurias...

—Aunt, please! Not him!

For a heartbeat Ashrayan hung on the edge of decision, studying the man before her. He was intelligent, if narrow-minded, and strong—virtues not to be wasted. If he was ambitious, ruthless and impatient as well, such things did not pass in the seed. *We should get his child...*

—Please!

"I am not accustomed to being refused, La-dy," Tian pressed, a touch of anger showing in his voice and the lift of his lip. A vein pulsed visibly in his temple.

Thin veins, Ashrayan realized. *Thin veins and high choler. Left to himself, he would likely die early of stroke. So would his children.*

"Very well. Only let go my robe, sir, and give me a moment to put it aside. I may not do as you wish while wearing it."

Tian gave a booming laugh, and let go the cloth.

Release the cord, Lurias.

The bushes whipped closed.

–Oh thank you, Aunt! Thank you thank you–

Control! Maintain the Illusion, child. This will be tricky work.

Ashrayan stood up as quickly as she could, groaning inwardly at the twinge of rheumatism in her knees. She hurried up the almost-invisible pathway to the brush-shielded image and paused a moment, sculpting the Illusion around her. *'Robing the bride',* she thought, with a tight smile. So long it had been... Well, she would make the most of it; there might not be another time. She picked up a wineskin from the diminished pile, took a deep breath, padded around the far edge of the bush and stepped out into Tian's sight.

"Ah, there you are." Tian smiled in genuine approval as he saw her: a small woman in a plain dark gown and belt-cord and pouch, with plain sandals on her feet and a wineskin in her hand. If anything, she seemed more beautiful without the trappings–like a drawn sword. Ah, this game promised to be intriguing as well as profitable. He made an elaborate bow and offered her his arm. "At your convenience, Lady. Where shall we walk?"

"Let us go a little further into the wood," she smiled. "It would not be politic for others to observe me at such sport." *Get him away from his soldiers.* But the only available paths led to the pass and the shrine. Not the shrine: he might see the other priestesses there. The pass, at least, was well watched and guarded. She led him that way.

I can threaten her with this, after. Tian walked with her between the trees until they came to a mossy path. It seemed to lead deeper into the forest. "Not too far," he cautioned, "Lest my men call for me and become... disturbed at not finding me." He added just the right hint of menace.

"There is a good place quite near," said Ashrayan, pointing.

Close it was: a small circle of white pines, the ground between them carpeted thickly with dropped needles. She pushed through the springy branches, Tian following, and stepped into the tiny shaded grove. "No one can see us here, but a shout can easily be heard," Ashrayan smiled knowingly.

Tian paused to listen. Yes, the revelry in camp was clearly audible. He could call for troops, and they would arrive in a moment. Perfect. He took the priestess by the arm, turned her quickly, and kissed her.

Strange: for a moment her lips felt thin and dry. Then they yielded, seemed to melt, let him enjoy them thoroughly. When he finally pulled away, she smiled up at him.

"So, you are indeed a prince." She settled

on the carpet of needles. "Come, sit here. I've some of our good red wine."

Tian sat, amused at her forwardness. The lady was no virgin, and had doubtless stolen away from her duties before this. *Charm further. The more I learn, the more I can use.* "I certainly mean to enjoy your... vintage," he grinned. "Will you not enjoy it with me?"

Ashrayan started to agree with both meanings, then flinched as she remembered. *The powder! I didn't take it! Quick. Pouch–* She fumbled in her belt-purse, drew out a pinch of the green-gray powder and hastily put it on her tongue. She could feel a twitch of amusement from Lurias, and wryly acknowledged it. If the girl hadn't been maintaining the Illusion for her, it would have slipped badly just then.

"Here, what's that stuff you're eating?" Tian asked sharply.

He's observant, and no fool. Take care. "Something to discourage fertility." Ashrayan gave him a sidelong glance that suggested much. "It would not do for my... occasional amusements to bear unwanted fruit."

Tian laughed. "That powder would sell merrily in many a lowland town!" *What commerce do they have?* "Many a jolly youth could avoid embarrassment thus."

"A man should not touch it," Ashrayan smiled back. "It would cause his generative parts to, er, shrivel."

Tian rolled his eyes. "Pray take off that pouch and put it aside." He reached for the wineskin and wrenched out its plug, pulled a plain soldier's cup from his belt and poured in the wine. "Ah, it's thick and red, like fresh blood. Is this used for your celebrations, Lady?"

"Some of them. For sacrifices." Ashrayan smiled faintly. "Also for rites of fertility, such as the maidens are doing now."

Tian sipped cautiously, and found the wine surprisingly sweet. "Yes, that seems fit to make lovers merry. Will you not drink with me, Lady?"

Ashrayan obligingly took the cup and drank a mouthful, letting him see the length of her throat working as she swallowed. She smiled as she wiped her mouth and handed back the diminished cup.

Tian drank again, deciding he liked the wine. "You grow fine grapes hereabouts. Do you make much wine every year?" *How large a crop?*

"We have no grapes; this is made of mountain berries. We make barely a tun a year, which is why it is reserved for celebrations."

"Ah. What do you drink on common days, then?"

"Milk, herb-tea, and barley-beer. Our little

land has but modest riches: enough to keep us well, but little to spare." Ashrayan gave him a deliberately knowing look. "We would be poor, Milord, were we compelled to pay such taxes as the lowlanders must."

Aha! "Is that why you stay hidden on your mountain, discourage visitors, and spread such fearsome tales of yourselves?"

"What tales?" Ashrayan asked, putting on an arch, mock-innocent look.

Tian laughed, coughed, and drank again. "They say in the villages below that only women live here, a tribe of witches who slaughter any man that invades your realm. They say that few men have ever come back from trying to enter your valley, and they were only those who failed to gain admittance: a few mountaineers who tried to climb the peaks, poachers who hunted too deep in these woods and were driven off with arrows, a few bold peddlers who came openly to sell goods and got no further than the meadow there. That much I know is true, for I've talked to some of them."

"It's quite true that we discourage visitors, at least the sort who will go away again spreading boastful tales of our supposed wealth."

"Ah." Tian took another mouthful of wine, noticed that he was sweating heavily, and

decided it was time to get out of his swelter-
ing armor. "Come, Lady; will you help me out
of these irons?" he asked, fumbling one-
handed at his belt. "It's quite a warm day."

"That it is," Ashrayan smiled, and complied,
thinking of how Myrweal would have been
shocked at the sight.

"The weather's no better in the lowlands,"
Tian grumbled, shedding mail. "Scorching in
summer, freezing in winter, poor soil and no
decent forests. My elder brothers got the good
lands; I got Riverfort." He drained the cup, set
it aside, and pulled off the sword belt for
himself. "Your valley is probably the richest
land in the whole province."

"That says little. In a bowl-shaped valley the
soil can't be washed away in spring floods.
Still, it must be endlessly tended..." Ashrayan
frowned, "And fertilized. Our wealth is slight,
and bought at great price."

"Well, industrious folk make fine subjects."
Tian poured himself another cup of the wine.
"You would be welcome additions to the
kingdom, sworn good protection and just laws.
As Baron of Riverfort I have the power to
adjust the taxes; I'll be happy to pledge you
the lightest of fees. You'll have a good bargain of it, I swear." *Carefully now...* "What
crops do you raise, what herds and flocks,
what goods do you make that your folk could

easily spare?"

"Not much," said Ashrayan, pulling off his boots for him. "We have some fruit-trees on sheltered ground. We raise barley and hemp, sheep and goats, a few cattle, no horses. We gather berries and pine-nuts, mushrooms and herbs from the forest. Sometimes we snare rabbits and birds. Occasionally we take a deer. We must be sparing of wood; we cut barely enough for house-timbers and furnishings, make our houses of stone, burn brush and fallen branches in our cook-fires, and are often cold in winter. There is hardly enough clay in the stream to make pots and dishes. We've found no gold, no silver, no gems, not even iron in these hills, I assure you—only a little copper. We sometimes trade barley and wool to peddlers for iron tools. That's all we have."

"Surely you could trade a little wool or bar-ley or berry-wine for the protection of a powerful kingdom." Tian smiled at her over the edge of his wine cup. *And even if your little tale of woe is true, you still have a treasure worth claiming: yourselves. I've never seen lovelier women. Imagine paying your taxes thus!*

"So far, Milord, we've managed to protect ourselves."

"Aye, with clever rumors, isolation and good

luck." Tian took a long pull from his cup. "But how long, think you, can such straws hold? In time, some army will come—led by generals far less reasonable and generous than I—who will discount the rumors as readily as I have, and what then? Such will take your valley by storm, and ravish all your women. Best to make alliance now, Lady: a good bargain with a good ruler. Surely you can see the sense of that."

"At the moment," Ashrayan smiled archly, "Since you have not yet seen and assessed our lands, nor we your taxes and armies, that would be rather like buying a pig in a poke."

Tian gave a shout of laughter, and raised his cup in salute. "Quite true, Lady. More must be seen. In three days I'll come and see your valley. Afterwards, you yourself may come with me to Riverfort and see my court and army there—if you wish, of course."

"Army? Then this is not all of it?"

Tian laughed again, and gulped the wine. "No, no: only my personal guard. We keep a thousand men under arms, not counting the local levies in wartime." *...But a wretched, ill-disciplined lot. Only my guards deserve the name of soldiers—but she need not know that. Women know nothing of soldiering; easy to hide such flaws from them.*

"If Riverfort lands are so poor, how can you

feed and clothe a thousand men to do nothing but wait for war?"

Clever girl. "Ah, the lands are also vast. A tenth of a poor land's yield can suffice, if there's enough land. Besides, we have trade; there are always the iron-mines of the west. That's where your tools come from. You see? Your folk need trade with us, and trade must be protected with laws and armies. Already you benefit from the good rule of Edris. You could benefit more."

"We have trade already, and have had for these last ten generations. It is enough for our needs. Why should we change?"

Tian meant to speak more of good government protecting trade, but caught himself. *TEN generations?!* The kingdom of Edris hadn't existed then. Three small kingdoms had warred for the south; Riverfort had been largely empty, tossed back and forth between the three combatants whenever one of them could spare enough troops to march in, demand allegiance and collect taxes. Nobody then had protected trade, or safety, or anything else. "Is *that* when you settled this mountain? How did it happen?"

Ashrayan clasped her hands in her lap and recited, as if from an old lesson.

"In the days of King Luothan, the word went out that all the lands should worship the sea-god Nodad as consort of the Great Mother. This the northlands scorned to do, as the sea was far from them and the priests of Nodad famed for greed. Then did the priests of Nodad suborn the king of the south so that he punished the northlands, laying waste the soil, slaying the men folk and ravishing the women. Those priestesses who yet lived went among the women, saying: 'Thus we have been served by the god, his priests, his king and his men. How shall we then serve him, or take new husbands from among his worshipers? Let us rather go up to the mountains with our children, and keep ever apart from such men.' Signs were shown that the Mother would provide, and so the women came away. They brought their children in their arms and the seed-crops on their backs, driving before them such flocks as still they had. By gift of the Goddess' visions, they found the mountain and the High Valley. There they set down their burdens and gave thanks–"

"So you're all the descendants of those refugees!" Intrigued, Tian sat up and pulled off his cloak. "And you still worship the goddess without a consort? Amazing relic! Well, I assure you, you have nothing left to fear from old Nodad. The founding of Edris broke the power of his priesthood, and he's quite a minor deity these days. Most people worship the Storm-

God Obdur now–and the old goddess still has her shrines, of course."

"Of course," murmured Ashrayan.

"Hmmm, but if the men were all dead, how did the women manage to leave any descendants?"

"There were some boys among the children. Also, it was then that we began the custom of lying with outsiders."

And raising crops of bastards. High time that custom changed. Tian took another gulp of wine to wash the bad taste from his mouth. "But then, you should have had enough men to go around within a generation. Why is this still called the Mountain of Witches? Where are your men?" *And how many of them?*

"The Goddess decreed that the men should live in a separate village, at the far end of the valley, far up on the slopes." Ashrayan judged that the truth of that, too, would do no harm. "The men's village was destroyed by an avalanche, two years ago."

"No men!" Tian almost laughed into the sunlight. *Nothing but a few boy-children, at most. What incredible luck! The women will welcome us as deliverers, as founding fathers–hell, as fertility-gods! My descendants here will worship me above Obdur!* He drained his cup and tossed it aside. "Come then, Lady," he grinned hugely, reaching for her. "I'll gladly compensate you for your two years without."

To Ashrayan's surprise, she enjoyed it. Tian was not a simple thrusting brute; he was thorough, flamboyant, and proud of his skill. This was another weapon in his arsenal, and he used it well. Had Ashrayan truly been as ill experienced as he thought, she might have been overwhelmed. *It's well that Lurias was spared*, she smiled wryly to herself. *As it is, I may as well take as much pleasure as I can. It has, after all, been years...*

After the performance, Tian rolled over and fell asleep.

Ashrayan lay on her back and wriggled her toes, feeling the last sweet echoes fade. The late sunlight slanted through the trees in bars of gold, much as it had on that long-ago day in the forest near the Men's Village, when she had felt this for the first time. *Sweet Evial... Dead now, under the avalanche. We were lovers, friends, for so long. A truly decent man... Gone. I'm old.*

A glint of sunlight on metal caught her eye. She sat up quickly and saw Myrweal crouched under the trees, bow drawn. *Fool girl!* Ashrayan hitched backward until her body shielded Tian's, then pulled on her dress, got up and stalked toward the Guard Commander, staying carefully in the way of the arrow.

"Get out of my line of sight!" Myrweal

hissed. "Let me take him now."

"With his men just down the path?" Ashrayan whispered. "Suppose they come looking for him and find him dead. Then what?"

"Then we'll have a battle, and we'll win."

"With 200 of our people, unarmed, in the middle of it? Would you risk such losses?"

Myrweal thought about that, and eased down the bowstring. "But they're not likely to come looking. They're all exhausted with rutting, and the wine is doing its work."

"You know very well that such business takes hours. They could get up and come looking at any time, and in what mood the Goddess alone knows. How many of our people do you wish to sacrifice to your glory?"

Myrweal took a step back. "N-not one, Aunt. I only mean to be sure."

"The slow way is sure. Go back to your station and wait. You are not to attack until and unless you see one of them actually assaulting our people with a weapon. That is my direct order, Guard Commander."

Myrweal whispered an oath, but lowered the bow and backed into the forest.

Ashrayan padded back to Tian's side and sat down to wait. He was still deeply asleep.

Then a sending came to her, strong and clear, from Lurias. *–Aunt, when should the* *powder be given?*

To whom? Specify! Ashrayan shot back, wondering frantically which of the women had forgotten the precautions.

—To a man, if one wishes to keep him.

There was a brief warm image of Lurias' sister, and of the point-rider—the one who rode with blunt spurs and was good to his horse.

We had not planned to... Ashrayan abruptly remembered Evial, and reconsidered. Yes, this was wise. The Men's Village needed repopulating, rebuilding. Why wait for a whole generation to grow up from this day's work? It could be done now.

When he has forgotten his father's name. Ashrayan sighed, committed.

—Thank you, Aunt. Lurias pulled away, trailing a last unguarded thought: *Rianna, question him constantly to make sure...*

Ashrayan lay back on the cloak and watched the sunbeams shift.

Eventually Tian woke. He rolled on his back, coughed, sat up and pawed about him for the wineskin. His motions were clumsy, and he spilled almost as much as he drank.

Ashrayan picked up his tunic and handed it to him. "Would you care for food now, Milord?" she asked, checking herself to be sure the Illusion still held.

Tian blinked at her in puzzlement for a moment, then took the garment and put it on. "Mmm, no. How long was I asleep?"

"Perhaps two spans. The sun will be down soon. Do you wish to go back to your camp?"

"No." Tian pulled on his leggings, boots and sword belt, and slung the wineskin on his shoulder. His forehead furrowed with concentration. "That's strong wine. I believe I'm drunk. Mustn't let the troops see me like that. Lose their respect."

"Then you will spend the night here? The weather is mild, but if you wish a tent, I'll-"

"No." Tian struggled to his feet. "I'll walk a bit. Clears the head. Join me, Lady?" He held out his arm, flashing his old smile.

"Certainly." Ashrayan got up and took his hand.

His grip closed on her like a trap. "Now, good lady, which way to the valley?"

"Milord, you've not yet passed a single night with us. Custom requires three."

"Time the custom was changed. All things change. Grow or die, that's the way of the world. Conquer or be conquered. Stuck with it." He plodded determinedly back to the path, towing Ashrayan with him.

"Cannot one balance growth and death?" she asked, hoping to slow him down. "Is there no way to avoid being conqueror or conquered?"

Tian shook his head, not up to philosophical discussions now. He pored for a moment over the pathway, and then turned resolutely away from the meadow, toward the gateway and the pass beyond. "I want to see the valley first," he insisted. "Before the troops do. Get some idea, strategy... Come back, tell them about it when they wake in the morning. When they get there, they'll see I was right. Respect. Have to win their respect every day, every moment. Bind them to me..."

"Well, then, you will see it." Ashrayan padded along beside him, indulgently stroking his arm. *He may as well go under his own power.*

"Best troops in Riverfort. Still have to win them over." Tian shook his head in disgust. "I thought it was such a prize when Father sent me here. I heard all the legends. Everyone has. Mountain of Witches. Chance to make my reputation..."

"The legends are well known in the south?" Ashrayan almost missed a step. *Then King Vernalt must have known! No army has ever come back–*

"Oh yes! I was the man to do it, he said. My great chance, he said. I thought he'd forgiven that brawl with my brother, saw that I was the better son... Oho!"

They had come to the end of the wood. On

either side of the path the rock walls closed in, ending in a narrow gap. Its sides were sheer, as if they'd been cut with a blade, of dark and strangely glassy stone, as if some titanic dragon had once breathed against the mountain wall and melted it through. On the scarps above the glassy channel, well disguised, were crenellated walls and fortified armories. Most, if not all, of the Guard were there, watching. Ashrayan waved surreptitious signals at them, hoping to the Goddess that the girls would see and obey and keep still.

"So this is the way in!" Tian laughed, stumbling toward it. "What a disguise! Hidden pass, fortifiable... Lady, you don't know what a treasure you have here."

"Ah, but we do."

"All you need are the men to build it up, guard it. We'll do that. Our own little kingdom, defensible as hell. Could entrench here, raise our own supplies. They'd never dig us out." His voice echoed off the narrow walls, carrying far.

"'They'?"

"Southland troops." Tian glowered at the glassy walls as he plodded between them. The rising wind through the narrow channel lifted his hair and snapped at his clothing. "Thousands. Well disciplined. Loyal to Father. Not like mine... Learned when I got here. Worthless rabble, won't fight 'til their own borders are overrun. Only my Household Guard worth calling an army, and they don't trust me. Bring them here, take the Mountain of Witches, then they'll be loyal." He raised his head, grinning wolfishly. "Didn't count on luck. Gods, what luck! Rich valley, natural fort, hundreds of pretty women, eager for men... Oh, we'll take good care of you, my princess. Good care." He patted her arm, not easing his grip.

From somewhere on the cliffs above came the faintest echo of sweet, cruel, girlish laughter. It was quickly hushed, and might have been the wind.

King Vernalt sent his troublesome fourth son here, Ashrayan pondered, taking Tian's weight as he stumbled on the stony path. *Sent him to us, priming him with dreams of glory, tales of our wealth and unconquered valley— and gave him no more troops than the king- dom could easily afford to lose. Oh, that old viper! And men call us cruel!*

"How bright the light is on the rocks," Tian marveled, stumbling again. "Oops! Sorry. I'm drunk. Is it much further?"

"Less than a quarter-mile, but if you wish to sit down and rest—"

"No, no." Tian leaned on her shoulder and struggled forward. "Want to see it before dark. My treasure. Core of my kingdom. Heart of glory. I'll be remembered as a god... So bright here! Like rainbows..."

"Yes, yes, you'll see it," Ashrayan promised, impressed by the man's sheer determination. "What is your father's name, my prince?"

"King Ver... V..." Tian slipped on the stony path and pulled himself up, hand over hand, climbing Ashrayan's thigh and arm. "Doesn't matter. He doesn't matter. Only me. ...And you, of course, my queen."

"Of course." *Now, if ever. Be sure.* "And once you have your kingdom, Milord, what will you do with it?"

"Do?" He was astounded at the question. "Why, rule it! Rule, of course. Make it grow. Make an empire. Command the world. Grow... grow or die..."

Like a cancer. Ashrayan pulled her hand away from her belt-pouch. "Yes, Milord, I see it. Any man may want power for what it can gain him: land, wealth, safety, freedom, the mate of his choice, the respect of others.

Offer him those things, and he'll gladly trade power for them. But some men—like you, my prince—are different. You seek power for its own sake, as a true priest seeks his god."

"Yes! Yes, you understand... like a god..." Tian struggled onward, eyes widening on his private vision. "That's the secret... unlocks magic... glory on everything..."

"Soon," Ashrayan murmured. *He drank two cups...* She paced her breathing, matching it to the surge of the steady wind, dropped a level and Reached for Lurias. There. Contact. *Child, how fare the others?*

—Aunt, the women are well. Lurias' reply was laced with fatigue. *The horses are being loaded. The invaders are down, raving or still. The few we selected have been given the powder and are being led to the pass behind you. The Web cannot be maintained much longer, not beyond sunset. Turaga has fallen out in weariness, and Binnell is weakening.*

Ashrayan calculated the risks, and decided. *Pull the women out. As soon as they've left the Apron, drop the Illusion for the fallen. Concentrate on the selected—and on Tian; he's still armed and walking. That should give you more time.*

Lurias paused a moment, roiling with indecision, then stiffened with resolve. *No, Aunt,* she answered, with a determination Ashrayan had never suspected in her. *We'll wait until the visions blind them. Let them die happy, seeing only pretty, willing maidens.*

Ashrayan blinked in surprise. *If the Gifted are weakening, we should conserve their strength.*

Lurias stood firm. *We can last, Aunt. We can afford a little effort not to be cruel.*

Ashrayan sighed, agreed, and pulled back from the contact. Yes, the girl was right. The victor could afford a little mercy. *Have I fallen so far from it, in all these years of battles and losses? Am I the hardened soldier Myrweal longs to be? Am I the Battle-Crone indeed?* She bowed her head and walked on.

Tian fell again, and lay panting on the stony ground. He noticed the wineskin as if for the first time, pulled it open and drank. "Good wine," he mumbled. "Tastes sweet... a little sharp. Wha's it made from?"

"Mountain berries," Ashrayan sighed, helping him to his feet, "Flavored with a little pale mushroom that grows in our woods. Come now, Milord. It's only a short way further."

"Yes... my kingdom..." He staggered on, leaning heavily on Ashrayan's shoulder. "Name's not Milord. It's... Ti..."

"Only a few steps more. Ah, there. There it is."

The path dropped before them, and the sheer walls fell away to either side, opening on a vista painted with sunset-gold. Tian paused and stared, wide eyes pinpointed in the falling light. "Beautiful," he whispered.

"Yes. Yes, it is." In a sudden spasm of pity Ashrayan Reached for him, probing only deep enough to see the valley as he saw it.

Paradise!

It was a vast punchbowl in the top of the mountain, round as a wine cup, rimmed with silver-blue peaks, filled with woods and fields of a vibrant green. A fire-blue stream wandered from a snow-peak down to a central lake that reflected the copper-gold sky, and on its shore nestled an exquisite little city of soft-blue stone. The air was filled with a chorus of sweet wind-voices, like elfin-lovely women singing welcome. Sky and earth shimmered with a glory of subtle rainbows.

My kingdom. Paradise.

Ashrayan wrenched her mind away from his, feeling her eyes burn with long-absent tears. She blinked them away and looked again, seeing High Valley as it truly was: a little circle of land in the top of a near-barren mountain, its soil thin and sandy, made fertile only with constant effort. Made fertile with sacrifices.

No, no paradise. Yet it is beautiful, and I would defend it with my life–and more. And I have.

"...So green..." Tian mumbled, staring. "Wha' makes it so green?"

"Constant fertilization," Ashrayan murmured. "With dung, with compost... With bone meal. With ground meat. With blood."

Right then she felt a tightening, a quivering in the Web that had surrounded her all afternoon. It was going to snap.

–Aunt! Lurias' urgency Reached to her. *Can't hold you! Too far, and we're too tired. It's going to–*

SNAP!

Ashrayan flinched and gasped with a pain that was purely mental. Her skull seemed to echo with emptiness. The Illusion was gone.

"...Lady?" Tian turned to face her.

Now he will see. Goddess, I can't help being cruel!

She took a deep breath and drew herself up to meet his eyes, waiting for the shock of horror and betrayal and whatever he would do then. She knew all too well what there was to see: hair almost completely white, skin like a dried riverbed, face all stark bones, body gaunt and knotty as an old tree–all the indelible marks of 60 years' hard living in a little mountain farming-village.

Let him look, and endure the consequences.

But Tian only smiled vaguely, his eyes unfocused and glassy. "Princess..." he mumbled. "...my lovely..."

Ashrayan bowed her head in gratitude for the Goddess' mercy. He didn't see her at all. His eyes were filled with poison-visions, false glories, and ecstasies of fever. There was less than an hour of life left in him, but he would find it utterly beautiful.

From the pass behind them came the shambling footsteps of the selected, spared men, still dazed with the aborted mushroom-poison, yearning now for nothing but sleep. They wouldn't recall now that the rawboned, coarse-handed farm-women walking beside them had ever appeared as delicate, aristocratic maidens. They would keep their lives and regain their strength, but never their memories. They would never remember their fathers' names, their lives before this, their lowland customs, or that they had ever been an invading army.

Our mercy to the enemy. Would the lowland men do as much?

Behind them, barely audible, came the slow hoof beats of the horses bearing the first load of the dead.

"...Mother..." Tian whispered, and fell down on the road. He twitched for a moment, and then lay still.

Victory, Ashrayan thought, shivering in the first evening wind. *Our inborn and carefully bred Gift—to read thoughts or send them. Our long memories and ready wits. A little pale mushroom that grows in the woods. Little enough to keep us free and safe, but they suffice.*

The sun slipped behind the far peaks, and from below came the quiet sound of approaching footsteps, the faint clattering of butcher-knives and the rattle of empty buckets and barrels and carts–the ugly, necessary end to dreams of conquest.

The replenished soil would yield a good harvest next year.

Sidestreets

Angelina Lobo–"angel-wolf": she didn't feel much like either of them as she waited in the backyard, crouched between the cardboard carton and the solid wood gate, chewing her nails ragged. Hank was coming up the alley, at last; she recognized the chugging engine even before she saw his car through the knothole. He didn't have time to tap the horn before she was tugging the disguised gate open. Lina dragged the box through, shut the gate fast and muscled the cargo into the back seat.

"Hurry!" he whispered. "I don't think anybody saw me turn in, but–"

Lina ran around to the front passenger door and piled in fast. Hank took off the minute she got the door closed.

"Got it disguised okay?" he asked, pulling the Ford out toward the end of the block.

"Sure." Lina fastened her seatbelt, pulled tangled black hair out of her eyes and started feeling around in her purse for a cigarette. "It just looks like household goods, after all." She felt much better about this now that she was actually in the car, surrounded and hidden by metal.

"So what do we say if the cops ask us what we're doing with it?" Hank peered left and right before pulling out into the street.

"Say we're moving it from my place to yours." Lina threw an automatic glance behind them as she lit the cigarette. "Why should they complain?"

"The booze, the tools, even the dried mush- rooms maybe we could get away with." Hank frowned at the traffic, looking for telltale red and blue lights. "But what're you going to say about the jewelry?"

"When're they gonna see it?" Lina pulled open her shirt with an almost lecherous grin, revealing line after glittering line of neck- chains strung with pendants and rings. "I keep my shirt fastened, they won't know what I've got."

Hank nodded, his dark-blond hair falling into his eyes. "Nice. Just don't move fast, or you'll jingle and give the game away."

"I'll be careful. How's Ralphie?"

"Rarin' to go. Just pet him and see."

Lina turned around, reached over the seat and patted the enormously shaggy gray dog curled up on the floor. Ralphie slobbered happily on her hand. She scratched his muzzle and neck, then moved her hand further down his back until she found the elastic cords completely hidden under the thick fur. A little further probing found the fake-fur sling stretched under the dog's belly. Ralphie didn't seem to mind it.

"Very nice," she agreed, sliding back into her seat. "Nobody'll find that. Which way're we going out?"

"Straight out North Avenue to the border." Hank's jaw was set as if to fend off an argument. "Quickest way."

Lina only frowned. "Not much trouble from thugs," she said, "But that's bound to run us into cops. Why that way?"

"Looks innocent." Hank relaxed a little, remembering that Lina didn't argue much, especially not when the action was starting. Before and afterward, maybe: not during. She was a damn good partner. "We go straight down one of their big patrolled streets, it doesn't look like we've got anything to hide."

"Just a backseat full of barter-goods, huh?"

Lina smiled through a curl of smoke. "Let's hope they're so busy on the street–and keep 'em bored enough with us–that they don't decide to holler 'Drugs-drugs' and strip us all down to the bones. But once we get past the turn-off for your place, where're we gonna say we're taking the goodies?"

Hank gulped. He hadn't thought of that. "Uh, some buddy's address..." he tried, knowing it sounded thin.

"Gimme the map." Lina pawed open the glove compartment and took out a worn city street-map. "There. Just over the border. Pick a street, claim it's your sister and brother-in-law's place, and we're going to visit."

Hank brightened. "Make it a good ways over the border," he suggested. "Too close looks suspicious."

He slowed to a stop at the red light on the corner of Vine and North, and glanced as far up the street as he could. No sign of cop-cars, but in this crush of traffic that didn't mean much. One could be hiding behind a truck or a bus.

"All right." Lina pondered over the map. "Let's say... 2251 Glendale Road. That's part of an apartment complex, rich enough to look respectable. Say they just moved in, haven't got a phone yet, so the cops can't check it out quickly. Say their name's Jackson; there's always a Jackson somewhere."

"Right." The light changed and Hank pulled the car slowly out onto North Avenue, west-bound. "You bring any hardware?"

"Just the slingshot. Legal-legal." Lina pulled up her shirt, now revealing a heavy slingshot tucked into the waistband of her faded jeans. "Got a bag of marbles in my pocket. Innocent, right?"

"Let's hope," Hank grinned. "You've got enough surprises in that shirt, girl."

"That isn't what you said the first time you took it off." She leered at him, showing off her teeth.

Hank ducked his head, blushing like a kid. He always blushed so easily. "Hey, that's all right," he insisted, "I'm not a tit-man. I like legs: nice long dancer's legs, just like yours."

"I like your butt, too," Lina couldn't resist teasing, just to watch him blush again. Hell, but he was cute.

Hank obliged. "Goddammit, woman, keep your eyes on the road," he huffed. "This is Cop Alley, remember? And I haven't got your talent."

"Right, right. I'll look." Lina sobered at that, remembering their mission. Nice to know, too, that Hank wasn't one bit jealous of what she could do. Her two previous boyfriends hadn't been so tolerant. Frankie had turned mean and bullying on her. Bog had retreated into religious carping and calling her a witch. She'd kept the nickname when she'd walked out on him. Hank was different; he loved her for it.

I'll do it anytime for you, lover... Lina smiled as she closed her eyes and blanked her mind. This came easier with practice: breathe deeply, be calm, see the white light... Now, *reach.*

It was like unclenching a fist in the front of her skull, like focusing an eye set in the middle of her forehead, impossible to describe but easy, now, to feel. She looked/felt ahead, behind, to either side, up and down the long crowded street.

"Anything?" Hank asked softly, flicking regular glances in the mirror.

"Shhh... takes time..." Lina reached out, hunting for a particular giveaway feel, an emotional tone somewhere in that sea of thought/image/feeling. There was a common buzz of busyness, automatic wariness, constant low-level resentment–the usual feel of usual minds in this city these days.

There! A crackle of predatory hunger/excitement. Lina focused on it. Sensations of greasy clothing, pavement underfoot, glimpse of dirty brick near at hand. Ah, just a mugger waiting in an alley. No threat to them. She stretched wider.

There! Lazy-predatory, bored, self-pitying,

arrogant/resentful. Sensations of car-seat, metal-weighted jacket, heavy gun belt. Sounds of radio-crackle, buzzing voices. Smells of stale smoke and gun-oil. View through a different windshield, recognizable knot of dirty shop fronts. Classic 43rd Ward white cops patrolling a black neighborhood.

Lina pulled back, shaking her head slightly as she drew her vision into her eyes again. "Patrol car ahead," she reported. "About two blocks. Just cruising, looking for anything interested. If we stay this far behind them, we're safe."

"And that's the closest?" Hank relaxed in his seat. "Okay, this just might turn out to be easy."

"Don't count your chickens..."

"Just keep scanning, Wolf-baby."

They crept through the traffic, lockstep, lockwheels, while the muggy Illinois sunlight hammered down through the roof and windows. Block after block rolled past without incident, and Lina began to hope that Hank's guess was right. She dared to turn the radio on, dial WCFL and turn the volume up to almost normal—enough for background noise, not enough to distract. She let her talent stretch a little, loose-focus, not enough to take real effort, enough for good warning-range.

One by one the big cross-streets crept by and the miles crawled back. A glance at the street numbers showed them halfway to the border. Ralphie yawned and grumbled in the back seat, nosed briefly at the box of goodies, found nothing of interest, and settled back down. Hank began humming/singing along with the radio.

"'Ooooh, I need a dirty woman…'"

"Fat chance," Lina started to retort.

There! Sudden shock of anger/surprise/fear/desperation, crossed with an alien wary/hungry/bullying joy. Dead ahead.

"Hank!" she gasped, sitting up fast. "Trouble ahead! Cops!"

"Where?" Hank tensed hard over the wheel, but resisted the temptation to throw the brakes on. "Focus on it, Wolf-baby. Where? And what?"

Lina clenched her eyes shut, reached and focused. Sights now, and sounds. Car crawling past a pinched inspection. A street sign.

"Pulaski Avenue," she interpreted. "Road-block. They're stopping everybody, general inspection, looking for the usual. They say drugs-drugs, but it's really nothing particular this time."

Hank drew a deep breath. "Okay," he decided. "Let's walk through it."

"You sure?" Lina gave him a hard stare. "We

could avoid it, I think."

"Maybe they've got cars on the side-streets, watching for that. Even if they don't, I take us out of our way, run us into street-thugs, and all we've got now is my knife and your sling-shot." Hank clenched the wheel in a hear death-grip. "Our chances are better this way."

"Make 'em better still, then." Lina thought fast, then turned up the radio. "Cops really hate a family fight. So argue with me. We're going out to visit your sister, right? Okay: last time there, you flirted with a neighbor. I'm nagging you about it, and you didn't do anything. Got it?"

"Got it." Hank reviewed the script and started practicing some impromptu lines. "Honest, I was just being polite to the neighbors. I don't even know the girl's name." He remembered to roll the window partly down to make the argument good and audible.

"The way you were looking at her, her name didn't matter." Lina raised her voice to a naggy whine that anyone who knew her would recognize as fake. The cops wouldn't know her.

They drove into the roadblock arguing, accompanied by an old Beatles song.

"I was only being polite, for godsake!"

"Polite, nothing! You didn't take your eyes off her all evening."

"Get back, get back, get back to where you once belonged."

The first cop came up to them and tapped on the window while they argued. "Lessee your license," he rattled off, one hand resting showily on his pistol-butt. Behind him, his partner casually aimed an Ithaca riot-gun at the driver's window.

"What?" Hank looked up and frowned, as if this were just one more irritation in a long, miserable day. "Ah hell, here it is."

In the time-honored Chicago fashion, he pulled out his wallet and handed the whole thing to the cop. The cash-compartment gaped submissively open, revealing a twenty, a ten and a five. The cop flipped open the card-section and peered through it.

"Now we're gonna be late, on top of every-thing else," Hank grumbled.

"Your sister won't mind," Lina whined. "*She* never minds if you're late. *I'm* the one who minds, but you never seem to remember that."

"Everyone who knows her says she's got it comin', But she gets it while she can," sang the radio.

"Destination?" asked the cop, fumbling qui-etly with the wallet.

"My sister's new apartment, 22... Ah, what's the rest of it?" Under his stage-perfect exas-peration, Hank threw Lina a desperate look.

"2251 Glendale Road," Lina answered tartly. "I swear, you'd forget your head if it weren't nailed on."

"Well, you're the one who forgot about the gas bill."

"I didn't forget the bill; you forgot to give me the money for it."

"Get back, get back..."

"What've you got in the car?" the cop asked, leaning closer.

"Some pickles," Lina tossed off, "And the hammer George loaned us last month, and a dress that might fit Suzanne–if she's really lost those five pounds, like she said."

"Peace offering," Hank elaborated, rolling his eyes heavenward. "After the way you carried on last time, I'm lucky I don't have to get her a new set of dishes. Real party-pooper, you were."

"Speaking of dishes," Lina carped, "If you hadn't made such a fool of yourself over that broad, I wouldn't have had to snap at you. It's your own damn fault."

"Get back, Jo-Jo!" added the radio.

The cop yanked the rear door open and looked in. As he pawed the box in the back seat, Ralphie growled at him.

"Down, Ralphie," Hank warned, sweating a little. "It's all right; he won't hurt you."

"Just doing his job," Lina echoed. "And

speaking of jobs..."

"Oh, come on!" Hank grabbed the offered lead. "I'm lucky enough to have three days a week, the way things are. Whaddaye want, I should push the Old Man before I've been there six months, and maybe get cut back to two days—or even fired?"

"Why've you got the dog with you?" the cop asked, withdrawing from the back seat.

"To watch the car, of course!" Lina snapped, knowing it was risky. "The way things are, you can't leave your car parked for five minutes but some punk tries to break into it. Ralphie may not be attack-trained, but he can bark like crazy."

"Besides, it's good for him to get out of the city every now and then," Hank added, reached over to pat the dog's head—and incidentally block the cop's view. "Give you a real big yard to run in, right, fella?"

"Let's see some ID from you, ma'am." The cop turned his attention to Lina.

The radio switched to a car commercial.

"Oh, all right." Lina opened her purse and pawed inside it, pulling out a compact, lipstick, comb, eye-shadow, tissues. Hank smiled fleetingly, knowing how little she used such stuff. "Damn, why is it that whatever you want is always at the bottom of the bag?" Lina rummaged deeper.

The cop picked up the tissue and sniffed at it. "Smells like drugs," he hinted, rapping his fingers noisily on his gun-butt.

"Burt Wyman Ford gives you the best trade-ins, the best rebates, the best deals on ethanol conversion–" the radio chirped.

"And you say I'm the one who can't find anything," Hank tried to divert the cop's attention.

Horns began sounding behind them. The cop frowned, pulled up as tall as he could, spread his feet apart, rolled his shoulders forward and stuck his belly out in the classic pose. "C'mon, lady," he rumbled. "We don't have all day." His partner shoved the shotgun-muzzle closer.

"Neither do I!" snapped Lina, pawing deeper. "I *know* it's here somewh–Ah, there!" She came up with a brown plastic wallet that made only the thinnest pretensions to cowhide. She handed it, open, to the cop. He began pawing through it.

"*Dollar-days special: only one hundred dol-lars down, until Friday! No money down on trade-ins! Trade for ANYthing! That's right! Burt Wyman Ford–*"

Horns sounded, louder, from down the line. The cop shrugged, tossed both wallets back through the window and turned away. "Move on, please," he said.

"Right." Hank shifted into gear and rolled out slowly.

"*You* explain to Suzanne," Lina went back to whining. "You get along with her so well, and I'm always saying the wrong things, huh? Well, *you* tell her why we're late…" Her eyes tracked the cop as he and his partner moved off to deal with the cars on the crossing street. The dozen or so other cops on the line moved sluggishly in time with him. Standard operation.

As soon as they were clear of the roadblock, Lina checked the wallets.

Sure enough, the twenty-dollar bills were gone from each.

"Bastards," she sighed as she shoved Hank's wallet back into his nearest pocket. "Drugs, guns, whatever excuse—hell, all these roadblocks are good for is a little squeeze. Only the squeezes keep getting bigger."

"Hey, we're through it," Hank grinned, speeding up as much as the traffic would allow. "They bought it. They only took some cash, and we're free."

"Until we have to come back this way." Lina slid down in the seat and glowered at the windshield. "How much worse do you figure it's gonna get? I mean, Anti-Crime regs getting worse all the time… Our ancestors would've had a war if anybody'd tried this crap on them! And the Recession never letting up, just getting worse... The politicians never even mention it anymore."

"Who knows?" Hank shrugged. "We'll find a way around it. People always do, one way or another. Look, if we can make enough on trade-runs to set up the machine-shop..."

"Yeah." Lina stared bleakly out the window. "And what do we do when the inspectors come around, wanting to see a dozen gobbledygook licenses we never heard of, or the tax-boys come wanting to sock us retroactively for the last five years?"

"So we hide the shop and don't let the bastards know." Hank squinted at the windshield. "Hell, half the economy's underground, anyway. Meanwhile, we gotta finish this run. It'll put us in a lot better shape, whatever we want to do."

"Yeah." Lina brightened, looked at the street ahead and stretched her talent out again. "No roadblocks after this, anyway."

"All the way to the border?"

Lina stretched a little further. "Beyond, too. I think... They road blocked out there just yesterday, and won't hit that street again for awhile—maybe a couple weeks."

"Then it's clear sailing, Wolf-baby. Smile, already."

Lina smiled.

They rolled on, unbothered, all the way to the town border and beyond.

There was nothing much to mark the end of the city, just a small sign to one side of the road and a row of specialized stores starting within yards of the sign. Subdued lettering announced sales on fuel-alcohol, liquor, fresh meat carcasses and quarters, smoking equipment, and–there, a small sign above metal-screened storefront windows–guns.

"There it is," Lina whispered. "Don't look. Drive past."

"Uhuh." Hank moved past without changing his speed one iota. His eyes raked the street for watchers and escape-routes. "I'm going to turn at the second block," he said. "Do you see anything?"

Lina watched the store slip past, talent reaching, eyes busy. It was a delicate business maintaining the particular mental detachment necessary for her talent to work while her eyes took in details. She sagged and rubbed her forehead when they were safely past.

"We used to say it was a passing thing, It didn't mean anything, But we were wrong," sang the radio.

"There's one local cop loafing around outside, and two Federals in the gold-toned car parked in front," she detailed. "The local doesn't like the job, and hates the Feds. He's watching them more than the civilians. The Feds're sore at having to sit in a car in the sun all day. They're getting a little sloppy, but I don't think they'd miss us going in."

Hank chewed that over while he pulled into the second street on the right. "I'll drive as close as I can on the side-street," he said. "Feel around. See if there's any thugs waiting."

Lina glanced at him, caught the tentative map in his head, and searched ahead on it. "There's one trap, on the parallel street. Two kids, waiting to throw rocks. Can your windshield take it?"

"Dunno." Hank frowned at the cracks along the side of the windshield. "Another heavy enough rock could get through."

"Okay. Do a surprise lunge at the one on the left. I'll shoot the one on the right."

Hank grinned, not prettily. "I love the way you say that, Wolf-baby."

They pulled onto the parallel street. It was technically residential and had once been upper-middle-class; now the neat little buildings had been turned into boarding-houses with far more inhabitants than they'd been designed for. Windows sprouted signs announcing assorted cottage industries: tailoring, shoe-repair, car alcohol-conversion, fuel-alcohol for sale, roof-greenhouses for sale, palmistry and fortune-telling. There were dozens of kids sitting on steps and running the yards, but no sign of the ambush.

"Next street," said Lina. "About halfway up. Can you avoid it?"

Hank thought for a moment, then shook his head. "Can't turn back to where the cops could see us. They'd wonder about the same car coming back so soon. We've got to stay on this street and walk around the corner."

"Okay then." Lina rolled her window down, pulled the slingshot from under her shirt and fumbled the bag of marbles out of her pocket.

"Say when." Hank eased through the intersection, going slow.

"Almost... wait, wait..." Lina reached ahead, peering with eyes and mind, one hand loading the slingshot. There was a formerly-white car... There. "There! Now!"

Sure enough, a face and hand appeared around a bumper. A rock flew.

Hank stepped on the gas and swung the car hard left.

The rock soared over the windshield, bounced off the roof and fell harmlessly into the street. The thrower screeched and ran— back between the parked cars, across the sidewalk, through the vegetable-garden beyond. An outraged bellow and the roar of a shotgun came from the house's porch. The kid reeled, screaming, clutching his suddenly ragged backside with both hands. He hobbled off at a respectable speed, a howling example of the classic fanny-full of rock salt. An old man in shirtsleeves appeared on the porch, holding a smoking shotgun and laughing like a loon. Obviously, shotguns were still legal in this town.

The kid on the other side should have realized something was wrong when the car abruptly changed speed and direction. If he did, he hadn't the sense to change his battle-plan. He stood up between the parked cars and prepared to heave his rock—the better half of a brick—just as if the driver and passengers had been totally occupied with the attacker on the other side. Lina got him smack in the face and neck with a half-dozen slingshot marbles. His head snapped back, followed by the rest of his body, and he collapsed against the curb with a copiously bleeding face. The half-brick fell on his own chest, but he didn't seem to notice.

Neither boy could have been more than ten years old.

Hank wheeled the car back to the center of the road, still racing, and zoomed down to the end of the street. He whipped right around the corner before throwing on the brakes. From here on down they'd have to move quietly and look for parking spaces.

"Does the gun-shop have a back door?" he asked.

Lina closed her eyes and felt for it. "There is one," she said, "But it only opens from the inside. Also, there's a state-cop watching it. He knows about the other cops. Hates 'em all."

"Okay. We park on the side street and go in through the front. Got the phony IDs?"

"Yeah." Lina pulled two cheap wallets out of the box in the back, handed one to Hank and stuffed the other in her purse.

Hank spotted a parking space beside a burned-out house, and pulled into it. He and Lina both transferred money into the fake wallets. Hank reached into the glove compartment for a baseball cap, mirror sunglasses and a false moustache in a plastic envelope. "I'll bring Ralphie," he said. "You bring the box. Just like we rehearsed it. Any problems?"

Lina thought for a moment. "No." She reached over the seat-back, pulled the dress from the top of the box, hung the dress on the car's coat-hook to block the window, took out a blonde wig and slipped it on, then folded the box's flaps down tight. Last, she stuffed the slingshot back under her shirt.

They got out cautiously, casting quick covert glances around them. Hank locked the front doors. Lina pulled out the box and hefted it in her arms. Ralphie hopped out on call and stood quietly while Hank snapped his leash onto his color. They checked the doors once more, threw a last look around them and headed for the corner.

They strolled up the street, looking like any young couple out on an errand, not even glancing toward the gun-shop. Lina relied on subtle guidance from Hank's hand on her arm, concentrating on her talent, stretching into the minds of the local cop out front and the two Feds in the car. The local spared them barely a glance; this town was large enough that he didn't know everyone in it, but the couple looked as if they belonged here. The Feds gave a bored once-over, assumed that the couple was headed on down the block, and allotted the pair only scant attention. A man in an old army jacket came up the street toward them, and the Feds fixed their eyes on him. Vets were always suspect; they knew too much.

"They're busy," Lina whispered. "If this holds…"

"Just a few steps more," said Hank. The re-assurance was unnecessary—she was stretched so wide that she could feel/hear it in his mind—but the words were nice to hear, any-way. Ten steps, then five, then one.

Smoothly and swiftly, they turned and ducked in through the gunshop's door. They were through it, with the door's warning-bell tinkling and the door swinging shut, before the Feds outside realized where they'd gone. Lina felt their sudden annoyance, turning toward accusations at each other. A glance at the shop discouraged them from getting out and peering through the windows; the door was solid, and the window-display was backed with a floor-to-ceiling opaque curtain. The Feds griped, took notes and subsided, cursing; their assignment was to take note of everyone who went in, and they couldn't just march inside without a halfway reasonable excuse.

Safe... Lina and Hank kept moving, away from the windows and doors, toward the back. The place was well lighted, displaying orderly rows of locked glass cases with assorted long-guns in them and–shockingly naked to inner-city eyes–polished black and silver pistols. Lina took a deep shaky breath. It was the sight of the things that drove all this home; somehow, until this instant, she hadn't quite believed they would do it.

Hank's hand tightened a fraction on her arm, guiding and warning. *Just as we rehearsed it, Wolf-baby,* she heard/felt him thinking. *I'll steer, you bargain.* She could feel him sweating.

As he led the way toward a counter full of old-fashioned-looking revolvers, she felt the eyes. The shopkeeper, appearance indistinguishable from the salesmen, watched from dead ahead. Four salesmen at other counters glanced almost casually, watching, calculating. They were all wondering the same thing, the thoughts beating on her like heat-waves: *Cop spies? BATFink entrapment bust?* Lina raised her head a fraction, knowing what she had to prove to them. She went to the counter and set the carton on it.

The shopkeeper watched her steadily. "You can't bring that dog in here," he said.

"Please, Mister," she said quietly, not taking her eyes off his. "He's the only protection we've got right now. We don't dare set foot outside without him."

The man blinked, thinking that over.

"He's a good dog," Hank added. "You can pat him if you want. You can pat him... down."

The owner considered that phrasing, flicked a ghost of a smile, and snapped his fingers at Ralphie. "Here, boy," he said. "Nice dog. I like dogs, myself. Good dog..." He eased around the counter, offered his hand for the dog to sniff and subsequently lick, then patted Ralphie's head. He worked his hands down to the collar, felt over the worn leather, encountered the first of the hidden cords and followed it. Eventually he found the empty sling. His eyebrows rose a fraction of an inch, and Lina felt his puzzlement as he drew away.

"Ralphie's a nice dog," she explained carefully. "He fetches and… carries things."

The storeowner straightened up, gave them both a puzzled look and stepped back around the counter. He glanced thoughtfully at the carton, and his curiosity rose a notch. "So, what can I do for you?" he asked.

"We'd like… a couple of black-powder revolvers, the antique-replicas. And ammo. Four boxes."

A ripple of almost relief flickered invisibly around the store. Lina ventured a cautious half-smile.

The owner replied with a slightly wider smile, knowing, still cautious. "Hmmm, you wouldn't have a local license-to-purchase-firearms, would you?" he asked.

Lina shook her head. "Didn't know we needed one for… antiques."

"You're right." The storekeeper grinned a little wider. "No, not for black-powder firing antique replicas. No waiting-period either, nor federal records."

Lina met his look and nodded once. There it was, the god-blessed loophole; to buy, let alone carry, a modern gun the state law demanded a permit-form signed by the local police. The local cops could refuse for any reason, for no reason, and did—to everyone but certain select friends. No one that Lina or Hank knew of had that kind of clout, had a permit-to-purchase, let alone a permit-to-carry; they didn't even have a model to forge copies from.

However, there was an exception to the law: antiques, including antique replicas. Black-powder guns, black-powder ammo. Bless the loophole.

Behind his eyes, the storekeeper made the connection. "You from around here?" he asked, still cautious.

"N-no." Lina added just the right amount of tremor. "Further out."

On the surface of his mind, the thought stood out plainly: *City people. Too poor to hire guards or bribe big-time. Ducking the ban, God help them.* And then another thought, part of the automatic caution that had kept him and his in business all these long and darkening years: *Or maybe just a damn good BATFink trap! Careful...* He frowned, hunting through his experience and knowledge for some test that would meet the possible threat.

"There's... another little problem..." said Lina, reaching for the cardboard box. "We... don't have much *money*..." Just the right amount of stress to catch his attention. God bless loop-holes, indeed: accepting barter wasn't a crime, but offering it was. She opened the box, showing the homemade liqueur with the berries floating in it, the small box of jewel-fine wrenches, and at the bottom the mushrooms. Most shopkeepers these days would recognize those mushrooms.

Behind her, Lina felt Hank tensing. If the man wanted to turn them in, now he could do it. They'd deliberately made themselves vulnerable.

From the flicker in the man's eyes, and the welter of thoughts behind them, he knew it well. *Could bust you kids… you know that… 'cheating the tax-man'… you'd get it, and not me… and those are psilocybin mushrooms or I'll eat my hat.* Click, click, and the balance shifted. *They're for real.*

"We really need to, Mister," Lina added.

The man smiled. His eyes narrowed again, but this time with simple tradesman's calculation. "Nice booze," he said, examining the goods more closely than the casual words implied. "Nice tools, too. Not much, though. Not enough for two guns and four boxes." *… even with the mushrooms… street-value a couple hundred bucks, maybe…*

"There's a couple of other things," Lina almost whispered. She reached into her shirt and pulled out the first chain of jewelry. It was thin, but it was real gold, and so was the pendant on it. One advantage to living in the big city was its flourishing jewelry trade. Money to jewelry to guns: small trade, low finance, as hazardous now as the silk-trade in the Middle Ages.

The storekeeper raised both eyebrows at the sight of the chain and pendant. If he'd had any lingering doubts about where the couple really came from, they were gone now. He leaned on the counter and settled down for some serious haggling.

Ten minutes later and three chains lighter, Lina picked up the two gun-boxes and the four small boxes of ammunition. She glanced at Hank and smiled. If he had any extra dealing to do, he could handle it on his own. "Excuse me," she asked sweetly. "Is there a bathroom?"

The storekeeper pointed to a door in the back, and didn't bat an eye when she took Ralphie along with her. At her back she heard/felt Hank asking for a book about black-powder formulas and reloading techniques. She guessed that he'd trade the big gold-and-onyx ring on his left hand for it. He'd bought the ring only yesterday. Easy come, easy go.

Ralphie inspected the plumbing while Lina pulled the guns out of their boxes and stuffed them carefully in his belly-sling. If their weight bothered him, he didn't complain. He rolled his eyes and whined as the ammo-boxes were shoved in too, but accepted the burden for the price of much petting and ear-ruffling. Lina checked the sling once more, just to be sure, then gave the toilet a good flush for appearances' sake.

She was about to come out of the bathroom when the sense of warning hit. She could feel every eye in the shop turning toward the front door.

Cops coming in.

She pulled back from the door, ducked back into the toilet-stall and pulled Ralphie in with her. Hank: where was he? Reach—

The thoughts/feelings came battering at her, hard and heavy, thick as syrup. There was the cop's lazy/arrogant basking in the fear and wariness of the civilians: *Shouldn't be selling to civilians anyway never mind their squawk about some damn rights they got no rights when it's a Question Of Crime the sooner they see that the better...* There was the watchfulness and calculation of the salesmen: *Just like last time just like we planned everything covered just make nicey-face give him no excuse...* There was the cool precision of the storekeeper as he snapped off some quiet instructions, whisked the box of barter-goods down behind the counter, swept up the onyx ring and pressed a book into Hank's hands, motion swift and smooth and sure as the best stage magician's sleight-of-hand, and one sharp thought: *Give them no excuse to holler 'drugs-drugs' or they'll tear the place apart and steal everything dammit Jay have you got the vid-cameras on him?* There was Hank's tight anxiety as he asked a couple of brief questions, then strolled, painfully casual, toward the bathroom door–mentally yelling warning. The nearest salesman bravely stepped up to the intruder and asked, ever so politely: "May I help you, sir?"

In the instant's distraction Hank made it to the door, through it, and into the bathroom. "Lina!" he whispered fiercely. "Cop came in!"

"I know. Over here."

Hank ran on tiptoe to the stall. "Everything hid?"

"Yeah. Got anything hot-looking on you?"

"The book." He opened the door and held it out to her. It was a trade-size paperback, the title and covers proclaiming its damning contents. Any city cop could call it 'suspicious', 'reason for a search'–wherein handy snippets of drugs could be 'found' or money removed. And Ralphie's sling wouldn't hold anything more. Oh, damn…

"Rip off the covers," she said. "Then roll it up and stuff it in your pocket. First chance we get, we'll buy some glue and a porny, and put the porn covers on it.

"Right," Hank grinned, sweating, as he

ripped the covers off the book. "But some kind of high-class all-written porno; no pictures, or the cops'll want to look. You're a genius, Wolf-baby."

"So're you, Hank the Hunk." Lina listened/felt for the front of the store, noting how the cop was preoccupied by the big guns in the front display-case. He intended only to buy some more ammo, but enjoyed the ritual fawning too much to let it go quickly. He'd be awhile at his game. "We've got a few minutes running time," she said, "But he's right near the front door."

"It's all right." Hank grinned again, bestowing his news like a gift for her. "The shopkeep said we could use the back door, and told me how."

"Okay." Lina took a deep breath, noticed that her hands were shaking and took another. "Let's go now, then."

Holding Ralphie's leash short, they slipped out of the bathroom. Lina took care to keep the door from slamming and attracting attention, and then they strolled–quickly, quietly, smoothly as dancers, to another door in the rear wall. A big, burly salesman was quietly guarding it, but he stepped aside to let them pass. He also pressed down a switch connected to some wires leading from the door: the alarm. The door opened soundlessly, and Hank and Lina and Ralphie hurried through.

"Fast, now," Hank panted. "There's still the state-cop watching this door."

Lina only nodded. They half-walked/half-ran down the alley to the street. She could feel the watching state-cop's attention zero in on them, feel his eyes raking them over for any sign of packages, and feel him debating whether to yell a challenge at them. Quickly now, quickly, while he was still wondering: around the edge of the building and out of sight with a sense of relief so fierce it was exhausting. And how much further to the car? She suddenly couldn't remember.

"I'm tiring out, Hank," she panted. "All that reaching..."

"Just a few steps more, Wolfie. It's right there. He can't see it from where he is. We're almost home free..." Hank kept up the whispered reassurances as they half-ran to the car, holding Lina up by an arm around her shoulders. "There. There we are..." His key was out and into the lock before she reached the car. He whipped the door open, bodily shoved Lina into the car and pushed Ralphie in after her. "Get down!" he whispered, sliding in beside them and pulling the door shut. He didn't slam it, but the sound of the lock engaging was intolerably loud.

"We made it!" Lina almost sobbed, whipping

off the curly blonde wig. "Let's get out of here!"

"No. Down." Hank pulled her down in the seat and shoved Ralphie into the back. "Just in case that joker comes looking for cars that take off suddenly. Stay down. Wait. … Can you change clothes in here?" He pulled off the false moustache and sunglasses, rolled them up in the baseball cap and shoved all three into the glove compartment.

"Maybe," Lina considered. "Gimme the dress."

On the floor, Ralphie scratched himself and whined. Hank automatically reached back to pet the dog, reward for faithful service.

It took forever to change clothes, crouched down the way she was. Dress over the head, shirt off, dress yanked down, pants off, dress pulled the rest of the way down: all the while doubled over in the foot-well, trying to be as small as possible and invisible through the windows. Hank watched up and down the street, but no pedestrians came by. The few drivers went past without stopping, slowing or looking.

When Lina was finished and wearily sat up, remembering to find the slingshot and hide it in her pants on the floor, Hank squirmed out of his own shirt and pulled a fresh one, still in its plastic bag, out from under the seat. He changed quickly, keeping his eyes on the street and the darkening sky. "Okay," he whispered. "It's been nearly fifteen minutes, and there's nobody around. We can go now."

"Okay." Lina slumped on the seat, leaned her head back and let her mind go blank. It was a fuzzy-exhausted blank. "Honey," she whispered, "I'm tired to death. I'm really worn out. Can't reach worth beans. How're we gonna get home?"

Hank rubbed his forehead for a moment, and then came to a tight-lipped decision. "Sidestreets," was all he said. He reached down and started the car.

"Omigod," Lina groaned. "There'll be thugs, ambushes, all over the place."

"But no cops," said Hank, pulling out into the street. "And now we've got guns. Thugs we can deal with. Get 'em and load 'em."

"God," Lina murmured, but she could see the point. She reached over the seat for Ralphie.

By the time Hank had the car pointed northward, Lina had both guns loaded. It was as easy as practicing with the plastic model back home; only the iron weight of the guns reminded her that this time the game was real. She handed one to Hank, who stuffed it into his waistband under the shirt. The other she slipped under her skirt, into her underpants. Sure enough, it didn't show. It was heavy, though; it would probably fall out if she tried running or walking far like that. She'd have to make some kind of holster eventually.

Hank turned the car onto a secondary street and headed east. He tensed as they passed the street where the border lay; no sign marked the law's edge here, but he could feel the difference.

"So damn stupid," he muttered, for maybe the hundredth time. "Stupid laws. Stupid politicians. Cross one street and get treated like a dirty animal. City's not a jungle-hell, that'd be fair and clean by comparison. No, it's a badly run zoo—and they're the zookeepers. We're supposed to be citizens, goddammit! How'd it ever get so crazy?"

"Power corrupts," Lina sighed, likewise for the hundredth time. "It's bad everywhere, honey, just in different ways. That poor guy who runs that store… Talk about walking the thin line!"

"Yeah," Hank considered. "Cops want his business for themselves, so they don't shut him down. Sure want to keep him from selling to civilians, though. All that goddam spying… They had four cops busy watching his store, who knows how many more on that roadblock—and meanwhile the side streets grow thugs like weeds."

"It's gotta change." Lina sat up straighter, a

little re-energized by a sudden thought. "It *is* changing. We… us, people like us…" She groped for words to contain the idea. "All of us: bartering instead of buying, making our own where we can, getting fed and armed and all that without them finding out, we're like… we're the water leaking out at the seams. The tighter they squeeze, the more we leak out."

"Yeah," Hank laughed, cheering up. "Like a leaky tub! What'd they used to call it, the 'Ship of State'? Leaky tub! Hahahahaaaa!"

"Okay. Right. Pretty soon, they're gonna rule only what they got their guns pointed at, any given moment. How long can they last like that?"

"Until even the people they've got their guns pointed at say 'screw the law', and shoot back." Hank glanced out the window. "Not long, Wolf-baby. Not long."

Right then, the first stone hit the windshield. Cracks rayed outward. Hank swore, hit the gas and pulled out his new pistol.

"Omigod!" Lina howled in a spasm of guilt. She'd been mind-blanked, had felt no warning and had given him none. She yanked the gun out of her pants and rolled the window down. She didn't need her talent to see the bodies leaping out into the street ahead, swinging chains and crowbars. "There! There!" She leaned out the window, aimed as she'd practiced all these long months with toys, and pulled the trigger. A chain-wielder went down, squalling. She aimed at another figure and fired again. Hank's gun boomed from his side. The car began filling with fine yellow-gray smoke. Figures in the headlights dashed away to cover, abandoning their battle-plan; they hadn't expected this.

"Get down!" Hank snapped, still accelerating. "Some of 'em might have—"

A gunshot cracked, not one of theirs. Lina heard the bullet thump against the door, but it didn't come through. The car had the advantage of speed and some armor; maybe the attackers didn't. She edged one eye over the bottom of the window, looked back and saw a man in tattered denims aiming over the back of a parked car. She fired one second after he did. A solid thump hit the back of the Ford, but the attacker went flying, loose-limbed, onto the sidewalk. Lina ducked down as the car raced through the cleared street toward the intersection. "Hank," she gulped, "What if they hit the gas-tank?"

"They didn't, and they won't. Too much junk in the trunk to get through." Hank hit the brakes as they made the intersection, took a fast look around, saw no close oncoming traffic, and hit the gas again. They roared up the next street, and a tottering drunk fell into the gutter jumping out of their way. "Reload," Hanks said. "God knows how many more traps we're going to hit before we get home."

Lina pulled out all the expended bullets, replaced them, stuffed the empty brass back into the box and then did the same for Hank's gun. "Gauntlet," she muttered, absently patting Ralphie's head. "We're running a goddam gauntlet. How many traps, do you think?"

"Maybe every couple of blocks." Hank shrugged. "Beats dealing with cops, doesn't it?"

"Yeah," Lina sighed. "Here, at least, we can fight back." She sat up straighter on the seat and peered ahead through the cracked windshield. With her talent exhausted, she knew, this really was the safer way home.

They made six blocks before they saw the bonfire in the middle of the street ahead.

Hank pulled the car to a stop near a parking space, and gave Lina a long grim look. "If it's just a bonfire, and just local thugs, we can handle it," he said. "If it's drawn the cops, we'll have to back up now and go around. Can you try, even a little, to tell if cops are there?"

"I—It'll take time." Lina pulled a deep breath, feeling the weariness in her mind. She'd never used her talent this much, this long, in one day. It might not work at all until after she'd slept. Still, there was nothing lost by trying.

She closed her eyes, relaxed completely, gathered all the energy she could find for the reach, and blanked her mind.

Ralphie hopped into the front and curled up protectively on her feet. Hank held so still he scarcely breathed. Through the fog of weariness Lina could feel their protectiveness, their care: wordless and simple from the dog, intricate and vast from the man, but not really that different. Ah, but that helped; it buoyed her up, offered a trickle of clumsy strength.

Could I... draw from them? she wondered, through the habit-enforced calm. She'd never tried before, never thought to, but what if it were possible? Not quite understanding how she did it, Lina reached and pulled.

Yes! Yes! The trickle of strength grew to a stream. She floated on it, laughing soundlessly in triumph. It was a marvel, a joy, the crown of this whole incredible day. *Their... love... is feeding me. The old story's really true!*

She could have floated there for long minutes, but practicality called. Crooning to herself, Lina pulled the borrowed strength under her, reared up on it, and *reached.*

There. There ahead. Heat and motion and angry satisfaction. Resentment crowning into defiance. Mixed, jumbled sensations: images of fire from a dozen pairs of eyes, all dancing, dancing.

Nowhere was there the characteristic feel of cop mentality. Nowhere.

Puzzled, Lina reached further outward, questing in a widening circle. An open fire, a dancing firebug crowd, simply had to attract attention. If nobody had called the Fire Department, surely a passing cop-car must have seen the blaze. That fire had been burning for nearly half an hour so far; surely the city's Official People had to notice!

There: cop-mind, unmistakable. Two of them, in a patrol car, slowing down for a look… And then, incredibly, driving on. Clear words through the radio: "Let it burn, Chuck. Let 'em burn themselves out."

Lina reeled back against the seat, laughing wildly.

"Baby? Wolf-baby?" Hank gripped her shoulders and shook her hard in concern.

Lina was laughing and hiccupping too hard to stop fast. She shook her head and waved her hands, trying unsuccessfully to explain.

"Hey!" Hank snapped, really worried now. "City-Witch, come back!"

The grim old nickname cut through the laughter. Lina hiccupped a few more times, swallowed, and got her voice back. "It's all right, Hank the Hunk," she grinned, showing teeth. "The cops know. That's the whole joke; they know, and they're keeping away. They're not gonna do anything! They're letting it burn!"

Hank relaxed, let his hands slide off her arms, but shook his head in bewilderment. "Great for us. I mean, we can get through the thugs ourselves, but… I don't get it. Why?"

"It means they've given up!" Lina whooped. "They've pulled back! The law doesn't extend beyond the big streets anymore. One block—just one block—away from North Avenue, and they won't go there! They hope the whole block burns down, maybe for cheap Urban Renewal—but don't you see what it means?"

Hank saw. He laughed like an idiot. That set Lina off again, and they sat braying in each other's arms for a good five minutes. Ralphie gave them a puzzled but unworried look.

Finally they kissed, long and thoroughly, and took up their guns. Lina pulled the ammo-box out of Ralphie's pouch and set it openly on the seat, where they could get at it fast. Hank killed the headlights, tossed Lina a last salute, and gunned the engine.

At the last minute, Hank hit the horn. Angry fire-dancers leaped, yelling, out of the way. The Ford roared through them at highway speed, scattering flame, sparks, and burning trash like fireworks through the street. Bits of burning cardboard wind-washed off the hood all the way down the block, lighting the track behind them but doing no harm worth mentioning.

At the end of the block Hank hit the brakes, only long enough to check for crossing traffic and to turn the headlights back on. He speeded up again as they tooled on down the side street, laughing and pounding his hand on the wheel.

"Home free, Wolf-baby!" he whooped. "It ain't much; it's poor as hell and full of thugs, but it's ours—and we're damn-near free! Only what they've got their guns pointed at, and they don't point their guns at near as much as they used to. All the rest is ours! All we can fight for—and bigod, Baby, now we can fight!"

"Helluva brave new world," Lina commented, looking at the grubby buildings around her. She was grinning, nonetheless.

"Ah, Wolf-baby, I know why I love you so much. You're my partner, my good buddy, fellow-warrior as well as girlfriend. Fight by my side, guard my back while I sleep, ride shotgun on barter-runs with me—"

"Any time, Hank the Hunk!" Lina caught his fire. "Say when!"

"You and me, Wolfie! We'll survive, we'll make it, while the world falls down around us. New age comin', and it's gonna be ours. Marry me, Lina! We'll be king and queen of the 43rd Ward, even if nobody else knows it. Marry me!"

"Set the date, honey... And look out; there's another thug-trap on the next block."

"Our kids'll be wizards and warriors, free as the goddam wind..." Hank lifted his gun and peered ahead for likely targets. "Free, bigod. Free!"

They went through four more ambushes before they got back to Lina's place. The Ford looked as if it had been through a small war, which was just about true, but they parked it openly on a side street and walked to the apartment as if they owned the world.

Two days later they bought wedding rings and began planning the next barter-run.

The Hounding

The Subject's dog started yapping in the backyard as Juste strolled up to the surveillance van. If the Subject didn't notice the noise, Juste's partner did. Koffle looked wide awake now, but Juste knew that but for the dog, if he'd climbed into the van ten seconds sooner, he would have caught his partner napping.

Juste scowled at the lone monitor screen and the motionless tape-reels in the back. Damned antiques, these were. Ancient equipment, bright-eyed Wonder Boy here for a partner, and this zilch-priority stakeout: Juste's career was definitely spinning its wheels,

and all because of that messed-up Militia case. Somehow he'd have to live that down. Somehow, here and now.

"The Subject's not home." Koffle not only looked like an over-eager puppy; he whined like one, even when giving his end-of-shift report. "I know I should have followed her, but you told me yesterday to stay put, and anyway I figured she went to just where she said she would–on the phone, I mean, when the vet called this afternoon."

"Great." Juste peered out of the one-way tinted window. "You taped the call?"

"Well, of course I did–and caller-ID'ed it, too. It was the vet, sure enough, calling to say her cat died and there was nothing they could do, so she went to pick up the body. You want to hear the tape?"

"Later, later." Juste reached into the tiny fridge behind the seat, pulled out a cold cola, and studied the Subject's house, seeing nothing new. Same old slightly rundown ranch house, in the same old blue-collar neighborhood. Same clear tape over the crack in the front window, where Juste had broken the glass two days ago hoping she'd blame the neighbor-kids' ballgame and maybe fight with the neighbors. Same bulging knob on the TV cable where she'd had to patch it after Juste cut the cord last week. Same old, same old. Despite all the little nudges the Subject hadn't moved yet, hadn't done anything bustable. No change. Depressing sight. Still, it beat looking at Koffle. Wonder-Boy's baby face was a constant reminder of his own sagging jowls, and sagging career.

"Any idea how long 'til she gets back?" Juste tried.

"Maybe twenty minutes. You mean to set more bugs on her place? Not much time…" Koffle was damn-near bouncing on the seat, like a hopeful little kid.

"Nah." Juste slumped into the passenger seat and eased his already aching feet out of his shoes. "Wait 'til she gets back, see what her morale's like, then I'll think of something. I don't suppose she said anything bustable on the phone, did she?"

"Nothing. She just talked to the vet, then called a girlfriend and cried about the cat, then took off." Koffle squirmed under his too-large Department Standard suit jacket.

"Dammit, she says lots of subversive stuff, but nothing really specific, y'know? She's nobody's terrorist, and she's sure not an illegal alien, and she hasn't *done* anything but bad-mouth the government. Nothing bustable, and it's been weeks. When're they gonna pull us off this dead end and put us on something juicy? Y'know, like Militia types or Urban Farmers, or 3D Fabricators, or something like that?"

Juste ground his teeth at the reminder, and

vividly imagined Koffle as a big dumb puppy—with his own well-shod foot kicking the mutt right in its wriggling rump. "This is as juicy as it gets," he snapped. "Those Militia types, I was on 'em all last autumn, and they were a helluva lot more boring than this broad."

"Aw, how could that be? She doesn't even have anyone in the house to talk to."

"They went to work all week, came home and did family stuff, and that was it. Yap-yap family, yap-yap work, yap-yap prices and taxes—like watching the same episode of a family sitcom, over and over. I mean, all week! Only on the weekends

they'd go out in the woods and shoot a few tin cans, then sit around drinking beer and talking crap, badmouthing the government. It took us four months—four long months, Junior—to finally get something on 'em. And then it turned out that we should've waited longer and gotten more, so don't talk to me about boredom."

"So what *did* you get? And how?" The kid's enthusiasm was disgusting, and he wouldn't give up the topic.

Hell, I can give him the good part, anyway, Juste considered. "We finally pulled something together. One of 'em bought diesel fuel for his power-mower, and another got some fertilizer for his rosebushes; put 'em together, and that's bomb-making material. Then a third one videotaped a program off one of the educational-TV channels, some biography of a famous demolition company. That was enough, we thought: bomb materials, videotape about demolitions, and they'd done plenty of bitching about the government. That's Conspiracy With Intent To Make Illegal Explosives–and that was enough." *Should have been enough, dammit.*

"So what happened, huh?" Yes, Koffle was definitely bouncing on his seat.

"We busted 'em on Christmas Eve." Juste couldn't help grinning; this was the best part of the story. "Right in front of their kids and neighbors and relatives, just in time for the ten o'clock news." *That should have broken their morale, got them to snap and confess to anything. Instead they got that smart lawyer...* "Sweet bust... But it took lots of work, and it was a helluva lot more boring than this. At least this dame talks subversive crap almost every day."

"Well, yeah..." Koffle abruptly switched gears. "But then, everybody knows that gun-nuts are dangerous. All civilians with guns are dangerous, y'know." He scratched thoughtfully at the spot where his shoulder-holster rubbed his neck. "But what's with this babe? She's just a middle-aged widow who writes poetry. We've never seen any sign that she's got guns or anything."

Juste decided that he hated the kid's whining worse than his puppy-eager enthusiasm. Still, it was nice that Wonder Boy had changed the subject himself, before the Militia story got to the sour part. "Her husband might have left her something we don't know about," Juste explained. "And we know she's got some fertilizer; that's one ingredient of a bomb, right? And she's subversive, anyway–showing up on protest marches, always bitching about the laws and the government. That's enough to Indicate Intent. Now unlike the poor city cops, county-mounties and state troopies, we've got a mandate to stop crimes before they happen. God bless the new anti-crime bills: we can bust subversive types for Intent, before they actually go out and do something. Is that enough for you, Junior?"

Koffle honest-to-god scratched his head. "But if we go after everybody who buys fertilizer, might own a gun and bitches about the government, well, jeez, that's half the civilians in the country!"

Juste grinned, very wide. "Then that guarantees our jobs until we're old and gray, doesn't it?" *Just not promotions.* Koffle got it. A perfectly classic look of enlightenment spread across his chubby cheeks. "... So we're never out of work," he breathed. "We can bust damn-near anybody, look good on the TV news, get more allocations out of Congress..."

"You got it," Juste finished, leaning back. With any luck, the idea would keep Wonder Boy too busy thinking to talk. Maybe the blessed silence would last until the end of shift-overlap, when Koffle would clock out and go home. Maybe the kid would never think of the next step in the argument: that to get promoted, get up to where the good assignments and good pay and good bennies were, you had to do more than routine surveillance—and you had to bring in a good, solid, unshakeable case. You had to get good, showy, solid busts—as that Militia case should have been.

Koffle pulled up his briefcase, opened it to reveal that damned laptop computer he carried everywhere, and started punching buttons. Juste looked pointedly away, and studied the street, watching for the Subject to come home.

Koffle didn't take the hint. Of course, Koffle never took hints. "Hey-hey-hey," he chirped, peering at the laptop's screen, "I got something. Y'know all those federal crime bills they passed—"

"I know 'em all, God bless 'em," Juste growled. "They're our meal-ticket."

"Well, one of 'em's gotta have something

we can use… Yeah! How 'bout this? If some citizen badmouths a politician while holding a weapon–any weapon–that's Proof Of Intent To Commit Assassination. If Intent counts the same as really doing it, if we can catch her badmouthing some politician while she's holding a bread-knife–"

"It's not that damned simple!" Juste snapped. Fury and frustration were building up to a solid pain behind his eyes; if he didn't do something about it, he'd have a king-size headache in another few minutes. *Hell, might as well tell the rest of the story. Let him hear it from me first, get my spin on it…* "You've always got to have enough to look good to a jury, because there's always a chance the perp will hold out for a jury trial. That's what screwed up the Militia case." Koffle paused, fingers wobbling above the computer keys. "I thought you guys got 'em all to plead guilty…"

"Most of 'em." Juste glared out the window and gulped more cola, wishing that all the damned unpredictable juries in the world had just one throat, and he had his hands on it. "Most of the perps were family men. We threatened to take away their kids, do Asset Forfeiture on everything they owned, and they came around. A couple of 'em, though, were single and no parents, either, no way to squeeze 'em. They had guts enough to stand up and slug it out in court, and damned if they didn't talk the juries into letting 'em go. Now the others have grounds for appeal, so the whole case is coming apart. Now do you understand, Junior?" *That's why I got shipped off to this nowhere assignment—with you.*

"Uh, yeah." Koffle tapped the keys again. "This dame, she's got no kids and her husband's dead. He left her the house and enough to live on. So we can't threaten her house or job or family, right?"

"Right," Juste sighed, wondering how many facts he'd have to hammer into the kid's skull to make him marginally bearable. "So we sit and watch, and maybe nudge a little, and wait for something to break."

"Nudging, huh?" Koffle scratched under his holster-strap again. "Is that why you busted her window, and cut her antenna, and poisoned her cat?"

Juste did a fast double-take. How had the kid figured that out? He'd done all those things when he was safely alone, after Koffle's shift ended. Maybe Wonder Boy really could see beyond the end of his pudgy little nose.

"Yeah." Juste managed to sound nonchalant. "Putting on a little pressure. Damaging Morale, they call it. Rattle her cage, see if she'll do something stupid. Then we get it all on tape, and move in."

"Well, jeez, then maybe you shouldn't have told me to stay put yesterday," Koffle smirked. "Maybe when she went out she mailed off another poem, or letter to an editor, or something else subversive. If I'd been there, I couldn't gotten into the mail and sent it back with a real-looking rejection slip, like I've done before." He patted the printer-port on his laptop. Juste said nothing but only glared, finished off his cola and pitched the empty can in the garbage-bag under the dashboard. Damn, but the kid really did have more than two brain cells. What else was he up to?

"Yeah," Koffle chortled onward. "I mean, if we can keep any of her subversive poems from getting printed, maybe she'll give up writing 'em, huh? Or maybe she'll get mad enough to pull out that gun you think she's got and Go Postal, and then we've got 'er. Right?"

"You're wising up," Juste admitted, hating to say it.

But the kid just couldn't leave it at that. "So what're you gonna do tonight, huh? I mean, you can tell me; it isn't like I'll be here to actually see it, y'know, if anybody asks."

"You don't have any Need To Know, Junior." Juste flicked a glance at his watch. "And you just went off-shift anyway. Beat it."

Koffle pursed his lips in a disappointed little kid's pout, but he obediently opened the van's door. Of course he couldn't resist throwing a last comment over his shoulder as he slid out. "Hey, maybe I could try Damaging her Morale during my shift, y'know? Maybe I'll be the one that gets to bust her, huh? Wouldn't hurt my record any." He slammed the door and trotted off to the car before Juste could answer.

Juste watched, unblinking, until his partner got into the unmarked car and drove away. Of course Koffle's jaunt to the car set the Subject's mutt barking again, but again, nobody noticed.

Juste muttered a few automatic curses and considered his options. No way was he going to let Wonder Boy get the collar on this case. Neither could he afford to let the kid do something stupid and get caught for Provocation; Juste might come out smelling like a rose if it didn't happen on his shift, but then again he might get splashed by the fallout if the kid really blew his cover big-time. Oh no, Mama Juste's little boy wasn't going to be tarred, or upstaged, on a case as easy as this. He'd find a way to nudge the Subject into doing something interesting, something bustable, this very night. It shouldn't be that hard. She'd be good and shaky after losing her cat...

And hey, there was the dame's car, coming

right up the street.

Juste crouched a little lower in his seat, though he knew that nobody could see in at that distance through the tinted glass. His eyes darted from the camera monitor to the windows to the mirrors. There she was, parking the car, now getting out of it. She walked slowly, carrying a small bundle wrapped in a towel. That must be the dead cat. There she went, into the house. The dog was barking again, sounding different: "Hello, hello!" instead of "Alarm! Alarm!" Juste could almost understand the mutt's language after weeks of hearing it.

He turned to the monitor and switched the view to the pen-sized camera hidden in the rose-trellis near the kitchen window. Its fish-eye lens gave a wide angle of view, but distorted the image; he could barely make out what the Subject was doing.

There: she set down the bundle on a table, patted it slowly, then took off her purse and coat. Now she was going to the tool-cabinet and taking out... What? A gun?! ... No, only a pair of heavy work gloves. Then she went back to the bundle, picked it up, and walked toward the back door.

Quick now, switch to the camera in the backyard—the one hidden in the hedge. Right: the Subject was putting on the gloves, now picking up the gardening shovel, now walking over to her backyard rosebush. Yeah, she was going to bury the cat there.

And here came the mutt, big shaggy-sheepdog, tail wagging, whining to be petted, sniffing at the bundle. Now what was the woman doing?

She'd set down the shovel. Now she was kneeling beside the dog, petting him, talking to him—too quietly for the microphone to pick up, damn this lousy second-rate equipment. Anyway, the dog's tail had stopped wagging.

Hey, what was she doing now? Unwrapping the bundle? Yeah, there was the dead cat, all right. She showed it to the dog, let him sniff at it, maybe trying to make the dumb mutt understand that his cat-buddy was dead. Funny how those two had gotten along, sleeping curled up together instead of fighting like cats and dogs were supposed to. The stupid mutt probably didn't even know it was supposed to chase cats. Stupid broad, too; the mutt wouldn't care, would probably just as soon eat the damn dead cat...

Right there, inspiration struck. Juste knew exactly what he'd do to crack the Subject, make her lose control and do something bustable, get him the collar and the commen-dation and start him back up the promotion slope, Koffle be damned.

He'd dig up the buried cat—maybe trash the roots of the rosebush while he was at it—mess up the body and make it look as if the dog had done it. That would wreck the broad's Morale for certain. Perfect!

All he had to do was wait for late night, silence the dog and plant the evidence. Easy.

Juste turned back in the seat and reached for the van's mini-icebox for another drink and a snack. He calculated that he could probably sneak in a couple hours' nap, too, before midnight. The machines would let him know if anything interesting happened be- tween now and then; the sound-activated tapes were ready to roll.

He flicked a last look at the monitor and noticed that the Subject had re-wrapped the bundle and started digging the small grave under the rosebush. The dog was sitting nearby, still sniffing at the dead cat. Then the dog pointed its shaggy nose skyward and began to howl. Maybe the mutt really had figured out that his cat-buddy was dead.

"So you've got nearly as much brains as Wonder Boy," Juste muttered, leaning back in the seat. He imagined the dog protesting its innocence all the way to the pound, and chuckled.

Then it occurred to him that he hadn't brought any more hamburger, or peanut butter. Damn, was there enough left to make any more dog-bombs?

Swearing to himself, Juste rolled out of the seat and went to check the fridge. Yes, there was still a little raw burger left, and some peanut butter too, and even some cough syrup: not much, but enough for two dog-bombs. Best make them now, and then catch forty winks.

Juste duly took out the hamburger, divided it into two fist-sized balls and poked holes in their centers. Into the holes he stuffed the remains of the peanut butter. Now for the tricky part. With the wetted handle of a plastic spoon he poked holes in the two nested balls of peanut butter, then carefully poured the last of the cough syrup into the holes. The hardest part was sealing up the peanut butter balls afterward, but he'd had enough practice. Finally he patted shut the holes in the outer shells of hamburger, and happily shoved the two dog-bombs back in the fridge.

In the backyard, the damned dog was still howling.

Juste frowned briefly as he stretched out on the seat for his well-earned nap. The noise didn't really matter. If the dog didn't shut up before Juste made his foray into the backyard, the mutt would absolutely shut up once it bit down on one of the dog-bombs.

He grinned, remembering the first time he'd tried it. The operation was simple: sneak up to the gate and toss the dog-bomb over the fence. The dumb mutt, of course, sniffed at the inviting lump of hamburger and then happily chewed into it. In less than a minute the dog's mouth was smeared with the sticky peanut butter, and a dog's tongue wasn't designed for licking the stuff off his teeth. The mutt sat down to concentrate on getting his teeth clean, and of course swallowed the cough syrup. Two minutes later, one dead-to-the-world dog. Juste had gotten over the fence with no trouble, and planted that back-yard camera in record time.

Yes, it worked like a charm that time, and the time after that when he'd cut the antenna-wire, not to mention last night when he'd filled that jar-lid with antifreeze and left it under the lawn chair where the cat would find and drink it. Dumb mutt never learned. Like Koffle.

Juste's alarm-watch discreetly woke him a little after midnight. A quick check of the monitor showed nothing but darkness; the Subject had gone to bed. The dog was snooz-ing on the back porch. A look at the tape-counter showed that the woman hadn't made

any phone calls. She was probably too de-
pressed. Good.

Now, do the commando routine. Off with
the jacket, on with the black sweater over the
dark pants. Leave all ID in the jacket on the
seat: if caught, stay mute until the cops would
give him his phone call, then call the Department to come bail him out. Now check the
gun.

Finally he retrieved the dog-bombs, stuffed
them in the sweater's belly-pocket, put on his
gloves and slipped out of the van. He was
halfway over the fence when the dog woke up.
Of course the mutt came running, and barking.

Swearing quietly, Juste got his hand into
the belly-pocket and hauled out the first dog-
bomb. He lobbed it over the fence in the
direction of the yapping. There was a moment's silence, followed by earnest snuffling.

Juste waited, perched awkwardly on top of
the fence, counting the seconds. All he heard
was a brief scuffling of nails as the dog
retreated. Right: the mutt was wandering off
with a mouthful of peanut butter, preoccupied
with trying to get its teeth clean, while the
cough syrup did its work. Another thirty
seconds, and nighty-night.

Juste counted the seconds slowly, then
dropped to the other side of the fence. No
sound came from the dog.

Softly now, over to the corner where the Subject had left her shovel. Best take the rake, too; a few rake-strokes would make the excavation look like the work of doggy toe-nails. Now where in hell was that rosebush?

Right, the big shadow by the hedge. He tiptoed toward it.

Out of nowhere, something large and hairy slammed into him, knocked him down and sank dagger-sharp teeth into his right hand.

The shovel and rake fell beside him, clang-ing loudly together. Juste flinched at the racket, even as he pawed at whatever was chewing into his hand. He managed not to yell, but now he could hear that the damned thing was growling.

The dog! The damned mutt hadn't eaten the dog-bomb!

Could the dumb beast actually have figured it out: eat strange burger, and bad things happen? Could the dog really have cared that much about its dead cat-buddy?

Juste tried to grab the beast's muzzle with his free hand, and got it raked by a flailing paw. Hell, the dog was heavier than it had looked! He could feel–worse, hear–the bones in his hand crunching. He tried to get his feet under him, and only kicked the shovel and rake again. They clanked with a godawful racket.

A light came on over the back porch.

Dammit, no! He couldn't let the Subject see him!

But the damned chewing, flailing, growling dog wasn't going to let go.

Lord, Lord, was that the sound of the back door opening?

End this, fast! Juste scrabbled awkwardly with his left hand, trying to pull the silenced automatic out of its holster. He had to roll over to reach it, and the damned dog came with him. He groaned as he thought of what his chewed hand looked like. There, there, thank God, he managed to pull the pistol out.

"Burglar!" screamed a voice from the porch.

Juste couldn't help it, years of training or no. He jerked his head around to look.

There stood the Subject, silhouetted in the porch light, looking straight at him. And the light was falling right on him. Hell, she'd seen his face!

For an instant he wavered between shooting the dog and shooting the woman. Then the dog's teeth met through his hand, and he made up his mind. He angled the gun toward the thrashing mass of fur, trying to get a clear shot at its fiercely tossing head.

The after-image of the woman's silhouette stayed in his eyes for an instant, and right there he remembered something odd.

He hadn't seen the outline of her arms.

As he wrestled the gun-muzzle toward the dog's thrashing head, one fraction of his mind finished the calculation; he hadn't seen the woman's arms because they were both pointed straight at him. Now why would she point both arms—

"Burglar!" the woman screamed again.

And then came the flash and the roar—and the impact, high in the back of his neck. The pain in Juste's hand stopped. All sensation stopped. He had time to recognize what had happened, and to bitterly acknowledge that it had been a good shot at that distance, in that light.

And dammit, this proved that he'd been right! He really had pushed her into doing something reckless, and she really did have a gun after all. This proved that civilians with guns were dangerous. When the cops found his federal ID and badge, the woman would really be in trouble for shooting a cop, and a federal at that...

Except, he remembered as the darkness closed down, that he'd carefully left his ID in the van. All the cops would find on him would be his gun and the other dog-bomb.

There was nothing to connect him to the van, the equipment, and the badge in the jacket on the seat.

The cops would write this off as just another foiled robbery. The dame wouldn't serve a day's time in jail. Hell, she might wind up as a local hero, claiming that armed civilians were good for fighting off crooks.

Worse, if they ever did identify his body, somebody would be sure to raise the question of what he was doing with a dog-bomb and a silenced gun in some civilian's backyard at midnight. It might even wind up making the Department look bad.

Hell, what a legacy!

The last thing he heard was the dog barking. This time there was definitely a note of triumph in the sound.

The Testament

Of Elitu

FOR OTTER ZELL RAVENHEART

The first new moon after equinox it was, when the stranger came stumbling out of the sunset—straight toward our well, our goats, and my sister Enotu. I gripped my spear and made ready to challenge him, for I saw that the stranger was a man, yet he seemed not to see us at all. He staggered past us without a word or glance, made straight for the well, and all but fell into the water. Enotu and I exchanged amazed looks as he drank noisily.

"What lies west of here, sister?" Enotu asked me, for as huntswoman I had ranged further into the wild lands than most.

"Scrub plains, then desert, with mountains beyond," I recalled. "I have never seen nor heard of any people living there, and I know nothing of the mountains."

"Is it possible he came from beyond them?"

"If so, he made a difficult journey across the desert. Perhaps one might do it with a large enough water-skin."

I stepped forward to examine his gear, but just then he groaned loudly and collapsed at the edge of the well.

Enotu, as could be expected of a healer, at once hurried toward him. I feared he might be diseased as well as tired and thirsty, but when Enotu turned him on his back we both saw that he was wounded. A long gash ran across his face, from right cheek to left forehead, just missing his left eye, as if a bear or lion had slashed him with a single claw. The wound was not new, but neither was it well healed: a half-moon old, I thought.

Enotu washed his face carefully, paying special attention to the wound. His face was handsome and young, but wasted with pain and privation.

"Long thirsted and hungered, hard-worked and ill-healed," Enotu pronounced, "But I see no sign of disease. We can safely take him to the village."

"Drive the goats home first," said I, "And bring others to help, if any will. I don't intend to drag him that far by myself."

Enotu laughed, then whistled up the goats and drove them toward the village, leaving me alone with the man, I leaned on my spear and studied him further, seeing much that was strange. His hair and skin were lighter than was common among our folk, yet darker than the northern hunters', and the bones of his face were longer than ours. Indeed he carried a large water-bag, and it was empty, as was the food-pouch slung from his other shoulder. His shoes were crude strips of rough leather, and were worn nearly through.

Oddest of all, instead of a simple breech-clout and cape as would have been sensible in mountain and desert land, he wore a long shirt of heavy rough-woven wool that covered him from shoulders to knees. Its ragged hem suggested that it had once been even longer: a most impractical garment in this land. I poked lightly at the sole of his foot, hoping he might rouse enough to tell who he was and whence he came, but he never stirred.

Dusk was thickening when I heard the hullabaloo of Enotu returning with friends.

She had brought our brother Ena—no doubt glad to escape household duties—her friend Masu with her heaviest small net, and Masu's sturdy mother Sosua who had thought to bring long carrying-poles.

I stood back and tended to my duty of watching for wild beasts while Ena and the women exclaimed over the stranger, then made a litter of poles and net and rolled him onto it. We made a chattering procession through the twilight, all the way back to our village, where we installed the still-sleeping stranger in the healer's hut. Enotu's teacher Nala went into the hut with him, while we siblings—much to our annoyance—were obliged to go off to our mother's hut for supper and to tell her the news.

Our curiosity remained unslaked for days, since the stranger slept the sun around and was too weak for speech thereafter. Enotu, at least, got to tend him when Nala slept, while I was obliged to take Ena out with the goats. Ena, of course, could not stop bruising my ear with speculations about the stranger.

"The folk who come trading from the north are only a little paler than he," Ena chirruped. "Perhaps he's one of their folk, come early,"

"Then why did he come from the west?" said I. "Also, they wear shirts and leggings of leather, while he wore a long woven shirt. He comes of another people."

"The Sacred Folk have told us the Earth is very wide, and there are many people we have not seen, but why would they not mention neighbors to the west?"

"Perhaps the Sacred Folk know nothing of the lands west of the mountains. They admit that they cannot see everything at all times."

Ena opened his mouth in what I knew would be the beginning of more fruitless speculations about the Sacred Folk, who fascinate him, but just then the goats caught scent of a wolf and bleated alarm. Thankfully, I hurried off to hunt the wolf, and escaped from Ena's chattering.

For the next two days I used the wolf for excuse to range far out beyond goats, and out of Ena's earshot. Often I looked to the west, wondering how many days' water one should carry to reach the mountains.

On the third day, as Enotu excitedly report-ed, the stranger grew strong enough for speech. His pronunciation was strange, and not in the fashion of the northern hunters, so that it was difficult to understand him. He did not help this by being very sparing with words.

"He seems almost afraid to speak," Enotu solemnly reported at dinner. "He says only that his name is Ka'eeneh, that he came from beyond the mountains, and that he knew of no other people than his own family before he came away."

Mother frowned as she ladled her bowl full of antelope stew, "Did he say why he left them?" she asked. "Probably to find a mate," Ena offered, making the sign for erect penis, which made baby brother Ukas giggle. "He looked old enough for that."

"He did not say," Enotu answered stiffly.

Mother raised an eloquent eyebrow. Of course, a single family would have to send its males elsewhere to find mates; that was the obvious answer. "Learn if he has any sisters," she said. "If so, we might send our excess men to them."

"But how did he get that wound?" I asked. "Are there bears or lions in those mountains? And might they come down to the plains and hunt our goats?"

"I did ask," replied Enotu. "He said he didn't remember."

Mother gave her a sharp look. "Nala told me," she said, "That his wound is healing well and cleanly. She also said it was shallow–that only the skin was cut, the bone not touched. That is not such a wound as robs one of memory. Did the stranger meet your eyes when he said so?" "He would not look at me at all!" Enotu burst out. "That is the strangest thing! I was beside him when he woke, and when first he saw my face he looked amazed and smiled greatly. But then his eyes fell to my body, and he looked horrified. Then he covered his eyes with his hands and would not look at me again. Is there something shocking or repulsive about my body, Mother?"

We all stared at her, wondering what upon Earth was the matter with the stranger. Enotu had fine big breasts, I admit to my envy, with wide brown nipples and flawless smooth skin. The soft fringes of her doeskin skirt revealed the wide swell of her hips, and her round thighs gleamed in the firelight like polished oak-wood. In truth, Enotu was far more beautiful than I—and I have had a good number of mating-offers.

"The man must be mad," snorted Mother. "Ask Nala again about that head wound." She then addressed her attention firmly to her food, and everyone else had the sense to do the same.

For myself, I felt a sourceless chill, as if from an omen. In that moment I knew two things surely: first, that the stranger's madness and his wound were not as child to mother, but both children of the same unknown cause— and second, that my sister was fascinated by this man.

I liked it not.

As the days stretched toward Solstice, I kept watch upon Enotu and she kept watch over Ka'eeneh. Within the moon-quarter, he grew strong enough to rise and leave the healer's hut. Also, he no longer covered his eyes in the presence of Enotu, or Nala for that matter, but he commonly kept his eyes averted–usually toward the ground. Enotu took this as evidence that he was painfully shy. Nala, when I could catch up to her, considered that it might be shame. Shame for what, she could not say. Ka'eeneh remained reticent concerning his past. He admitted now that he had come east seeking a mate, but he would not look at Enotu as he said it. Now he claimed that he got his wound in a fall, but Nala privately doubted that.

"Unless he was grazed by a single thorn as he fell, I see not how it could have happened," she said. Then she laid a finger beside her nose and winked. "Solstice comes, and the Sacred Folk will appear. Perhaps they can coax the true story out of him."

I felt that sourceless chill again. The Sacred Folk are said to have amulets and rituals that can see into one's soul, but I never heard that the experience was pleasant. Did the stranger deserve that?

Further strangeness appeared when we first took Ka'eeneh down to the seashore to bathe.

When we cast off our shoes, skirts and clouts to run into the water, he dug his heels into the sand and stared at us with an expression of sheer horror. Then he turned right around and tried to run away. Of course he promptly struck his foot on a stone and fell flat. I hurried up and stood over him, spear ready, in case he might do something dangerous.

"What ails you?" I snapped at him, none too kindly. "Do you fear water? How then do your people wash? Or don't they?"

"Not water," he groaned "They are… *naked!*"

Given his strange way of speaking, it took me several heartbeats to understand his meaning. "'Uncovered'? Without skirts?" I puzzled. "Why should that frighten you ?"

"The *sin*," he panted. "The first *sin!*"

I did not understand that word at all. Before I could ask him its meaning, Enotu came running out of the sea, scattering water on the sand. She tried to comfort Ka'eeneh, and he wouldn't look at her.

She tried to hold him, and he shivered away from her. She asked what had frightened him, and after panting for long minutes he told her a bizarre story.

He spoke many strange words with obscure meanings, so that we had some difficulty making out the tale. Even when finished, it held so many absurd parts that Enotu thought we had heard it wrong,

Apparently Ka'eeneh's mother and her man had long ago offended some particular male Sacred Person, whose name was strange to us. This Sacred Person was so angry that he ordered the mother and her man to leave their home and go out into harsh lands, where they had to work hard to feed themselves. Worse, the Sacred Person had put a curse upon the mother which caused her great pain in child-birth. As if that were not enough, there was also some obscure curse regarding the moth-er's man, so that she would lust for him even when he behaved badly.

I looked thoughtfully at Enotu when he said this, and felt as if a cloud had shadowed the sun. I glanced up and met Nala's eyes behind Ka'eeneh's back; she too had come out of the water and heard his story, and liked it as little as I.

"Therefore," Ka'eeneh finished his strange tale, "My family took oath not to be uncovered again. Never have I seen a person uncovered before I came here. The sight reminds me of my family's offense, and their punishment."

"Just what was your family's offense?" I insisted,

Then he told us, if you please, that his mother had stolen and eaten fruit from a tree that the Sacred Person wanted for himself.

"All that, for stealing fruit?!" I could scarcely comprehend it.

"For disobedience," Ka'eeneh corrected. "He told them not to." Even Enotu looked askance at that, Nala signaled silently to me, and we walked away to where we had left our shoes and skirts. As we dressed I could hear Enotu crooning words of comfort, and Ka'eeneh apologizing.

"Did we hear the story aright?" I murmured quietly to Nala, "Or is my sister enthralled by a mad liar?"

"There is another possibility that I like even less," she whispered back. "The Sacred Folk have always behaved kindly and wisely toward us, but I have never heard of this particular one... Lao'ue, did Ka'eeneh call him? Might it be that one of the Sacred Folk is so ill-tempered as Ka'eeneh says?"

Again, I felt that cloudless chill. "If so, could he be an outcast from their tribe for that reason?"

"These waters are too deep for me to swim alone," said Nala. "I think it is time we went to see Great Grandmother."

And to that I could only agree.

Great Grandmother was not truly mother to all the families in the tribe, and neither was she extremely old; we gave her that title for courtesy, because she was very wise and because the Sacred Folk would speak privately with her. She had a very grand hut, very big and made of whole timbers, near the top of the hill where the Sacred Folk commonly appear. She was there when we arrived, painting story-pictures upon an antelope-skin. We patted the image carved into her door-yard tree and waited for her to finish.

She put away her hide and brushes and looked up at us. "You've come about the stranger, haven't you?" she said.

Of course she would know. Nala and I sat down and told her our tales. Great Grandmother filled a drinking-horn with one of her potions and sipped thoughtfully.

"We know two things, then," she said at last. "This man is afflicted with shame, and it has something to do with this unknown Sacred Person, Lao'ue. The other Sacred Folk have never mentioned him, but I will surely ask them when they come at Solstice. Bring him here to meet them." She took another long drink. "We must learn the source of his shame, but that is the very thing he will most surely conceal. You will have to trick him into reveal-ing himself,"

"What of Enotu's infatuation?" I insisted. "I fear he may harm her."

Great Grandmother chuckled, not kindly. "Infatuation cannot be discouraged," she said, "But only burnt out. You must keep in her confidence by not conflicting with her passion. Indeed, you should encourage her to disport herself with this Ka'eeneh, to take him into her hut, to beguile his secrets out of him–and to tell you everything. Do you understand?"

I understood, and liked it not. No more did Nala.

"My apprentice may be hurt," she insisted.

"No one lives long without being hurt," replied Great Grandmother. "If you remain her friend, you can comfort her afterward."

We could find no argument to that, and soon after took our leave.

A moon-quarter later, Enotu built a new hut for herself and moved Ka'eeneh into it. Now it was Mother who had misgivings, and Nala and I took pains to remind her of Great Grandmother's words. Enotu seemed happy enough, and confided freely with me. Her only complaint was that Ka'eeneh was most inept at mating, as if he had never done it before.

But soon enough, Ka'eeneh revealed more strangeness. He utterly refused to go tend goats, not with Ena nor with anyone else. Neither was he much of a hunter nor fisher.

He could gather plants well, but brought home no meat. When Mother scolded him for this he replied, with an odd defiance, that he could herd plants as we did animals–and he set out to prove it.

First he took seeds from fruit, some nuts, some yams Enotu had gathered, and then he buried them all in the ground near Enotu's hut. Then, if you please, he went out every day and pissed upon the ground where he had buried them. We all thought he was mad, but were too polite to tell him so. He went on like this for nearly half a moon, while everyone snickered behind his back and Enotu grew increasingly sullen.

Then the first sprouts showed above the ground.

Ka'eeneh all but crowed like a cock, and showed the sprouts to anyone he could catch. Nala and Sosua confirmed that these were indeed the sprouts of fruit trees, nut-bushes and yams. Enotu glowed, vindicated. I sent for Great Grandmother.

Great Grandmother duly arrived, bearing a skinful of one of her berry potions and a pouch-full of joy-leaf. She studied the sprouts, then clapped Ka'eeneh on the shoulder and proclaimed: "You're right, boy. Let's celebrate."

Mother provided the fire-pit and a young pig from our herds. Masu and Sosua came with salads, Ena brought out some mats he had woven, Nala fetched some new berry-juice, and I provided the firewood. Enotu, shining with happiness, played the drum and sang. She sat at Ka'eeneh's right hand, and Great Grandmother took care to sit to his left. I noted, as the feast progressed, that Great Grandmother took care to fill his cup with her potion. I made a point of sitting beside Enotu, and Nala likewise sat herself beside Great Grandmother.

Ka'eeneh enjoyed himself hugely. I had never seen him so relaxed, or so confident. Indeed, as Great Grandmother plied him with the potion and tossed joy-leaf on the coals nearest to him, he became even more relaxed and confident—and talkative.

"It's a skill I learned in my family's land," he explained. "The seed—the nut, the root—is the... the mother of the plant. You put it in the ground, you give it water—especially piss—you keep other plants away, and it grows. It grows! From the seed comes the tree, the shrub, all green things..." He belched, and grinned sloppily.

"You were right," Great Grandmother nudged him. "It's much like herding goats and pigs. Put them where you want them, feed them, and encourage them to breed."

"Better," Ka'eeneh snapped. "Even a fruit-tree—" Belch. "—gives you food sooner than a sheep grows to give lambs. You can dry and store fruits, nuts, roots, even herbs, longer than you can store meat. I showed them that; I proved it. I could feed our family longer and better than my brother could. You'd think that Lao'ue would be grateful..."

He stopped suddenly, his face gone fearful.

"Who was ungrateful?" Great Grandmother queried, with just the right amount of sympathetic indignation.

"Uhmm, excuse me. I must go piss." Ka'eeneh struggled to his feet and stumbled off toward his plant-patch, leaving the rest of us to look at each other.

Mother smoothly steered the conversation toward the usefulness of Ka'eeneh's invention, keeping the others occupied, while Nala and Great Grandmother conferred quietly. All I could do was flatter my sister, which needed no falsehood, since Ka'eeneh's skill was indeed wonderful.

Ka'eeneh did not return to the celebration, but tottered off to Enotu's hut and went to sleep. We found him there later, snoring soundly.

"Well," muttered Nala as I walked her home, "That was precious little repayment for all of Great Grandmother's work."

"At least we learned," I considered, "That this Sacred Person is ungrateful as well as bad-tempered."

"Also that there was some competition between himself and his brother. Hmm, the
Solstice cannot come too soon to suit me."

The next strange news came from Enotu
herself. She came stamping back to Mother's
hut, eyes streaming angry tears, to report that
Ka'eeneh had been most shockingly rude to
her.

"He refused to sweep out the hut," she
wailed, "Refused outright, saying that such
work was for women and not him. He ordered
me to do it—commanded, as if he were my
mother's-brother instead of just my man.
Mother, shall I throw him out?"

"No, bide here," Mother rumbled, getting to
her feet. "I'll see to this."

I noted that she picked up her big leather
tanning-flail, and made haste to follow her. I
knew how Mother could wield that flail, and I
wanted to see this.

Mother was once a huntswoman, and she
can move quietly when she wants to. Almost
soundlessly, for all her bulk, she came up on
Ka'eeneh as if she were a stalking lioness. He
was in the plant-patch, bending over to tend
his sprouts—presenting a perfect target. He
knew nothing of her approach until her flail

gave him a resounding WHACK across both buttocks.

He screeched like a hawk, jumped a good body-length and came down half-turned, clutching his rump.

Mother promptly gave him another WHACK across both thighs–from which his coarse shirt did not protect him–and followed that with a hailstorm of blows almost too rapid to be seen.

Ka'eeneh screeched again, and took off running. Mother followed, fast as a charging aurochs cow, still raining blows on him. I followed, slowed only by my helpless laughter.

Through the whole village we ran, entertaining all the neighbors, and out to the field where Ena and Ukas were tending the goats. Ena, seeing the merry chase, rightly concluded that Ka'eeneh had done something to deserve it. He ran in front of Ka'eeneh and made a smart jab with his herding staff.

Ka'eeneh went down all asprawl. Mother, being right behind, fell on top of him. Ukas hopped up and down, shrieking with excitement, and the goats all bleated in bewilderment.

It took several moments to straighten out the jolly tangle, with Ka'eeneh pleading to know what *sin*–that word again–he had committed. Mother, barely restraining her flail, promptly told him. Ka'eeneh, if you please, had the temerity to look confused and even indignant.

"But- but I am her-" He used a strange word: 'house-bound' was all that I could make of it. "It is right that I should (unknown) over her, as my (unknown) does to my mother. Lao'ue said so!"

Mother caught enough of the sense of that to be furious. "I part my buttocks and fart at your bad-tempered Lao'ue!" she roared. "He's far away, and no one here has ever seen or heard of him. Here, you fool boy, you live by the customs that our Sacred Folk give us-or else, by Moon's horns, I'll whip you all the way back to your mother's hut! Do you hear me, boy?"

Ka'eeneh, rubbing his sore buttocks, allowed that he did.

Mother took him by the collar of his ragged shirt and marched him back the way we had come, still shaking her flail, lecturing him all the way. "Don't you forget it again," I heard her bellowing. "And while you're at it, wash more often; you stink like a bearded he-goat. And burn that ragged shirt; it's falling apart, and probably full of lice. Get some sensible clothes. And another thing-"

I stayed behind with Ena until I had laughed myself out. I also congratulated my brother on his fine jab with the staff. Ena grinned, and admitted that he'd been practicing a bit. Ukas volunteered the knowledge that Ena wanted a sling to drive away wolves, and Ena blushed. I promised to make him a sling myself, and train him into the bargain.

For a moon-quarter thereafter Ka'eeneh sulked and moped about the village, telling his tale of mistreatment to whoever would listen to him, trying to win pity. None of the women gave him any, so he tried with the men. Sosua's brother reported that Ka'eeneh had wailed his complaints at a feast in the un-mated-men's house, and was roundly laughed out of the hut.

What Nala and I did learn from these tales was some sense of the meaning of Ka'eeneh's strange words. 'House-bond' meant a man who bullied his mate. 'Rule' meant to command and bully. 'Father' was the difficult one; it meant that a man had some strange relationship to his woman's children, whereby he could bully and command and even punish them. Sosua's brother was especially annoyed over that; clearly, this concept took prerogatives away from the mother's brother, opposing the ties of blood.

And all of this, like Ka'eeneh's odd fear of uncovered bodies, was traced back to the commands of the mysterious Sacred Person,

Lao'ue.

"I like it not," said Great Grandmother, when Nala and I related this to her. "It suggests some conflict among the Sacred Folk, which bodes no good for us. I must speak to them at length, come Solstice...and perhaps consider what not to tell them, also."

That was something no one had thought before, and it worried us.

As we walked back to the village Nala told me of yet another worry. "Ka'eeneh was not ashamed of his family's strange customs," she said, "Yet he seems of two minds about this Lao'ue, and he still conceals some great shame about something. We have not yet discovered his mystery."

"It is not, I think, only an inheritance from his family," I considered. "I think it is related to his skill with plants, for he tends them with an almost defiant pride."

"For a huntswoman," Nala smiled, "You have grown expert in hunting the motives of men."

For the next moon Ka'eeneh behaved himself, being no worse than sullen with Enotu, spending most of his time determinedly tending his plant-patch—which truly did thrive. We took care to compliment him on his diligence and his clever invention, for indeed he did deserve praise for that, even if we had not as yet seen any fruit from his plants.

Also, he did agree to burn his ragged shirt, wash daily in the sea and wear sensible garments. Still, he always bathed alone or with only Enotu, always avoided looking straight at people, and always wore his cloak outside the hut—even as the air heated and the sun climbed toward Solstice. His wound healed cleanly, leaving only a narrow scar. He cut many saplings and withies, and made a sturdy fence all around his plant-patch to keep out wandering animals. He still would not herd beasts, and was totally useless at hunting, but I patiently taught him to set snares and he did manage to catch enough small game to fill the pot. He also became competent enough at net-fishing to help Enotu bring in fish and crabs. All seemed well with him, at last. Surely Enotu had no further complaints.

Then one morning my sister came trotting up to Mother's hut, smiling so wide I feared it would split her face, and announced that she was pregnant. Of course we all rejoiced, and Mother happily planned a feast for the next day. Ena and Ukas wanted to kill and cook the fattest goat in the herd for the occasion, but Mother made them see sense and only kill one of the yearling bucks. I hurried off to pick flowers for wreaths and necklaces, delighted that my sister was proven fertile and our family would continue.

All our friends were invited, including Nala, who took care to invite Great Grandmother. Great Grandmother arrived early, bringing the gift of a bone flute for Enotu, and bearing another skinful of berry-potion. During the feast, she took care to ply Ka'eeneh with her drink. Sure as sunrise, he became relaxed and merry as the feast progressed. Then he became oddly smug. Then—at about the fifth horn-full of potion—he became strangely possessive about Enotu's child.

"My son," he called it, as if he had some omen about the child's sex, and as if he were its mother's-brother—or even the mother himself.

Ukas looked indignant, Ena embarrassed, and Great Grandmother sniffed at her potion with puzzlement. Mother tried to change the subject. Nala and I traded looks.

"The child could as easily be a daughter," Enotu tried to cover for him. "Let us think of good names for a daughter, too."

"Right, good name for my daughter." Ka'eeneh sounded noticeably less enthusiastic. "What's a good combination of 'Enotu' and 'Ka'eeneh'?"

For a moment, no one could think of any-thing to say. Ena blushed furiously, and I could see him groping for polite words.

"How does 'Enatu' sound?" Great Grandmother spoke up. "It's a good combination. Let us drink to it."

Ka'eeneh frowned slightly, but accepted the potion. "Not enough of my name in it," he mumbled around the spout of the skin-bag. "But if it's only a girl... suppose it won' matter..."

Everyone else was very quiet, staring. Mother signaled for the others to play music, quickly. Ukas dutifully pounded on the drum, and Enotu thought to take up her new flute and play. Sosua, always quick with words, promptly invented a simple song to go along with Enotu's playing. Everyone else clapped along, as if they were seriously listening to the music.

Great Grandmother leaned closer to Ka'eeneh. "Eh, would you be disappointed if Enotu had a daughter?" she nudged.

"Better than nothing," Ka'eeneh slurred. "Could trade her, I suppose. But a man needs sons..."

"*Your* sons?" she clarified.

"Mine." Ka'eeneh belched. "Know it's mine. Enotu wouldn't (unintelligible) me. I keep her too busy. Heh! ...Pour me some more."

Great Grandmother obliged. "Just how is the child yours? I don't understand."

"Man makes child, of course." Ka'eeneh hic-cupped impatiently. "My father told me. Plants seed. Like in my plant-patch. Woman... Earth... grows it. Din' you know?"

Mother threw him an utterly filthy look. Enotu badly fouled a note on her flute. Sosua choked briefly on the words of her song. Ena almost missed a beat on his drum. Everyone else smothered explosive whoops and giggles. Ka'eeneh noticed none of it.

"We know," Great Grandmother said careful-ly, "That the man opens the womb. A woman who never mates will never have children. But do you say the man makes the child? The woman has nothing to do with it?"

Half the women around the campfire all but smothered themselves keeping quiet. "Man plants seed," Ka'eeneh blearily insisted. "Wom-an grows it. My seed, my child." He belched again,

Great Grandmother gave him a poisonously sweet smile, one I recognized. "But isn't it so, as you've said before," she purred, "That a seed can grow only its own kind? Nuts grow nut-bushes, fruit-seed grows fruit-trees, and all the rest?" Ka'eeneh nodded earnestly, taking a sloppy drink. "Why, then," she pounced, "How is it that a 'man's seed' can grow female children?"

Ka'eeneh blinked, coughed, put down his

drinking horn and thought about that. He thought long, with no answer.

In the stretching silence, Ukas giggled. Then Ena laughed. Then all the women joined in.

"But-but-" Ka'eeneh sputtered as the laughter grew, "Lao'ue told us, told my father-"

"Oh? What means that word?" Great Grandmother asked innocently.

"'Father'-male mother...uh, man who plants child-seed..." He shook his head in exasperation, got up and stumbled off into the darkness.

We watched him go, then looked at each other. Ena had the sense to take up the drum and start pounding it again, covering our subsequent words. Nala and I looked at each other, then at Great Grandmother.

"I suppose," Great Grandmother murmured, "That his mother bred no daughters."

That started everyone laughing again, and soon they went back to singing, much relieved.

All save Nala, Great Grandmother and myself. We had much to think upon.

To Ka'eeneh's credit, he did not repeat his stupid tale when he was sober again. He behaved himself and tended his plant-patch, which flourished, and he promised that we would see food from it by autumn Equinox.

But now Solstice drew near, and our tribe prepared for the festival. Ka'eeneh was at first bewildered by all the activity, as if the Sacred Folk never visited his home at Solstice. He spoke to Enotu about it, and came away silent and thoughtful.

On Solstice morning we all rose before dawn, put on our wreaths and flower necklaces and prettiest garments, filled the animal-pens with enough cut grass to last them all day, and made our procession to the Sacred Hill.

We gathered by families of course, eldest first. Mother led our family, her daughters next, then the men folk. I noted that Ka'eeneh hung back, trailing after Ukas, and I determined to keep an eye on him. Fortunately, Nala's family joined the procession right behind us. I caught Nala's eye and signaled her to watch Ka'eeneh for me, which she acknowledged with a nod and a keen look. He didn't see it.

Up the Sacred Hill we went, torches dimming against the growing sunlight. Great Grandmother, in her beautiful feathered cape, stood waiting for us just inside the ring of stones. We took our places, family by family, between the stones, and sat down to wait. Ukas had the honor of fetching Great Grandmother's stool for her, and as she sat so did we all. The food and water-skins came out, and we chatted happily as we waited for the Sacred Folk to arrive.

I noted Nala signaling to me. Using the excuse of my huntswoman's duty, I took my spear and got up, and paced around the outside of the circle to where Nala was sitting.

"What ails Enotu's man?" she said quietly over her shoulder. "He seems less than happy to await the Sacred Folk."

"If he has never met any but this Lao'ue, he may not think well of them," I considered. "Has Enotu said further to you than she has to me?"

"She mentioned one thing," Nala replied. "She said that her man did not seem to think that the Sacred Folk were real—at least, not in the same sense that his Lao'ue is. She questioned further, but could get no more answers from him."

"Then today's events may surprise him," said I. "Let us watch."

I stepped a pace away from the stones then, and took a place where I could observe Ka'eeneh and see his face. At the moment, he seemed only bored.

Then Masu, who has the best eyesight, shouted and pointed toward the sky. Everyone looked there, and in a moment all of us could see the boat of the Sacred Folk—small as a gnat in the sky, but growing larger, closer, by the heartbeat. We all stood up and cheered.

I glanced quickly at Ka'eeneh, and saw that he was the last to rise to his feet. His face was as still as a mask.

Lower and larger came the boat, like a great shining yellow coracle with a domed lid on it, humming softly as a swarm of drowsy bees. We shouted and sang our welcomes and tossed flowers as it settled, light as a thistle-down, near the center of the circle of stones.

I glanced again at Ka'eeneh, and saw him edging slowly toward the back of the crowd. His face was still motionless, but I saw sweat gleam on his cheeks.

The humming faded away, and the boat's doorway opened like a flower. The soft light behind it brightened, and the Sacred Folk came out.

At first they wore their Forms of Light: featureless human shapes that glowed almost too brightly to see. When all three of them had stepped away from the boat and its door had closed again, they changed into their Totem-Forms: the lioness, the stag, and the small fruit-tree with a woman's face. Everyone cheered again and cast more flowers, delighted with the display. Finally the Sacred Folk took the shapes of two tall women and a man, all dressed in shining-white shirts and leggings and wonderfully soft shoes, with hair and eyes the color of the sun.

Now everyone made the arm-gesture of respect, shifted into a long line and began to shuffle forward in order. Great Grandmother was first to greet them, reciting the words of welcome while the Sacred Folk held up their various amulets to bless her. She stepped back to her stool, and the line of people moved forward.

That was when I thought to glance at Ka'eeneh again, and saw him not. The grass was bent in spots resembling footprints, from behind the stone in a line leading down the hill. I hefted my spear and followed swiftly after.

At the edge of the acacia-grove I caught up to him. Doubtless thinking himself safe under the screen of the trees, he slowed down a little–enough that a thrown spear could reach him. I confess that I hesitated for a heartbeat before reversing the spear.

The cast was strong and clean, and the butt of the spear caught him smartly between the shoulder-blades. By the time he got back his breath and rolled over, I had the spear again and pointed the head directly at his throat. His eyes grew wide when he saw it, and he turned as still as a stone.

"Enough lies, sister's man," I said, quietly but very firmly. "Tell me why you run from the Sacred Folk."

"They're real," he panted. "I thought they might be only common folk, dressed in play-garments to fool others... Lao'ue never told us there were any others like him! But see: they change shapes–like him. They are his folk, in truth."

His face hardened like clay in a fire.

"And they are not your friends, mate's sister! Be sure, they have their uses for you; but see how well they love you when you try to please them–and guess wrong."

I saw that his secret was very near the surface, could I but cast my net true and catch it.

"How say you so?" I frowned. "The Sacred Folk have always given us gifts and knowledge, and asked no more of us than to hear all our news and watch our celebration. It is said that they first taught our long-grandmothers the secret of fire-making, and net-tying, and basket-weaving, and herding animals–and then they rejoiced to see how we elaborated upon what they taught us. Hmm, I think they would be pleased to learn your invention of herding plants."

Ka'eeneh burst into laughter, laughed so hard that for a moment I thought he might have fallen into a fit. "Lao'ue was not!" he whooped. "He made it clear that he preferred blood-sacrifice! First from the herd-beasts, and then... Oh, Earth, Sun and Moon, where he meant it to go next!"

"'Blood... sacrifice'? Did I hear you right?" It was important to understand his every word now. "Do you mean, giving the inedible portions of our food beasts to Earth?"

"No, I mean the blood—the life—to him. Through his fire." Ka'eeneh wiped his eyes and breathed more slowly. "He wants lives. Can't you understand? He thirsts for blood!"

"He seems much different from our Sacred Folk," I said carefully. "Tell me of him."

"Earth, Sun and Moon," Ka'eeneh groaned, "Lao'ue demands obedience, and is cruel, and is very generous with curses."

I recalled the story of Ka'eeneh's family, and the breeze of inspiration blew through me. "He cursed your mother for stealing fruit, you said. Now tell me; what curse did he throw at *you*, and why?"

Ka'eeneh howled as if my spear-point had struck him, and clawed at the healed wound on his face. I reversed the spear and poked him with the butt, hard enough to knock him breathless for a moment. "Tell me!" I shouted in his face.

He slumped on the ground as if his bones had turned to melted fat. "Yes," he muttered, "Best you hear it first from me. I had an elder brother once..."

I said not a word, but kept the spear ready

if further prodding were needed. "My father adored him... Ah, you don't believe in fathers. No matter. My... mother's man ruled the family, and he loved my brother far more than me. Mother loved me best, but that mattered little in the end.

"Lao'ue spoke only with my father, not with the rest of us. He instructed my father on herding, weaving, other skills we needed to live, and then Father would tell my mother, or my brother, what was needed. He spoke little to me. Most interesting it was to see my father shout and slap and bully the rest of us, yet bow and whine in fear to Lao'ue. My mother would never crawl and whine, no matter how much my father beat her."

"He ...*beat* your mother?!" I felt my jaw gaping, then silenced myself and waited for the rest of the tale.

Ka'eeneh seemed not to have heard me. "Mother remembered the useful plants from the good days in the better land, and she taught them to me. I was glad to learn, glad to get away from the hut... and from my father and brother. My brother tried to copy Father, you see; he could not bully Mother, so he played at it with me. Do you wonder I avoided him?"

I only gestured "No, go on".

"Watching the plants, I saw how they flowered—and then the flowers fell away and left the seed-case. Being curious, I watched what happened to the seeds. Did you know that squirrels and even beetles will dig holes in the Earth and bury seeds there? I saw it. Perhaps I was the first person ever to see it. I marked a squirrel's hoards, once. The squirrel had many hoards, and did not empty all of them before the hard season ended and the rains came. I saw what became of the hoards he missed."

Again, inspiration breathed. "They sprouted new plants? Like the seeds in your plant-patch?"

"Yes!" Ka'eeneh struck the ground with his fist. "I saw! The seed is—is mother to the plant! I learned this, by myself, not told by Lao'ue or my father or anyone! I did that."

"Did you tell anyone?" I asked.

"Only Mother. It was our secret. She helped me gather seeds and bury them. We learned, from watching, that they must have water. We learned to clear ground and put the seeds where we wanted them, to help them grow, to make food that would not wander away nor be eaten by wolves. For the first time, we had abundant food. Father noticed, and was even grateful. I think..." Ka'eeneh hitched his shoulders, as if expecting a blow. "I suspect he bragged of it to Lao'ue."

"And this Sacred Person was not pleased?" I

could scarcely believe this. "Did he tell your...
'father' to beat you, too?"

"Nothing so simple." Ka'eeneh grimaced.
"Instead, when we grew old enough to seek
mates, my father came home one day after
speaking with Lao'ue and told us to prepare
for a great honor. He told us to fetch the best
of our work, of our making, bring it to the
sacred place and offer it to Lao'ue. Then, if
the Sacred One accepted the gift, he would
speak directly to us."

I wondered what sort of person, sacred or
not, must be bribed even to speak to people.

"My brother took a lamb–the biggest he
could easily carry. I remember how forlornly
the mother sheep bleated as he carried her
child away... For my gift, I picked the best
fruits and nuts I could find. Mother gave me a
basket to carry them. Then we all went out to
the sacred place, even my mother trailing
behind, although she told me she had no wish
to speak with Lao'ue ever again..."

I did not doubt it. Had anyone done to me
as this Lao'ue had done to her, I should not
speak to them either.

"Father had made a great hut for the Sacred One, on top of a high hill. It was much
bigger and finer than our hut, and had sheepskin curtains hung over the doorway. I thought
of how many sleeping-mats we could have

made from all those sheepskins...

"In the dooryard stood a platform of flat stones, chinked and smoothed with clay. The top was greasy and scorched, as if much had been burned there. Father stopped before it, with us behind him, and began a long speech to the Sacred one—full of amazing flattery, speaking of us as if we were no more than worms. My basket grew heavy in my arms as we waited for him to finish, and my brother set the lamb down. He kept a tight hold on its ear, which made it bleat.

"Then the curtains parted slightly, just a finger's width, and I saw a light flash there. Father stopped his speech and hastily waved us forward, whispering at us to place our gifts on the platform.

"I set my basket there and waited, with my eyes politely cast down. My brother heaved the lamb onto the platform, but it wouldn't stay. It bleated and struggled, trying to get to its feet and escape. So my brother...

"I saw this, and could not believe it even as I watched.

"My brother grew angry at the lamb, so... he took out his knife and cut the little creature's throat. Its last bleat was horrible..."

"He did not think to stun it, strike it on the head?" I couldn't help but ask. "Hadn't he thought to bring cords and bind it? How did he know that the Sacred Person wanted fresh meat, instead of a live herd-beast?"

"You don't understand," Ka'eeneh sighed. "He killed it simply because it angered him. I knew that, even as I stood and watched the blood spill all over the platform. I wondered then what he would do if ever he became angry with me, or with my mother."

I shuddered, wondering if the family's curse included madness.

"As I stood, staring, the curtains parted a finger's width more—and I saw something dark and glittering, something like your Sacred Folk's amulets, sticking out of it. Then came a sudden humming, like a bee close to my ear. Then..." He shivered. "Fire leaped up on the stone platform. It flamed upon the body of the lamb, so that the hair crisped and the blood sizzled and...and in a few heartbeats the whole lamb had burned to ashes and soot and black grease.

"And yet, my basket of fruit—not an arm-length away—was not so much as scorched. I never before or after saw a fire do that."

"No common fire," I agreed, wondering if the bee-humming sound had been the same as I had heard from the Sacred Folk's boat.

"The rest of us did nothing but stare," Ka'eeneh went on, "But my father gave a shout of joy, and capered about beside the platform.

'He accepts!' he cried. 'The Sacred One accepts the gift!' Then I knew why the top of the stone platform was dark with soot and grease, and I wondered what my father had set there before. I wondered if plants or baskets would leave the same marks when they burned."

"I doubt it," I said. "Plants usually have not much grease in them."

"When I thought to look at the curtains again, they were no longer parted and I could see nothing shining between them—but a voice came out from behind the curtains, loud and deep and echoing, a fearful thing to hear. 'Let Ahb'el enter into my presence', it said, and nothing more. Father capered again, and shoved my brother toward the hut. I remember how flushed and eager they both looked. There was darkness behind the curtains, and my brother stumbled a little on the way in.

"When the curtains fell closed behind them, I watched after them for a moment. Then I looked at my forgotten basket of fruit on the platform. Then I looked at my mother—and saw her face streaked with tears, her teeth bared in rage and sorrow. I picked up the basket and took it to her. 'Here, Mother,' I said. 'If the Sacred One doesn't want them, we will eat them all ourselves'. She wept and hugged me."

"Indeed," I murmured, remembering that his mother had been punished for stealing fruit, which now that Sacred Person didn't want.

"So we walked home together, and sat down and ate every bit of the fruit and nuts, and then set the roots on the fire to roast. While the roots were cooking, my father and brother came in. Brother was smiling and looked tired. Father seemed annoyed, and demanded of my mother why we had left the sacred place. She replied that the Sacred One had no further use for us, so we had come home to make dinner, and she pointed to the yams in the fire. Father had no answer for that, so he and my brother sat down to wait for the yams."

"I don't suppose they had brought any food back with them," I noted.

"Oh, no." Ka'eeneh smiled thinly. "My brother made some joke about my roots having to content themselves with common fire. I replied that this fire, at least, would leave something for us to eat. He reached out and smacked me, as he had never before dared to do in my father's presence. Father did nothing, seemed not to notice. Mother scolded my brother for the blow, to which he replied loftily that he didn't have to listen to her anymore because now he was a man and the Sacred One spoke to him. I saw, though I hope Mother did not, the fleeting look of nasty pride on my father's face. In that moment, I despised him."

"So would I," I said, wondering what sort of mother this 'father' had, that she would let him grow up with such a character.

"But Mother sat up and said that, man or no, he was still her son and she would beat him if he misbehaved. Then Father bellowed that for every blow she gave his son, he would give her two. 'So be it!' she shouted. 'Then I'll strike him twice for every blow he gives his brother!' And she raised her hand to do just that, but my brother bawled and ran and hid behind Father, and Father bellowed, and I got up and ran out of the hut before it could come to any more blows. By the time the shouting stopped and I dared come back into the hut, the yams were burnt and nobody got much to eat from them."

"I can imagine," I couldn't help smiling. I hoped the two bullying men had gone to bed with empty bellies.

"The very next day came ruin," Ka'eeneh's voice sank low. "I was tending my plant-patch when my brother came and ordered me to leave it, to come with him and tend the sheep. Knowing that the plants needed no further help for the day, I humbly went with him. He ordered me to chase sheep for awhile, then sat down to eat a bird he'd snared that morning. It looked half raw, and I wondered if he'd cooked it himself. As he ate, he boasted...

"He told me what the Sacred One had told him, and it chilled me through the heat of noonday. Lao'ue wanted blood, he said: blood and lives, and strong men to fetch these things for him. There were other people in the world, he said: folk who knew not Lao'ue and were therefore weak and foolish, and so we could rule over them. We would go to them to fetch mates, and also take sheep and anything else we wished, so we would never need to do any other labor. If we proved we could readily shed blood, he said, no one could refuse us anything."

I could not believe I was hearing this, "Robbers? The Sacred Person wanted you to become robbers?!"

"And worse." Ka'eeneh fixed his eyes on my spear-point. "He said that we could kill any who refused to do as we said–that their spilled blood would be a gift to Lao'ue."

There was silence for a long time as we both thought about that.

"He wanted me to help him," Ka'eeneh resumed. "He said I must learn to kill sheep, and then come hunting with him, so I could also learn to hunt these other people. If I did this, he said, Lao'ue would be pleased and might be willing to speak to me."

"Why should you wish to?!" I burst out.

"That is exactly what I thought, but dared

not say it." Ka'eeneh picked up a small stone and tossed it away. "I remembered him killing the lamb, simply because he was angry, and knew that this was why the Sacred One loved him. I did not want such love as that."

"Wise of you!"

"But I also knew that if I would not do as my brother said, would not rob nor kill folk, that he would become... angry with me. He was filled with his dreams of blood and ease and robbery, and would not see his hopes marred. I would mar them, sooner or later."

"And sooner or later," I realized, "He would grow angry at your mother."

"Yes." Ka'eeneh gazed down at his empty hands. "I saw that I had no choice. I even wondered if this was just what Lao'ue had intended. He wanted me to shed men's blood. He wanted blood from our family. Mine or my brother's. Did he care whose blood he got? Was his message of slaughter meant for my brother or for me?"

"He made your brother into a rabid wolf," I realized. Such creatures must be killed, swiftly, from a safe distance, or many folk would die terribly. Our Sacred Folk had taught us that, long ago.

"So, the next morning, I took up my best knife and my axe. Then I woke my brother and said to him: 'Let's go hunting today. I am eager to learn whatever I must to gain Lao'ue's favor'. I remember how he smiled then, and how swiftly he agreed. He led me out toward the hills where we found many antelope tracks, and speculated on where the beasts had gone. I said: 'Let us see if there are any near the sacred hill. It will be a short journey, then, to take any beast we catch up to Lao'ue's house and give it to him.' My brother laughed, saying that I hoped to win favor as he had done, and I claimed that he was right.

"Still laughing, he led me up the hill. We found no tracks, so I said: 'Let us go to Lao'ue's hut. Then you can tell him what we plan, and ask him where the nearest game may be, for surely the Sacred One will know.' He thought that a good plan also, and perhaps was eager to speak to Lao'ue again, so he led the way up to the hut and the stone platform before it. There he hesitated, seeing no sign that the Sacred One was at home, and wondered how to summon him. 'We should have brought a sacrifice,' he said.

"'We have brought a sacrifice,' I said. Then I struck him on the head with my axe."

Why, I wondered, hadn't I guessed it before?

"He fell against the stone platform, splashing his blood on it." Ka'eeneh spoke through grinding teeth, his hands clenched together. "I heaved his body onto the platform and cut his throat, just as he had done with the lamb. Then I called out: 'Lao'ue, behold: I have learned your lesson. Here is man's blood for you. Now, as you will, I shall take my brother's place. Do you accept the gift?'

"Then I waited for an answer. And waited, and waited, while my brother's blood spread over the platform and dripped down its sides, and still there was no motion nor answer from the hut.

"Perhaps the Sacred One was afraid," I considered.

Ka'eeneh gave that bitter laugh again. "No, nothing so marvelous, as I soon learned. I grew tired and angry with waiting, so I thrust the curtains aside and went into the hut without invitation."

"What did you find there?"

"More and less than I expected. No one was there. Lao'ue was gone, busy with who knows what tasks. All I found was a large rug of sheepskins, a mound of sheepskin pillows—far finer than anything Father had ever made for us—and several tall benches filled with strange amulets."

"The amulets of the Sacred Folk are usually strange..."

"They were hard to see, for there was no light save what came through the parted curtains. They were too large to wear or carry easily, and seemed to be made of very shiny polished stones. Red lights, like embers, flickered on them. I had no use for the things, and knew not what they might do, so I left them and came away. Flies were already gathering for my brother's blood. I left him on the platform and went back to my plant-patch."

"What happened when Lao'ue came home?"

"He came to me, first. I was startled to see a man-shaped form of light walking hurriedly through my plant-patch. I knew at once who it had to be, so I bent down as I had seen Father do and thanked him greatly for revealing his presence to me. I believed, for that moment, that he had accepted my sacrifice and now would favor me as he had my brother. Instead, he cut short my words with an impatient gesture, and snapped: 'Where is your brother Ahb'el?'"

"So he didn't know?"

"Just so. In that moment I understood that Lao'ue did not know nor see all things. I also understood that he, like my father, cared nothing for me but only for what I might do to please him. Just to be certain, I asked: 'Am I to be my brother's herdsman? And herdsman of other folk also? Shall I steal their fleece and milk and offer up their blood to you? Is that what you wish from me?'"

"And what did he reply?"

"He only said: 'I see that Ahb'el has spoken to you. Where is he?' My hope sank then, for I saw that he would always prefer my brother and hold me no more than second-best, ever. 'He awaits at your sacred place,' I said. 'There I left you the sacrifice you asked for.' He looked at me for a moment, then made the air to shimmer between us and hum like bees, and then he was gone.

"I went back to tending my plants. I worked another hour there, filling my basket, and then saw Mother come out of the hut and walk toward me, carrying a full water skin. I knew that she, at least, would be pleased with the fruit I'd gathered.

"Then the air shimmered again, and Lao'ue appeared before me. He was still a form of light, but no longer so dignified; now he bounced up and down on his feet, like a small child squalling in a tantrum. His voice also was ragged and shrieking.

"'I found your sacrifice!' he howled. 'His blood was all over my altar, and stinking up from the ground! What made you do such a thing?!'

"Behind him, I saw my mother halt and turn pale. She understood; she knew everything.

"'You yourself showed me that you prefer

blood-sacrifice,' I said to him, 'And my brother told me to spill the blood of men.'

"Lao'ue did not speak, but screeched. He struck out at me, with something that gleamed in his hand.

"What next I knew, I was lying on the ground with blood streaming down my face. As I sat up, I saw that Lao'ue too was sitting on the ground, rubbing his head. A stone lay beside him, which had not been there before. Behind him stood my mother, picking up another stone. As Lao'ue looked around at her, she lifted the stone but did not throw it.

"'You cursed me for disobedience,' she shouted at him. 'Will you now curse my son for obeying you?'

"Lao'ue fumbled at where a belt would be on a common person, and his brightness increased so that it was hard to see him. He climbed to his feet, muttering strange words: 'You fools don't know what you've done. His genes were perfect. Perfect! Now I'll have to start over, give the she-ape more fertility drugs...' Those are his very words, I swear. Then he looked at me and shouted: 'Get out of here! No, I won't kill you, but now you'll be marked everywhere you go as a kin-slayer. Out! Out'.' Then he turned to speak to my mother, but she hefted the rock again, so he thought better of it. Instead he fumbled once more at his belt, and the air hummed and shimmered, and he vanished.

"I went to my mother, and we embraced, and did nothing but weep for a long time. I told her briefly what had passed between me and my brother, and asked what she would do when Father came home, for I feared he would beat her again. She said she would tell him to go ask Lao'ue, but surely I must be gone by then. She took me back to the hut, washed my wound, gave me the biggest water-skin and filled my pouch with dried food. We embraced again, quickly, and I set off for the mountains to the east. The rest, I suppose, you know."

I pulled up my spear and leaned on it, and thought for a long while. For certain, Great Grandmother must hear of this—and before the Sacred Folk did.

"Go to the herders' hut on the edge of the fields," I said. "Stay there until morning. If any ask, say that you suffered from sour gut and were in no condition to attend a festival. I will see what else may be done."

Ka'eeneh only nodded, got up and plodded off toward the fields. I trotted back to the sacred hill by a circuitous path.

By the time I returned, the celebration had reached the stage of dancing and music. The Sacred Folk sat beside Great Grandmother, watching the dancers and waving their amulets in blessing. Everyone else was either at the dancing or feasting in a ring among the standing stones.

Seeing that I could not reach Great Grandmother without being seen, I went to Nala instead, took her aside and told her the whole tale. She looked very somber when I had finished.

"If any word of this is true," she said, "Then for the first time in creation we must keep secrets from the Sacred Folk—at least until after we can speak to Great Grandmother. "

"Has she already mentioned Ka'eeneh to them?" I asked, "And did they behave in any way differently from before?"

"She has not yet spoken to them privately, and I could not hear all she has said to them so far. I know that something was said of the new invention of herding plants, for the Sacred Folk did tell us in detail how it is done. They also gave us seeds from many useful plants, with instructions on how to grow them."

"Hmm. Would they have done so had Ka'eeneh not already brought us the knowledge?" I considered. "Yet how else would they have thought to bring us seed?"

"The only other new thing the Sacred Folk did was that this time they did not ask us about Lost Buto." Nala gave me a worried look.

"They have asked us if we have seen Buto the Serpent-Woman for as long as I can remember."

"My mother says they started asking for Buto the year before I was born," I recalled. "Perhaps they have found her, after all these years. How soon can we talk to Great Grandmother?"

As it fell out, the Sacred Folk did not leave until well after dark, and spoke privately in Great Grandmother's hut for over a hand-span of the moon's course before leaving. By then, she was very tired and wished to rest until late next morning. Enotu finally caught up with Ka'eeneh, believed his story of sickness, and plied him with such curative potions as were to keep him constipated for the next moon-quarter. It was not until noon next day that we reached Great Grandmother and told her the story, and she frowned and was silent for long moments.

"There is no sense in sending for Ka'eeneh, to make him repeat his story," she presently said. "If he lied, he shall have had time to perfect his lie. If he told true, he would not care to repeat the painful tale. We must deal with what he has told us already."

"What, then, shall we do?" asked Nala.

"What shall we tell, and ask, the Sacred Folk when they return at autumn equinox?"

"We must learn more. We must confirm his story. Elitu—" Great Grandmother looked sternly at me. "Could you retrace Ka'eeneh's path? Could you travel beyond the western mountains and find his family?"

I agreed that I could, and we discussed the journey. I thought I would most probably need two large water-skins, much food and sturdy garments, and all the weapons I could carry. The journey might take as much as two moons, which meant I would miss the festival when the northern hunters come, but then the festival might distract attention from my absence. We agreed not to reveal the true direction and purpose of my journey to anyone else, lest word get back to Ka'eeneh, whereupon who could tell what he might do.

Subsequently, I told Mother only that Great Grandmother had sent me on a quest to gather more seeds, and I might be gone for as much as two moons. There was the usual worrying and advising, and the family provided me with food and gear for the journey. Thus it was that on the morning of the next full moon, I set out into the western scrub-desert and the mountains beyond.

In truth the journey was not terribly arduous, for I found enough small game to supplement my travel-food and could follow the game-tracks to sources of water. Neither was it overly long, though I usually traveled by night and slept in the heat of the day. A moon-quarter's travel brought me to the foothills, where water and game were more plentiful, though the passages were more difficult and the winds fierce. I had cause to be grateful that I had worn sturdy tall shoes, my breast-harness and cloak. By morning of the last day of the old moon, I came upon lands where I saw unmistakable sign that goats or sheep had pastured there recently.

I had had much time on my journey to con-sider the character of Ka'eeneh's family and their worrisome Sacred Person, so I did not approach directly. I hunted stealthily through the brush until I saw, at a safe distance, a large herd of sheep with a man tending them, He wore a cumbersome long shirt, much like Ka'eeneh's original garment. He had also let his beard grow to a most unruly length, and I wondered if it ever snagged on thorn-bushes. I also wondered, when the wind shifted and I found that I could smell him above the smell of sheep, if the man ever washed. This, I guessed, was the land of Ka'eeneh's family.

I avoided the man and took care not to

climb any high hills lest I come across Lao'ue's hut, for I had no wish to meet either of them. Instead, I followed the animals' tracks back to their pen. There, near the pen, I saw a collection of wretched-looking huts with smoke winding up from the largest of them. I saw three young girl-children trotting about, gathering sticks and carrying skins to and from the single well; all of them were different ages, and all of them wore not only the same long shirts but head-covering cloths as well. This I found intriguing, for Ka'eeneh had never mentioned his sisters. Had they meant nothing to him? I went quietly to the largest hut and looked inside.

There sat a worn-looking woman, visibly pregnant, hanging a haunch of meat in the smoke of her hearth-fire. She too wore the same cumbersome long shirt, though she had cast aside the head-cloth. There was no gray in her hair, though her face seemed much lined with marks of sorrow, and there was a bruise about one eye.

"I believe the meat would cure better," said I, stepping into the hut, "If you hung it in a small hut of its own, and made the smoke much more thick,"

The woman squeaked in surprise and almost dropped the meat.

"I didn't mean to startle you," I apologized,

"I am Elitu, the huntswoman of Aurochs Clan, Shore Tribe. Who might you be?"

It took the woman several tries before she could speak, and when she did so her accent was much like Ka'eeneh's. "I am called Ehweh, of... right here. You are a hunter... woman?"

"That I am," said I, pulling a fresh rabbit-carcass from my game pouch. "Do please accept this as a guest gift, and tell me about this land to which I've come,"

As I expected, the gift of food loosened her tongue. She was quick to put the carcass on the fire, eyeing it greedily as if she rarely tasted meat, then poured for both of us gourd cups of cold blackberry-leaf tea. I was careful to keep my cloak wrapped around me, remembering Ka'eeneh's strange aversion to the sight of bare skin, and complemented Ehweh on the tea. Soon enough, she was gnawing on a barely-cooked rabbit foreleg and babbling like a mountain stream.

"We never see strangers here," she said between bites. "For ever so long we believed we were the only people, until the Sacred One told us otherwise. ...No, actually, he told my son otherwise, and my son told me... I'm sure my house-bond will be delighted to hear of other folk nearby. We will need mates for our children, and there's no one else here."

"Be assured," said I, "My folk live half-a-moon's journey to the east, and we have many young men who will soon need to come seeking mates. But tell me, how many people can your lands feed? Could you support even another three men? And what of your daughters' children?"

Ehweh glanced at the open doorway, then spoke urgently. "No, we cannot feed more children. We can barely feed ourselves. In truth..." She took a deep breath, as if about to plunge into cold water. "I would be thankful if, when you return to your folk, you would take my daughters with you."

This was an astounding idea. "You would send your daughters away? But then, who would work this land after you?"

"My next son shall have it," she said bitterly, "Unless he too has the sense to leave. This is hard land, not worth holding."

"It did look sparse to me," I admitted. "Are there no good lands closer than half-a-moon away?"

"Oh, yes." Her gaze grew distant. "There is excellent land, only two days to the northwest: an excellent forest full of trees, and clearings filled with sweet herbs and berries, and ever so many animals..." She shook herself. "But we can never go there again. Not ever."

Of course I pressed her to tell me why not.

"The Sacred One forbade it," she said. "He

surrounded the land with a great wall, and set a fearsome creature to guard the gate, and he watches us to be sure we remain here. No one can ever go there again, and neither can I leave this wretched place–but please, help my daughters to escape."

What could I answer to that, save to agree? And if she would trust me with her daughters, I thought, it was time to trust her with my knowledge. "Did you have a son named Ka'eeneh?" said I. "A young man, with a scar, so, across his face."

"You have seen him?!" She seized my arm. "Does he live? Is he well?"

"Indeed he is," I assured her. "He came to our lands some three moons ago. My sister took him in, and he showed us the means of herding plants. In truth, it was he who told me the way here, and bade me to tell you he is well."

Only that last part was a lie, and it cheered her. She wept quietly for long moments, then came back to herself and poured some more tea.

"And...did he tell you much concerning us?" she asked cautiously.

"Yes, he told us everything," I said, patting her hand. "'It is a most sorrowful story."

"Oh Earth, Moon and Sun!" she cried. "How long have I waited to hear some person say that!" And she wept afresh.

I waited until she was not quite finished before I said: "This Lao'ue seems most cruel and bad-tempered, not like our Sacred Folk at all. I would learn more of him, to hear if he is a danger to us."

Ehweh looked about wildly, and clapped a hand over my mouth. "Don't say that!" she whispered. "He can walk unseen. He might hear us, and what then?"

I thought quickly. "You know yourself that he cannot be everywhere, nor know every-thing. Seeing how little regard he has for you, I think that if he is not in his own house right now, he is busy watching your man. I am certain he is not here, for I have good hearing and I hear no humming as of bees."

She gripped my arm again. "You're right, you're right," she whispered. "We have some time; let me speak quickly. You said there are other Sacred Ones? Others besides him? Is this true?"

"Yes, I've seen them myself many times, and they do not behave as Lao'ue does."

"Not alone," she murmured. "We're not alone, he's not alone... Oh, he lied! He lied to us from the beginning!"

"Tell me of the beginning," said I.

And indeed she told.

There was the good land, where fruits and nuts grew all year around, abundant for the picking. There were beasts so tame that one might stroke a lion like to a puppy. There was the man, a little older than she, and they grew up together among the fruitful plants and tame beasts. And always there was the Sacred One, whose name she now dared not speak for fear of drawing his attention. At first he taught the two children, showing them how to speak and make shelters and weave baskets and gather fruit. He appeared to them every day, always wearing his Form of Light, always giving instructions, always watching over them.

And then there were the two trees. They grew, tall and beautiful, in the middle of the good land beside a meandering stream. The first day the children so much as saw the trees, they hurried to tell the Sacred One about them and to ask if their fruit was good to eat. His answer surprised them, for he scolded them furiously for even going near the trees. They were dangerous, he said. Eating their fruit would sicken them worse than the green apples; if they ate that fruit they would sicken until they died. They knew not what that word meant, so he showed them, by striking a bird out of the sky with his fire. The children had never seen a dead creature before, and were very frightened. They kept away from the trees thereafter, and played happily elsewhere.

Then came a time when the Sacred One stayed away from them for days, appearing only once every moon-quarter, and the children wondered why this was so but dared not ask; by now they had learned to fear his anger, and did not want to see anything else die. Once, when he came to speak to the children, there was another strange being with him; it looked like a common grass-snake, but was very much bigger. This being seemed to converse with the Sacred One, but did not frighten the children as he did.

"A great snake, you say?" I interrupted, remembering Solstice. "Did you hear the being's name spoken?"

"Not then," said Ehweh, "But they used many strange words—like 'genes' and 'mutagenic' and 'instinct'—which we understood not. If the serpent's name was mentioned, we could not note it among the other words. But I did learn its name later.

"One morning after the Sacred One had left us, I was bathing in the stream when the serpent appeared. It spoke without moving its mouth, but I understood it clearly. It said its name was 'Buto', and it wished to ask me some questions about our land. Seeing no harm in the creature, I spoke to it."

"What did it ask?" said I, seeing a pattern half-formed,

"It asked me about the fruit-trees, and if I ate fruit from all of them. I mentioned the two poisonous trees that we must avoid, and Buto became most interested. It asked where those trees were, and I dared to show it the place. Then the serpent went up to the trees and..." She shivered again. "It took a Form of Light, the way Lao—the Sacred One does. Buto walked around both trees, muttering to itself about 'tailored viri' and 'mutagens' and other such words, and waved an amulet about the trees and their fruit. Finally, this Buto picked fruits from one of the trees, and returned to me, and resumed its serpent form. 'Look,' the creature said—and it ate the fruit'."

"Did the serpent die?" I urged,

"No, not though I watched for many long moments. Never did it so much as sicken. 'You see?' Buto said then, 'This fruit is not poison-ous. Lao'ue has told you a bad story. He knows that if you eat this fruit you will certainly not die, but just the opposite. You will become immortal, even as we are. He does not want that, not until he has made you into his totally obedient servants. This is what he's been planning, keeping secret from the rest of us.'"

"So!" I whispered, seeing a large part of the

pattern emerge,

"I asked then, 'What shall we become if we eat fruit from the other tree?' Buto said more strange words: 'That one will start your fertility, so that you can have young ones, as the other animals do. There is also an information packet which I cannot decode yet. I think it will give you knowledge of your own breeding, but I can't be sure.'

"Then we heard a faint humming, as of bees. Buto looked afraid, and said quickly: 'I must go. Think of what I've said.' Then he vanished quickly into the bushes. I was afraid, and ran away from the humming sound."

"Did the Sacred One find you?" I asked.

"Not then, no. I realized we could outrun him, and hide from him. I told my man this, and later told him about the forbidden trees. He was still afraid, but I thought about all the animals I had seen with their young... lovely kittens and fawns and cubs... and how they grew to be like their mothers, and... I so much wanted company! I had no one to talk to but my man and the Sacred One, and I could not find Buto again... Oh, I wanted children!" She pressed her face into her hands.

"So you went back to the tree, and stole the fruit," I finished.

"Yes, yes... I went back to the trees. I thought of taking fruit from both of them, but the fruit on the fig-like tree was out of reach, and I dared not take the time to climb it, so I just took fruit from the tree that would give me children. I thought my man might want some too, for he often snatched food away from me, so I carried it away with me instead of eating it there. I ate some of it before his eyes, and he saw that I didn't die, and he was always greedy for new foods anyway, so..."

"Ah, and it changed you?" I had often wondered what brought on the changes of adulthood, but I had never heard that eating fruit did it.

"That night," she whispered, "We were racked with strange dreams and feelings. In the morning we were too weak and hot to rise, so we slept and dreamed again. For three days this went on, and we barely had the strength to gather food and eat. And on the fourth morning we awoke strong and clear-headed again, but... we were changed!"

"Changed how?" I could guess, but needed to hear it.

"Different!" Ehweh wrung her hands. "I had... these..." She cupped her breasts, which were very full. "...and both of us had... hair..."

"Ah, on your mating-parts?"

"Yes! Yes! And our smell was different, and we were taller..."

"All the changes of adulthood, in three

days?" I marveled.

"And the feelings were worse! We suddenly knew how those hairy parts were supposed to be used, and we felt a frantic itching desire to do that, but also a terrible fear and—and shame, and..." She drew a deep breath. "Suddenly our bodies seemed ugly to us, especially the mating-parts. We felt horrible. We wanted to cover them up."

I remembered Ka'eeneh's fear of bare skin. Was the fear passed in the blood? What else might Ehweh's blood conceal? Was it wise to take her daughters back to my people? ...Yet Ka'eeneh had learned better, with time.

"Of course we could not hide from the Sacred One forever," Ehweh went on, her voice bitter "My man admitted that we were ashamed of being naked, and the Sacred One guessed the rest of it. His anger was terrible—especially, I think, because we saw that we had not died as he said we would."

"Ha! You caught him in a lie!" So that was where Ka'eeneh had learned to lie so well. And what other lessons had this Lao'ue taught him?

"He raged and ranted and frightened us terribly, and waved amulets at us that caused us terrible pain, and learned from me that I heard about the fruit from Buto." Ehweh cringed. "So he left us penned up in a strange little hut inside his big hut... it's difficult to explain. I saw him gathering up amulets from a small platform, and heard him muttering about 'spying for the team' and 'ruining the experiment', and then he went away and left us with no food for two days."

"Less and less I like this Lao'ue," I considered.

"When he came back he was much calmer. He took us out of the hut and marched us through the forest until we came to a high wall made of smooth stone. There was a gate in the wall, and we stopped before it. He took another amulet and poked the backs of our necks with it, which hurt and left a hard spot. Here: see?"

Ehweh pulled back her hair to reveal a small discolored spot on her neck. I felt it, and found something small and hard, like a tiny stone, under the skin.

"Then he thrust us through the gate, and he pronounced his curse on us. You heard of that from my son? Yes? He also promised that he would continue to watch us, so we could not 'sin' again without his knowing of it. Then he closed the gate behind us and left us standing in the brush, wondering what to do. My man bawled and cried that he was sorry, and he pounded on the gate, and then..." She shook her head, wide-eyed. "Then this... shiny thing came out from beside the wall. It had a whirling blade in the front of it, and it looked very fearsome. We were frightened and ran away. We looked for water and found a stream, and we followed it to this place."

"But you didn't escape from Lao'ue?" I made some guesses about the pebble in her neck. Great Grandmother had once mentioned magic like that.

Ehweh shook her head. "Once every moon-quarter, he would appear. He taught us to spin fiber and make garments, and to herd animals... and how to slaughter and eat them. I cried over that, especially for the young ones, but my man was so eager to please the Sacred One that he hardened his heart to everyone's feelings but his own."

"Hmm. And did this Lao'ue order your man to beat you, and to build his fine hut for him, and build that sacrifice-platform also?" I felt my anger rising, and fought it down with effort.

"Yes." Ehweh looked away. "And he taught my sons to kill, also."

I calculated as quickly as ever I had on the hunt. "When did your man last go to visit Lao'ue's hut? How long, think you, before La'oue appears again?"

Ehweh looked up, eyes bright with sudden hope. "He went but yesterday," she said. "Think you that the Sacred One will not appear for another six days?"

"So I expect. Now tell me again, and leave nothing out; by what path did you come here from the good land? Also, describe carefully those two trees,"

She remembered well, and described in good detail. We might have spoken longer, but that a voice came shouting from outside the hut.

"Woman," the man's voice bellowed, "Is my dinner ready yet?"

"Oh, Earth!" Ehweh whispered, scrambling to her feet. "It is my house-bond." She hurried to the door and called out: "Not yet, not yet! We must fetch more, for we have a guest!"

"A guest?" cried the man, sounding aston-ished and frightened,

I hastened to get up and go out the door, to let him see that I was no Sacred One but only a common person. Fortunately, I remem-bered to hold my cloak wrapped around me.

There stood the man, staring at me with his jaw hanging down. He looked no better than he had from a distance, and smelled worse. I saw several expressions chase themselves across his face: fear, curiosity, joy—and a strange kind of greed. I took care to introduce myself properly, and noted the change on his face when he realized that I was a woman. He fumbled and mumbled a bit, clearly wondering how to greet me properly–and trying to peer at my breasts through the cloak–until I took pity on him and suggested we come in out of the hot sunlight. He agreed, hastened into the hut and sat down at the fire, leaving me to follow as I would.

At once his eyes lit on the remains of the rabbit, for Ehweh had eaten only a forequarter of it. He happily picked up the bowl that Ehweh had set out for herself, cut off a haunch of the rabbit and plopped it into the bowl. As an afterthought he invited me to cut some too. His next words were a bellow at Ehweh to fetch more food. She glanced sadly at the meat, and went out.

I took care to cut the other haunch for my-self, at which he scowled, but didn't eat. To distract his attention, I asked for news of his lands.

He was almost as eager to talk as he was to eat, and he ate like a pig. Between mouthfuls of food–and often through them–he railed of how hard his life was, how difficult it was to tend sheep and shear them, and how his women would never spin and weave the wool fast enough to suit him, and the weather was so often miserably hot, and there was never enough water.

During this recitation, Ehweh and her daughters came in. They brought baskets filled with nuts and greens, silently set them down nearby and waited to be noticed. The man made no effort to notice them, so I did.

"Good mother," said I, offering her the bowl with the rabbit's other haunch in it, "Please accept my guesting-gift for you and your children." Then I cut off the loin and remaining forequarter of the rabbit, and handed them out to the girls.

The man stopped eating to stare, though his mouth still worked. Ehweh had the presence of mind to thank me and hand over her basket, and the girls hastily copied her. I made a show of handing out the nuts and greens, keeping only a fair portion for myself. Ehweh and her girls tore into the food as if afraid it might vanish. The man glowered at them, but hesitated to say anything.

To forestall him, I traded him news of my people and their land, giving particular stress to the abundance of game and water. I saw the man's eyes fill with honest longing, and something close to regret, but he said nothing. I mentioned how many people there were in my tribe, and everyone looked astonished. I spoke of the other people who came to trade with us, and the man almost dropped his bowl. "Other people... so many..." he murmured. "He never told me..."

"If life is hard here, why not come back

with me to my land?" I offered, thinking of how well this rude oaf would fare among civilized folk, and wondering how Ka'eeneh would feel about seeing his family again. "Food is abundant there. You could hunt and fish and gather, as well as tend sheep."

Ehweh and her daughters stared at the man, not daring to move or speak. He thought over my offer for long moments, and then sadly shook his head. "No," he almost whispered. "The Sacred One condemned us to stay here."

"Then ask our Sacred Folk to intercede for you," I dropped the words on him. "Surely they could persuade him to let you go."

Then the man did drop his bowl, and his jaw, and stared at me as if I had sprouted antlers. "'They'?" he repeated. "Your Sacred... Folk? There are others?!"

"Why, of course," I smiled sweetly. "Three of them visit us every year-quarter, and the people who trade with us speak of others who visit them. There seem to be very many of them. Indeed the world is very wide..."

The man jumped up and ran out of the hut.

I turned to look at Ehweh and her daughters, and asked: "Does he do this often?" The girls looked at each other, and burst into nervous giggles.

Ehweh tossed her clean-picked rabbit bones into the fire. "He has gone to consult with the

Sacred One," she explained, glancing at her daughters. "We did not know there were other Sacred Folk, not before you came."

The girls huddled together and whispered urgently among themselves.

"Perhaps this one will be pleased to learn of others," said I. "Perhaps he would like to go and visit them." But I didn't think so.

"This is not his sacred day," Ehweh considered, glancing nervously at the shadowed ceiling. "Perhaps the Sacred One will not be at home."

I guessed he would not. Seeing that the woman and her children would do nothing further until the man came back, I regaled them with stories about my lands and people—and about our Sacred Folk, and how kindly and generous they were. I also took care to mention how our women hunted and fished and traveled as they would, and the girls' eyes grew big and round.

As darkness fell, the man returned to the hut. He looked weary and bewildered, but said nothing. He only sat down at the fire and poked about for any remaining food. Ehweh, catching some signal I had missed, rose and gathered the children.

"Come, girls," said she, ushering them toward the doorway, "It's time for bed. Ah, Elitu, you may share the sleeping-hut with them."

I started to rise, but the man abruptly raised his head and gave me a look I liked not. "No," said he, "Let our guest abide here, and go you with the children."

Ehweh threw me a frightened look, and hurried the girls away. I quietly took a firm grip on my spear.

"Ah, you wish to learn more of my land?" I asked innocently.

"Rather would I learn more of you," the man said, grinning. "Come lie under me tonight."

It took me a moment to realize what he meant, for my folk do not commonly mate in that fashion. Once I understood, I was hard put to keep my feelings from reaching my face. I would sooner have mated with his sheep.

"I thank you for the mating-offer," I said pleasantly, noting how he winced at the direct word, "But our Sacred Folk, who sent me on this journey, forbade me to indulge in such pleasures until I return."

The disappointment on his face was as pouty as a small child's. "You never did say why you came here," he grumbled, not politely.

"Why, they sent me—and other hunters of our folk, too—out to gather seeds from every useful plant, for they have promised to show us the way of herding plants, as you herd sheep."

He flinched, eyes suddenly speculative, and

I wondered if I had given away something important. "Oh, we've known of that for years," he hurried to say. "But you won't find many useful plants here."

I saw his eyes fix on the gap of my cloak, and knew it was time to leave. "Still, I must gather what I can," said I, getting to my feet. "I wish you a good night."

I got out the doorway before he had time to react. He shouted after me: "Send my woman in here, then!" and I wondered if he had ever spent a night without Ehweh to warm his sleeping-mat.

It took me several moments to find the sleeping-hut. When I approached the doorway, I heard Ehweh whispering urgently to her children. They started up guiltily as I came in.

I gave Ehweh her man's message, which made her hurry out, then looked about for a sleeping-mat. There was only one, made of several sheepskins sewn together, though there were several straw pillows and a big covering made of that same woven wool–all obviously made, with love, by Ehweh for her children.

I set down my gear, unfastened my shoes and cast off my cloak–whereupon the children squeaked and giggled frantically. I saw that they covered their eyes, even as Ka'eeneh had first done, when I pulled off my breast-harness and breech-clout. "Why, what's the matter?" I asked. "Don't you take off those shirts, even to sleep?"

The girls giggled frantically, and the oldest dared to whisper: "No, no, we must never be naked. Father said so."

"How silly," said I, lying down on the mat. "You certainly can't wash with your garment covering your hide."

The girls giggled louder, and I realized they did so because they were afraid. I lay down at one end of the mat, tossed and mumbled awhile, then feigned sleep. The girls cautiously lay down as far from me as they could get, and whispered softly among themselves. After a time, I felt a small hand creep up, poke my near breast, then retreat fast—followed by more whispering. I wondered if the girls had ever seen a bare breast since they stopped nursing.

From the main hut came the sounds of the man shouting, then the woman weeping, and the girls grew very quiet. I lay still, looking up at the close darkness, and considered much. Though the sleeping-mat was soft, I never spent a less restful night.

Before dawn I rose, dressed and gathered my gear. The oldest girl wakened, saw me, and asked in her habitual whisper where I was going.

"One must rise early for successful hunting," I whispered back. "I shall be gone some few days. Be sure to tell your mother that when I return I will do as she asked. Can you remember that?"

The girl nodded without speaking, her eyes very round.

I crept out of the hut and quietly hurried away, keeping to ground where I would leave no tracks. At dawn I found the stream Ehweh had spoken of, and began following it to its source.

The journey was not long, no more than two days' easy travel before I saw the edges of a small forest ahead of me. Ehweh's description had been accurate; I found the rock wall just before sundown. It was very smooth and high, and no one could have climbed it. I spent the night curled up in a tree, and with dawn came down to explore the wall.

Soon enough I saw the gate, and its guardian. I might have mistaken it for a smooth boulder bearing a long twig on top, save for the whirling thing that projected from its belly, for it stood very still. It was certainly no animal nor person, but looked like a shining pointed stone mounted on smaller stones. It stood directly in front of a gate made from some strange dark substance, like smoothed wood, and it watched the forest. At one point a low-flying bird darted through the clearing before the gate, and the strange guardian moved forward, rolling on the stones it used for feet. The top of the thing turned like a head, with its wand following the bird's course. After a moment it moved back to its first position and stood as still as before.

I wondered if a well-cast stone might break that wand and damage the creature, but didn't want to gain its attention if I were wrong. I slipped back into the thin forest and proceeded back along the wall.

In time I found what I had hoped for: a tree close enough to the wall that one of its higher branches reached over the top. I climbed carefully, watching all the while for any sign of the guardian, and listened for the sound of bees. But nothing noticed me, and I gained the top of the wall.

The wall was narrow enough to straddle, and as smooth on the other side as on its outer face. Beyond lay a much thicker forest, but I could see in the greenery signs of blight and drought. In truth, it seemed to be dying. Ka'eeneh's plant-patch had looked better kept. If this was Lao'ue's private land, he had neglected it sorely.

I marked the position of the branch and

crept along the wall until I found another tree, this one inside the wall, which grew close enough for me to reach. It was of a kind I recognized not, and I would have collected its seeds had there been any. A moment's climb brought me to the ground. I marked the tree, and set out to explore.

For nearly a moon-quarter I searched the land inside the wall, for indeed it was thickly planted but not large. I saw no animals such as Ehweh had mentioned, and wondered if Lao'ue had killed them all, or let them escape, or left them to die of hunger or thirst or sickness. Many of the plants were dying, while others had overgrown and choked out their neighbors. Some I recognized, while others were strange to me, and I dutifully tried to collect seeds from those I knew not. Twice I came upon dried streams where plants had once grown thickly, and I wondered why the streams had ceased to flow. Did Lao'ue control the water?

Always, I marked the way back to the tree over the wall and my escape.

On the sixth day I found a stream that still flowed. Its source was a strange spring that came up from the ground through a peculiar stone shape like a twisted clay pot. There was a humming sound about the spring, not quite like the sound of the Sacred Folk's boat, but enough like it that I kept my distance. Clearly this was Lao'ue's doing. Why had he kept this spring flowing and let the others dry out? I followed the stream away through the woods, into a nearby clearing.

In the clearing stood the two trees.

There was no mistaking them; they fit Ehweh's description exactly, save that they were larger than she had remembered. I wondered how many years they had grown since she saw them last. I circled the clearing with great care, listening for any sound or sign of Lao'ue's presence or devices, but detected nothing. Finally I darted forward, reached the shade of the trees, and examined them.

The first, with dark leaves and branches low to the ground, was some manner of olive. Yet it was not like any olive I had ever seen, for its fruit—and it was indeed fruiting—was very large, oily and dark. This was the fruit that gave fertility, and the knowledge of mating and death, and a powerful fear and shame and horror of one's own body.

I took care not to touch it, but turned to the other tree.

This one was a great mulberry-fig, its clusters of dark red fruit showing ripe on the branches. In truth, some of the fruit had already passed ripening and had rotted on the branch, ready to fall. This was the tree that, according to Ehweh's memory of Buto's words, gave the very opposite of death.

I strapped my spear to my back, and climbed the tree.

Seen close, the ripe fruit was large and luscious, and smelled faintly of honey. I picked as much as I could reach, stuffed it into my food-pouch, climbed back to the ground and hurried back to the wall. Up the inner tree I went, along the wall, down the outer tree and away into the thin forest. Only when I reached the stream and the outer fringe of the wood did I sit down to examine my prize.

I saw that the fruit had been bruised, even by its brief journey in my pouch, and would rot soon if it were not eaten sooner. There was no way I could take the fruit home for Nala or Great Grandmother to examine. It would not last the journey even to Ehweh's hut. If I wanted to learn the properties of the fruit, there was only one way.

Three days to change, Ehweh had said.

I filled my water-skins, set out all my food in easy reach, dug a waste-pit nearby and made a bed of grass and branches. Then I took the least bruised of the figs, and ate it.

It tasted like an ordinary mulberry-fig, save that it was slightly more salty and had the faintest tang of mold. The seeds inside were tiny, and I couldn't help but eat them, too. I considered that if I wanted to breed trees from the remaining figs, I must bury the whole fruits. I put the rest of them back in my pouch, lay down and waited.

Weariness and fever came soon.

More than three days it lasted, for I used up all my food and drained the water-skins almost dry. How much longer it was I couldn't tell, for I spent most of the time in aching fever-dreams and never knew how long I slept.

When I finally woke, weak and cold in the summer sunlight, I knew I was changed. An old scar was gone from my arm. Despite hunger and weakness, I felt more sound and healthy than I could remember ever being. When I cast my gaze around the forest, I found that I knew things—the names of plants, the nature of the soil, the uses of stones—that I hadn't known before. Also, my memory was as clear as spring-water; I could remember all that had ever befallen me since the hour I first drew breath. I had much to marvel at, while I rested and regained my strength.

In the pouch, the remaining figs were beginning to rot. I had not much time remaining.

I took out the mess of figs, spread their meat thin upon a rabbit-skin stretched on a stone in the sun, and left them to dry. It would not save the fruits, but it would preserve the seeds. I knew that the drying would take some three or four days, and I had some notion of how to spend those days while I waited.

First I gathered several days' food. Then I went back to the wall, climbed the tree and went over it. This time I had another goal in mind.

I searched the dying land, spiraling in from the wall, until at last I found a cluster of strange huts. They too were made of that smooth stone, very large, shaped like halved eggshells, and some forty paces out from them lay a narrow trench with the sound of bees in it and a shimmering of the air above it. I found another tree with an overhanging branch and crossed safely above the trench.

From hut to hut I crept, listening at the walls until I came upon the sound of someone moving about. I searched further until I found a round doorway, like to that in the Sacred Folk's boat, but closed tight. I concealed myself among some flowering bushes nearby, where I could watch the door, and I waited. The sun moved three hand spans down the sky while I watched.

Finally, near dusk, the door flowered open and Lao'ue came out.

He was wearing his Form of Light, just like the other Sacred Folk, and I could see nothing of him beside his general shape. I watched further, saw him enter one of the other huts, rattle about there briefly and then return. I saw him gesture to his door as he approached it, saw the door flower open at his unspoken command, and took care to remember his motions. Then I retreated further into the bushes and made my bed for the night.

Next morning, when the sun was two hands high, Lao'ue came out again. This time, as soon as he had entered another hut, I dashed for the hut he had left. As I approached the door I made the gesture, and indeed the door opened like a flower for me. I dashed inside, and the door closed behind me. I ducked down beside the door and listened to hear if Lao'ue had noticed. I heard nothing but a bee-humming sound outside, much like the sound of the Sacred Folks' flying boat, but fading away.

Long moments passed with no sign of Lao'ue's return, so I knew I was safe for the while and looked about for a better hiding-place.

The furnishings of that great hut were very strange. Wherever I looked I saw platforms, like Great Grandmother's stool but much bigger, laden with odd devices, all as smooth and shining as wet river-stones. There were many flat sheets with pictures on them, like Great Grandmother's painted antelope-skin—but the pictures moved. There were sheets studded with shining beads, which twinkled and gleamed with colored light. There were many strange amulets lying about, and I took care not to touch them.

There was also a platform draped with a large hide or fine-woven cloth, which hung down to the floor, covered with recognizable bowls and dishes–many of them unwashed. I darted to the platform, looked under the cloth, and saw that the platform stood on slender legs with sufficient room between them. I ducked under the cloth and sat down beneath the platform to await Lao'ue's return. I also pulled out my axe, and kept it ready to hand.

Sun-hands of time passed. At length I heard a loud bee-humming noise pass overhead, again, much like the Sacred Folk's boat. I realized then that this must be the seventh day, when Lao'ue paid his visit to the sacred hut in Ehweh's lands, and this was the sound of his boat returning. I crouched lower beneath the platform, and listened carefully.

A few moments later, the door flowered open and Lao'ue came in. He stamped through the blossoming door, which closed behind him, and paused to fumble with his belt. At once, his Form of Light disappeared and I saw him as he truly was.

The sight was not beautiful. He was bald and spindly, with pale gray skin like a fish's belly, small of ear and mouth and nose, with large dark eyes that lacked a center. In truth, he was exceedingly ugly. If this were his true form, I could see why he never revealed himself to common folk.

He went straightway to one of the stools near the benches, and sat down. There he fumbled among assorted strange amulets, muttering angrily to himself. At length he seized upon a particular amulet, held it close to his mouth and spoke to it as if to a person. I took care to remember his words.

"4287 point 8 mark 4," he said, in a voice that creaked and whined. "No sign or report of the visiting nomad. Subject A still alarmed by the new knowledge, complains that the females are rebellious and keep asking questions. There's no way now to keep them from knowing about the rest of the team. Excrement! All I can do at this stage is tell him those others are evil, dangerous, lying, less powerful than I am, and that he should keep away from them. At least the she-ape's pregnancy is advancing normally, and this one will be another male. I'll take more care conditioning this one..."

He paused, then actually smiled. I saw one hand slip between his thighs, then move back and forth, and I realized that the Sacred One was rubbing his mating-parts.

"I'll start him early..." Lao'ue's voice grew speculative. "Keep him away from hunting this time, but make him practice on the sheep. Insist that he slaughter them only on my altar, so he associates food with sacrifice. When he's old enough, look for other nomads he can practice on. Let him steal livestock, then a woman.

"If he'll mate with his sisters, meanwhile, make sure the offspring are male. He'll need to raise a war-party soon. Or possibly use the sisters as bait for other nomads, get them under his control...

"Excrement! I thought I had more time, but the nomad stumbled on the test-site, and there's no telling who'll come next. I'll have to teach Subject A how to capture and enslave any strangers who wander in..."

He paused, still rubbing at himself.

Just then an odd chiming sound, like struck quartz-stone, rang from another part of the bench. Lao'ue jumped as if bee-stung, snatched his hands away from his crotch, punched at his amulet and then poked one of the shining beads on the nearest moving-picture skin. Its picture changed; though I could see but little, I could make out part of a face.

"Who is it?" Lao'ue snapped at the picture. "You know I'm busy here."

"It's Hau'a, your mother," said a woman's voice from the image. "Has it been so long that you don't recognize me?"

"I'm too used to seeing you in your human form," he answered, sounding not much pleased. "I've been very busy. What do you want?"

"I thought you might like to know," said she, "That we found Buto."

Perhaps his mother's image did not see him flinch, but I did. "That's good to hear," he said, almost too casually. "Where has she been all this time?"

"Crawling–literally crawling–through the wild lands to the south." The woman's voice sounded very cold. "Eventually she came upon a human settlement, where the locals took her in and built a temple for her. Our local observer came out on a routine visit, found her there and brought her back."

Lao'ue hesitated just the tiniest fraction of a heartbeat before speaking. "What," said he, "Had she lost her com-unit all this time?"

"Her com-unit," said the woman, stone-voiced. "And her projector, and her arms and legs and tongue, and much of her memory."

"Shocking!" cried Lao'ue, though I saw him relax ever so slightly. "Was it an accident? Or did the natives do it? I've warned you they can be dangerous–"

"It took us these last three local months," the woman cut in, "To regenerate her tongue, repair the skull-fractures, and regain her memories. Regenerating her limbs will take another half year."

Lao'ue made no answer but a tsking sound of concern. I saw him cross his legs, out of sight from the picture-skin.

"She remembers," the woman said slowly, "How she got her injuries–and what came before."

Lao'ue didn't stir nor speak.

"Boy, how could you do such a thing?!" the woman roared at him. "Why?!" Lao'ue jumped to his feet, clenching his fists. "Did she tell you what she did to me first?" he yelled back. "She ruined my experiment! She corrupted the subjects, made them mature too early. Twenty years of work, ruined! I was lucky to salvage anything. She did all that, just for spite. I had a right to be angry!"

"Angry?!" snapped the woman. "You came as close to murder as anyone has in a thousand years! I've always known you were childish and arrogant, but this–"

"She ruined my work!"

"Your work? Oh indeed, let's talk of your great experiment! Buto told us all about it, everything you showed her, and more that she learned by herself. Just why did you graft the immortality gene into a local fruit-tree? Just what were you planning to do with it?"

"I planned to give it to the experimental humans, once they'd evolved enough. I needed an available reservoir of the gene–"

"So you put it in the fruit of a local plant, where any creature could stroll up and eat it?"

"I kept it protected! Even the humans wouldn't go near it, not until Buto interfered."

"Did they eat those figs?" the woman shouted at him.

"No, no, just the olives," Lao'ue insisted, cringing. "I got them away before worse could happen,"

"And what was in the olives?"

"Uh, just a fertility-inducer. I'd kept the humans from breeding until then–"

"What else? Buto said there was a coded-memory packet. What was in it?"

"Wh-why, just basic sexual information..."

"There was more than that. Buto saw it, but couldn't decode it. What else was in that fruit, boy?"

Lao'ue was silent. The look I saw on his face was like unto that of a stubborn child who refuses to admit to eating berries when the stains are all over his face.

"Just what have you been doing with your experimental pair of humans?" the woman ground on. "Buto says they were unusually docile, unquestioning, but otherwise childlike—even though they had long passed the age of puberty. What had you done to them, Lao'ue? What were you planning to do?"

"Excrement! You know excrement!" he howled, bouncing up and down like a child in a tantrum. "You think they're innocent and rational and sociable, don't you? You think that in a thousand years or so they'll be ready to join the Great Harmony as respectable citizens—just one more trade-partner, like all the other races—don't you? Well, you're wrong! These are pack-predators, no different from wolves or lions or zagrils, and they're ambitious! Greedy! Eternally curious! Give them half a chance, and they won't be content to stay our equals—they'll become our masters! They will! They will, unless we change them. We have to make them docile, obedient, controlled—"

"Make them slaves or they'll be our masters?" said the woman.

"Yes! Yes! Can't any of you see it?! That's why I took a breeding pair to experiment on. If I could alter their genes, train them, control their breeding—"

"What did you put in the olives?"

"Fear of breeding! Fear enough to control them! You can't just let them breed as they like. They—"

"Did it work?"

There was a long, bitter silence. "Not yet," Lao'ue grudgingly admitted. "There were some unforeseen side-effects..."

"Why were you planning to give them the immortality gene?"

"To keep the best bloodlines producing for as long as possible, so we could breed out the wild strain. Just one fertile male could alter the entire species if he lived and bred long enough."

Right there I knew that even the Sacred Folk could lie to their mothers. Lao'ue hadn't mentioned what he'd done to Ehweh's children, how he'd planned not to suppress their wildness but make them into thieves and killers of men. He wasn't going to wait for his precious bloodline to work its way through all the folk of the world. He also meant to kill all those who would not consent, not be bullied, not serve him.

The wild strain: my people, and me.

I saw also that Ka'eeneh had been half right; the male provides half the seed of the child. Indeed, one long-lived male could spread a curse in the blood very far, and very wide.

"But Buto learned the truth, and disagreed," said the woman.

"She sabotaged my experiment," Lao'ue panted, glaring at the image.

"So she told us." The woman's voice grew very cold. "She told us everything, including what she'd learned of your plans. All the teams conferred, and concluded that your experiment is unethical, and will be terminated."

"What?!"

"I called you in the thin hope that the story was false, but I see that it isn't. There is no more tolerance, and no more time. It's my duty to inform you that the main ship will reach your location within a standard hour, with orders to destroy every remaining life-form within your boundaries. That will include you, if you remain."

"They can't do that!"

"Child, this is the last indulgence I will ever give you. Leave while you can, or die with your creation."

With that, the image-skin turned as blank as the wall.

Lao'ue screamed inarticulately at it.

I readied myself to leap and run.

Lao'ue grabbed his first amulet, jabbed at it and spoke into it quickly. "Supplemental: the council has sent the ship to destroy my laboratory. They still don't know about the secondary base or the breeding colony down-stream. I'll beat them yet! I know how to manipulate the humans, make them fear, make them obey. I'll send my colonies out to conquer and interbreed. I'll teach them to fear and hate all the rest of you fools, including you, Mother! They'll worship me, and won't listen to anyone else. They won't be your equals; they'll be my loyal servants–and when they finally do go out and conquer the whole Harmony, I'll be ruling them. You just wait and see, Mother! You just watch!"

With that, he snatched up the amulet and hurried toward the door.

I scurried silently out from under the platform, right behind him.

The door had just blossomed open when he heard or felt my presence, and started to turn. I brought the axe down, hard, on his head. He fell flat in the doorway.

Remembering that humming trench, I took hold of his body–which felt most unpleasantly soft and clammy–dragged it across the dooryard and threw it over the trench like a log bridge. The shimmer-hum snapped and vanished. I leaped the trench and ran for the boundary wall.

It seemed to take years to find the climbable tree, mount the wall, scramble to the next tree and down. Still longer did it take me to find the stream and follow it. I found the rock where I'd spread out the fruit, and rolled up the skin and stuffed it into my food-pouch. Then I ran on, down the stream-bed, until my legs fell out from under me and left me gulping air.

It was while I was climbing back to my feet that I heard the loud humming overhead. I could not tell if it was the boat of the Sacred Folk going to destroy the doomed land, or Lao'ue in his own boat making his escape. All I could tell was that a few moments later I heard a great roaring behind me, and saw light flaring above the trees.

After that there was no reason to hurry. I took my time going back to Ehweh's land, and also took care not to be seen.

On the next morning, from concealment, I saw Ehweh's man leave the hut and gather his sheep and drive them off to graze. I waited until I saw the girls go out to fetch water, then hid my pouches and cloak under a bush and made my way to the hut.

Ehweh was wearing a fresh bruise on her face, but this time showed no surprise at seeing me.

"Gather up your girls and all the gear you would send with them," said I. "I've come to take them away."

Ehweh barely flinched at the sight of my bare skin; the girls must have told her much. "It will take time," she whispered fiercely.

"What if my man comes back before we're finished? If he sees you–"

"I will deal with him," said I. "Summon the girls."

I left the hut two steps ahead of her, and made my way out to the sheep-field. On the way there, I sought out and cut a sturdy branch from a redbud tree, and stripped it of leaves as I walked.

The man was more than surprised to see me. He jumped half his length, and made an elaborate sign of warding-off-harm. "Away, away you liar!" he yowled at me. "The Sacred One warned me of your lies, your disobedience, your wicked ways, your–"

"Did he tell you that I found your woman's son, Ka'eeneh?" said I, striding up to him, the branch hidden behind my back.

"I have no son!" he wailed, covering his eyes. "No son but what the Sacred One has promised to give me. Away, you evil female!"

"Ah, but your woman has a son," I insisted. "He lives and is well, and a good woman has taken him into her household. And she has a mother, and that mother has sent you something."

"A gift?" he said, peeking out from between his fingers. "Is it food?"

"No, this." And I swung the branch as hard as I could into his belly.

He whoofed loud, and down he went. I swung next at his buttocks, thighs and back, as hard and fast as ever my mother had, whipping the dust out of his woven-wool shirt from his calves to his shoulders. He howled and struggled, but never could manage to climb even to his knees. His stinking shirt gave him no better shielding than its like had given his woman's son.

I shouted to him above his bawling: "This my mother's daughter gives you, for all the blows you gave your woman! How many blows, you stupid, greedy, fearful, bullying man? How many, in all your years? For each blow you gave her, I bring you two!"

I don't know if he even heard me, for he wailed as long as he could. By the time my arm was too tired to lift, he was down to blubbering and whimpering. He would not rise and go running after his woman any time soon—but just to be certain, I took out my knife and cut the filthy long shirt off his back. I dragged the pieces out from under him and carried them off, leaving him welted and naked among his curious sheep. Then I stuffed the rags well under a wide thorn-bush, laughing aloud as I thought of him trying to hide his nakedness among the sheep.

When I reached the hut Ehweh was loading the girls with bundles and water-skins, and they were crying and clinging to her. They all looked up, half-fearful, as I came trotting toward them.

"He surely won't be back before nightfall," I said, shouldering my recovered cloak and pouches. "Are you all ready to go?"

The girls nodded eagerly, looks of hope stirring in their eyes. I turned to their mother.

"What of you, Ehweh? Will you not come with your daughters?"

She paused to think for so long a time that I truly believed she would agree. But at the last she turned her head away. "I cannot leave," she said. "I tried to run away before, but he always found me and brought me back."

"If you mean your man," said I, "He'll be in no condition to follow you for a good hand of days. If you mean Lao'ue, he has troubles with his own folk–if indeed they've not killed him already."

The girls gasped in shock. Ehweh gave me a long look.

"I do not fear Lao'ue anymore, "she said. "As for my man... No, I cannot leave him. He would die, left alone."

I saw then that she still loved him, still re-membered him as the child he was long ago, in the good land that now was burned away.

"Good luck to you then, Ehweh," said I. "I'll tell your son you live and are well. Come, little wolf-cubs; it's time to go."

They wouldn't move until Ehweh had kissed and embraced all three of them, and then pushed them toward me. I led them away toward the mountains, and as often as I looked back I saw her standing by the hut, watching us go.

I took my time leading the girls through the mountains and the desert beyond, and not only to avoid tiring them. I needed to know, before I brought them among my people, just how deeply the curse of the poisoned olive-tree had worked into their blood—and how much of their slavishness was learned, and could be undone.

By the end of the first day, they were willing to cut the sleeves off their long shirts to make wrappings for their sore feet. Within another day, they agreed to cut the bottoms off their shirts to make proper breech-clouts and breast-harnesses. By the end of the moon-quarter, when we were well into the scrub-desert, they agreed to cut off the remains of their shirts and make cloaks of them. I also taught them to make and set snares to catch game while we slept, and the cord for the snares came from their shirts also. By the time we reached my village, they looked and walked like proper women. There was hope for them.

Midday it was, and everyone not out bathing or tending the animals was asleep in their huts, so our arrival caused no great fuss. I led the girls to Nala's hut, found her awake, and introduced them as Ka'eeneh's sisters. She cooed over them, fed them, and kept them busy while I hastened off to see Great Grandmother. We conferred until dark, for we had much to consider and many plans to make. Next morning I took the girls to the plant-patch, to see Ka'eeneh. They ran to him, shouting his name. He stood frozen for a long moment, then bent down to hug them soundly. Then I took them all down to the beach to meet Enotu and learn the fearful joys of bathing in the sea. At length I took Ka'eeneh aside to give him his news in private.

"Your mother is well and expecting a child soon," said I. "She sends you her blessings."

Ka'eeneh dropped his face into his hands, and said nothing.

"I also met her man—and your Sacred One—and gave them both a good beating."

"What?" He stared at me as if I had announced that I was Moon herself. "True. I hit Lao'ue on the head with my axe—" Ka'eeneh flinched.

"—but I fear the Sacred Folk may be hard to

kill, so perhaps he lives yet. If so, his own folk intend to make life difficult for him, for they learned what he did to your family, and were not pleased."

"I must ask them about that at equinox," he dared to smile.

"You shall have to make a journey to do it," I went on, "For it is true that there is a curse on your family, your... bloodline. You cannot stay here, nor your sisters either."

Ka'eeneh heaved a great sigh, as if he expected no better.

"I think I can persuade Enotu to go with you, and soon enough our village will send young men to make offer to your sisters, so you'll not be alone. Still, your sisters and their children—and the children of any woman you mate—may carry the curse. You must go make your own village a safe way from us, and we will see what comes of it."

Ka'eeneh sighed and looked out to sea. "I have heard of some good land a day's walk north along the beach, where a stream comes in," said he. "We can be happy there. It's more than I could have hoped, truly. Will you take care of my plant-patch?"

"I will indeed," I promised. "In truth, I may plant some fruit of my own." Ka'eeneh squared his shoulders. "And I will speak to your Sacred Folk, tell them everything and beg for their help in lifting the curse. Perhaps they will grant me that."

"Pray so," said I, clasping his hand.

So it was that Ka'eeneh's family went north, and Enotu went with them. They founded a village there, and Ka'eeneh made another plant-patch. At equinox they all came back to meet the Sacred Folk, and truly told their whole sorry tale.

Only I left out mention of my finding the trees, and of eating the fruit. Nor did I mention that I had planted seeds of the immortality tree—and not just in Ka'eeneh's first garden. Their location, as Great Grandmother insisted, must remain secret until we know all that will come.

The Sacred Folk conferred long, then took Ka'eeneh and his family—and Enotu and her big belly—into their flying boat. They flew them away, then returned them a day later, pronouncing them "most probably free from the curse". We thought it best that the family should remain at the northern village for generations yet, until we were certain the curse was truly gone. Even so, Ka'eeneh's relief was so great that he cast off his clothes right then and ran, whooping, naked into the sea. His sisters followed his example, and they spent all that afternoon playing happily in the water.

The Sacred Folk were not so cheerful. They said that they might not visit us again for as much as a year, since they had much work to do. From this I guessed that Lao'ue had escaped from the burning of his land, and they meant to hunt him.

This, I thought, did not bode well for us.

In time Enotu bore a son, and Ka'eeneh named him Enok. He also named the new village for the boy, claiming that it was fitting to name the place after the first child born there. By then he and his sisters no longer feared to undress and bathe, they all wore sensible clothing, and Ka'eeneh never again tried to bully anyone nor make exclusive claim to a child. Mother gave them some pigs, and they all hunted and fished, herded plants and animals, and seemed happy.

Slowly and carefully did Great Grandmother and I spread the knowledge that women do not make children by themselves, that mating does more than simply open the womb, that the man does give something of his blood to the child. This has not taken prerogatives from the mother's brother, but has made men more fond of their women's children, so the knowledge was for the best after all.

I saw less of Enotu and the others after

that, because that year I first became pregnant. The child was a girl, much to Mother's delight. The next, the year after, was a boy. Being slowed with pregnancy and nursing, I could not range so far out hunting anymore; for that and other reasons I spent more time working the plant-patch. Ka'eeneh had been right; the yams grew a dozen more yams from each planting, and the trees soon bore good fruit.

Only the mulberry-figs were slow in growing; it was a good ten years before they bore their first flowers, then fruit. By that time, even Mother noticed that I showed no signs of age. Great Grandmother, who has now also stopped aging, gave me some suggestions for keeping the secret.

Secret it must be, lest any word get back to the Sacred Folk—or, worse, to Lao'ue. I fear he still lives, and breeds the children of Ehweh and her man, for we have heard disturbing rumors in recent years of folk who rob and even kill people. I fear what Lao'ue would do with the trees, or with us, if he knew. I am certain that he never intended our 'wild strain' to gain immortality.

For that matter, I know not what the other Sacred Folk would make of it, either.

I must be careful where and to whom I give the fruit.

I also pledge to Earth, Sun and Moon that if the Sacred Folk never do catch up to Lao'ue and punish him, someday I will.

Revocare

Facilis est descensus Averno...
Sed revocare gradum superasque evad-
ere   ad   auras,
Hoc opus, hic labor est..

—*Virgil*, The Aeneid

Langspur Caverns are no deeper than treachery, as I found to my cost. It was a classic triangle–my money, my best friend, my supposedly-loving spouse–and I suspected nothing. I thought a weekend spent cave-climbing would be fun for all three of us; after all, I'd first met Lee at the Cavers' Club, and Jan often said she was willing to try anything once. I had no idea that there was anything more than friendship between them, or how far they were willing to go to have each other and my money too.

I trusted them completely, right up to the instant they cut my rope.

We were crossing the Johnson Chasm, usually called Bottomless Bend: Lee ahead, Jan in the middle, me on the end. The other two crossed and waved me on, so I fixed my line to the piton-ring and started across, concentrating on placing hand over hand, watching the rope. My only warning was that the beam from Lee's helmet-lamp jiggled–and I never imagined that it was from the motion of his arm as he sawed his knife through my line.

The very next thing I knew was that the rope had gone slack in my hands, and I was surrounded by rushing wind and darkness. I realized what was happening just in time to throw my head back and look up.

There I saw the fast-disappearing edge of the chasm with two helmeted heads peering over it, smiling like hell as they watched me go down. The only yell of surprise and shock was my own.

Then the smooth wall of the chasm began its long curve, and its rushing stone rasped against my backpack, and the ride became very rough very fast. I vaguely remember curling into a tight fetal ball, then impact after impact as I bounced and slid down the sloping wall, and I know I lost consciousness before the slide stopped. I have no idea how long I slid and skidded down the curve, or how long I was out cold afterward, or what miracle kept me from breaking more than my left arm.

I'm fairly certain I slipped in and out of awareness several times before the pain woke me completely, and then my only thought was to roll off that aching arm. It took me three tries before I managed it, and the arm still hurt. I lay still awhile longer to see if the pain would go away, but it didn't. Sometime later I noticed the sour smell of oil- smoke in the air. Eventually I opened my eyes.

My helmet-lamp was smashed, of course, but the darkness wasn't total. There was a dim reddish glow in the air above, not enough to let me see the roof of the cave, no more light than false dawn. It was enough to let me see my workable hand silhouetted before my eyes: enough to stir a thread of hope.

Then thirst competed for attention amid the sea of other pains. I remembered that I had a canteen, managed to sit up and fumble at my belt until I found it. The canteen looked and felt as battered as I was, but it didn't leak and had plenty of water. I drank until my throat felt a little less raw, then slowly began taking inventory of myself.

Besides the damned insistent broken arm, I had bruises and scrapes everywhere that I could feel. Everything moved stiffly, and everything hurt. I still had my helmet, pack and belt. I was alive and could still move.

Thoughts worked sluggishly through the constant haze of pain, but I constructed a good guess as to how I'd survived the fall. Johnson Chasm is an ancient volcanic vent, glassy with obsidian, too slick-walled to climb. Nobody had ever measured its full depth, and surely not the way I had, but the few explorers before me had noted that after the first hundred feet the chasm bent slowly to the westward. If that curve continued, it would eventually level out. If so, I'd gone sliding down the curve and come out at the end in this cavern, like a bowling-ball down a chute. I'd been falling feet first, and the opening must be somewhere behind me.

I looked back—slowly, stiffly—but saw only darkness. The dim red false-dawn glow came from somewhere ahead. So did a faint breeze, tinged with that burned-oil smell. That meant there was another opening, a way out, ahead of me. Best to go that way; even if I could find the chute where I'd come down, not likely in the dark, I'd never be able to climb that smooth chasm wall.

There was no point in waiting for rescue. I doubted that Jan and Lee would hurry to report me lost, or tell exactly where in the cave I'd gone down. It was anyone's guess if the police or even the Cavers' Club would send an expedition, or how long they'd take to arrive, much less find me.

My broken arm twinged for attention again. I rocked and groaned with pain for long moments, trying to think clearly about cleaning, splinting and bandaging. Eventually I gathered enough nerve to grit my teeth and work my way out of the backpack.

At that point I saw how I'd survived the long, sliding fall. The pack had been snagged, scraped, torn, and generally sandpapered clean away. There was nothing left but the straps and the scoured-bright frame. By some miracle, I'd skidded all the way down the chute on my back. The pack had kept my spine and ribs intact, the now battered and lightless helmet had done the same for my aching skull, and the gods of all cave-climbers only know how I kept from breaking both legs and my other arm. I was, all things considered, amazingly intact.

However, I had no food, lamp, radio or medical kit. All I had were the scraped backpack frame, the dented helmet, two long pitons on my belt, the canteen and the clothes

I was wearing.

I pulled my wandering mind together long enough to rip off my tattered shirtsleeves, tear them into strips, improvise splints from the pitons and a rough sling from the rags that were left. My left hand worked well enough that I could tie the knots. Once splinted and slung, my arm hurt less.

Now all I had to do was get myself out of here—with a broken arm, no rope, and no light.

But there was some light down here, now that I fixed my mind on it. The dim reddish glow seemed brighter ahead to my left, apparently behind the edge of a dark ridge. *Volcanic vent,* I guessed, wondering if this were some live remnant of the ancient eruption that had made the cavern.

I was too dazed with pain to think of possible danger; I simply knew that I needed light, and it was over there somewhere.

Likewise, I didn't stop to question why I struggled back into the remnants of my pack; I only knew that it had saved my life once today, and abandoning it would be downright ungrateful. I buckled the frame back on, staggered to my feet and went lurching like a last-stage drunk toward the dim red light.

It took a surprisingly long time to reach and cross the ridge, for it was much further off and bigger than I'd expected: more like a low hill than anything that belonged inside a cave. I was in no condition to ponder what this implied about the size of the cavern, but it made me uneasy.

So did the faint sounds that prickled at the edge of my hearing: soft rattlings and clickings, like falling sand... or claws on stone. I couldn't be sure I really heard them, but I had a worrisome feeling that I didn't want to hear them any clearer or closer. I made effort to hurry.

At the top of the ridge I got my first sketchy picture of the territory. A long stony slope stretched down and away from me; at the bottom was another sharp rim of silhouetted rock, and beyond that flickered the tips of sullen red-orange flames. It had to be some sort of burning gas-vent within a small crater; the air was too cool for it to be magma. It was approachable fire.

Now that I looked, far beyond the crater I could see other faint pinpricks of red light in the dark distance: probably more vents. I still couldn't see the roof of the cavern, and the walls were hidden in darkness. I could, however, see that the stones on the slope below me were bedded and twined with thick pale lichens or molds. There was life down here. I thought I heard the claw-clicking sound again.

Perfect love, they say, casts out fear. So

does perfect misery. Feeling only a sour annoyance above the surface of the gnawing pain, I went on down the slope.

Halfway to the crater's edge I stumbled over something that looked like a patch of pale and anomalous rock. Curiosity blooms at the damnedest times and circumstances–and just as well. I hunkered down to look at the odd rocks.

But they weren't rocks at all. They were bones. Big bones.

...Definitely animal life down here, was all I thought as I poked stupidly at the bones. There was a big thick one as long as my thigh. There was a roughly-round one that had to be a skull. I picked up the skull and looked at it for a long time while the facts trickled slowly through my pain-dulled brain.

What kind of animal has a skull as big as a bear's, a beetling brow, an ape-like jaw, and three horns?

Not an animal I wanted to meet. Not in the dark. Not empty-handed.

I noticed that there were toothmarks on the long bone. I remembered the faint clicking noises, wondered what this creature could have looked like when its bones were all connected, and how big it was, and what could have killed it. I decided that I needed a weapon, and right away.

The only likely materials I could see were the bones themselves. I picked them up and shuffled hurriedly toward the fire-vent.

It was a small crater, right enough, but it surrounded a pool of waxy, gummy material. The gum/wax/whatever was solid near the crater's edge, softer toward the middle, and liquefied at the center where the flame danced about a spur of spongy rock. It was like the top of a huge candle, a sullen mineral candle that might have been burning for half a billion years. The rock in and around Langspur Caverns is some of the oldest in the world...

The light was perhaps as strong as that of a large campfire, and it revealed that I was the only living creature within the crater–but it hadn't always been empty. There were some very odd footprints at the margin where the gum softened to liquid: tracks of something like a very large, thick-footed bird. At one side of the pool, amid a cluster of the tracks, was another pile of bones. These bones were different, somewhat smaller, all of them cracked, split or chewed.

I sat down with my back against a steep bank of the crater's rim, drank some more of the water, and considered the big shank-bone and the three-horned skull. If I could attach them, they'd make a serviceable mace. Tying would do, but I had no rope and couldn't spare any more of my clothing, thin protection though it was.

Then I thought of my hair. I'd always let it grow long, however fashions came and went, and it reached below my waist when unwound. The coiled braid made good padding for my cave-climbing helmet; it had probably helped save my life on the trip down here. With luck it could provide me with a weapon, too.

I uncoiled my braid, pulled it as far forward as I could, and chewed it off, strand by strand. It took a long time, and tired my jaws. It took less time to tie one end through the eye-holes of the skull and the other end to the shank-bone just below the swell of the joint. There were some small stones near the rocks of the crater's rim, and I stuffed the skull's cranium with as many of them as would fit.

The end result of perhaps two hours' painful and tedious work was a crude but reassuringly heavy bone-stone-and-hair Morning Star. I practiced swinging it, and managed to avoid hitting myself in the foot.

I was armed. Now what?

I struggled to my feet and walked to the edge of the crater facing the breeze. Yes, there were more of those dull flame-lights ahead, like distant red stars. There was also too much suspicious darkness between them, too much desert between oases of light. I didn't want to meet the local wildlife in the dark.

Maybe a torch...

I went to the pile of chewed bones and rummaged among them until I found a promising piece: a straight shank, hollow, with only one end broken off but the marrow totally gone. I didn't stop to wonder how the unsplit bone had come to be empty; it would be enough for me to avoid whatever had done that.

I poked strings of the pale lichen down the hollow of the bone, leaving an inch hanging out. Then I crawled laboriously to the edge of the liquid-gum pool and submerged the bone until it filled to the top. I managed to reach the end of the torch to the central fire, where the wick caught and burned well enough. The thick oil/wax/gum burned slowly, and I hoped it would last me to the next fire-pit.

Finally I tucked the torch upright into the lamp-catch of my helmet, set the helmet on my head, took the Morning Star in my right hand and set off into the wind.

I hadn't gone a quarter of the way to the next fire-pit before the clicks and rattlings came again. This time there was no mistaking them for the sound of falling sand.

I made a point of turning right and left every few steps to shine the dim torch-light around me. Whatever made those sounds didn't care for the light, and kept well beyond its reach. Still, whatever it was could move fast. Twice I felt certain that something was sliding up behind me, and I swung the Morning Star low and hard to discourage it. I caught nothing the first time. The second time, though, I felt a solid impact.

There was a surprised-sounding squeal, and the whatever-it-was clicked and rattled away before I could see more than a large shadow, shaped something like a deformed weasel. There was no way to guess the thing's true size.

I kept the Morning Star swinging and twitching in my hand as I walked on. That and the torch seemed to discourage the creature, or creatures, for I didn't hear that noise again.

More than halfway to the second fire-pit, I felt the ground change under my boot-soles: no more roughness of mixed stones or coarse cushion of pseudo-lichen, but a smooth hardness softened by dust. I bent my head to lower the torch, looked, and saw a broad bare path crossing my course. It was as wide as a small city alley. Down the middle ran two deep parallel depressions, like inverted rails.

It took me a long moment to understand that they were wheel-ruts. This was a road.

I stood up and looked both ways down the

road, hope stirring sluggishly through the relentless pain. Roads meant traffic, people, a way out of here. I wondered only for a moment what manner of people made or used a road at the bottom of Langspur Caverns. Most likely they were wildcat miners, doing a little illegal digging for gold, silver or gemstones. No problem: I could deal with such. I thought no further than that; it was enough to know that a ride was possible. I looked up and down the road, and waited.

In time I saw, off to my left, a tiny moving light that hadn't been there before. As I watched it resolved into two lights, then grew larger and closer, accompanied by a growing sound: rhythmic creaking, as of wagon-wheels. There was also an odd irregular hissing, but I ignored that. I stuck the Morning Star in my belt and stuck out my thumb in the time-honored signal.

As the creaking wagon grew closer, I noticed two things. First, it carried two tall torches set at its leading corners.

Second, the creatures that pulled it were not horses, oxen, mules, nor any kind of animal I'd ever heard of. They were scaly-skinned, high-shouldered, long-legged lizards— lizards the size of large ponies. The odd hissing came from them.

I blinked stupidly at them, pain-stunned

past wonder, thinking only that beasts in harness are, by definition, tame.

The wagon was a simple two-wheeled cart with a flat bench for the driver's seat, and the wheels stood taller than my head. The driver, as well as I could tell in that torchlight, was a huge and heavily ugly man. He wore scaly gauntlets and scaly armor, probably made from the hide of driving-lizards, plus an unmistakable sword-belt–if you please–with what I assumed was a hefty weapon in it, and a three-horned helmet that came down almost to his eyes.

Considering the signs of animal life that I'd seen down here, I wasn't surprised that he rode armed and armored, no matter how old-fashioned his gear. He'd probably be suspicious of strangers, but I didn't think he'd begrudge me a ride. I stepped forward and held up my thumb.

The cart pulled up beside me and stopped. The driver leaned over to get a better look at me, and I stepped further into the light to oblige.

Right then I saw that he was at least seven feet tall. And he wasn't wearing armor at all; that was his skin. The helmet was part of his head.

As he looked at me, his jaw dropped. His mouth was full of splintery gray fangs.

Mutant? I wondered, blinking owlishly. *Troll? Alien?*

He gave a grating brassy cry, turned around and tugged furiously at whatever was hanging on his sword-belt. There was no mistaking that action.

Without thinking, I yanked the Morning Star out of my belt. His weapon cleared first. I saw it swing up to strike: a long bar of dark metal.

I had no shield–except my pack-frame.

I swung far forward, and the swordlike bar came down across my back. It clanged heavily on the metal pack-frame, the impact enough to stagger me but not knock me down. I came up swinging and smashed the Morning Star upward into his elbow, knocking him backward. He screeched like grinding metal. I could almost sympathize, knowing intimately how a broken arm felt, but I didn't think I should give him time to recover; he had, after all, hit first. I swung the Morning Star again, this time catching him in the face. He tumbled bonelessly out of the cart.

The draft-lizards hissed in worry; I stuck the Morning Star back in my belt and shushed them with a tug at the reins. Then I bent over the downed driver, noticing that his weapon was indeed a coarse kind of black iron sword. I took it for myself and stuck it in my belt beside the Morning Star. He also carried a pouch of some greasy-looking meat and a skinful of suspicious-smelling fluid that I didn't think I should trust, and a small bag of lumpish metal coins that looked like nothing I'd ever seen. I left him the pouch and skin-bag, took the coins for reparations, and left him lying in the road.

As I turned away it occurred to me that his head looked very much like the three- horned skull of my Morning Star. In that case, I knew, there were creatures hereabouts that could kill and eat his kind. I didn't want to meet them on foot.

The cart was comparatively low-slung and not too hard to climb into. I put out my own torch to save for later, took up the reins and slapped them on the lizards' backs, which they didn't seem to understand. Beneath the seat I saw an unmistakable drover's whip, so I took it out, tucked the reins into my left hand, and slapped the whip experimentally over the team's rumps. It didn't seem to hurt their scaly hides, but they understood the signal and moved on.

The cart had no springs, and its action was rough and jolting, but it beat walking. The cool breeze blew against my left cheek, reminding me of my original direction. Considering the reaction I'd had from the driver, I didn't think his associates down the road would treat me any better, much less help me get home. I turned the lizards into the wind, off the road, which they were reluctant to do until I laid on a little harder with the whip.

The wind blew steadily, the lizards hissed complaints as they padded over the rough ground, and the cart creaked and jounced over the lichen and rocks. There was no other sound, and the gnawing pain threatened to soak up my mind if I didn't fix my attention on something. I tied the reins to one of the poles and explored the cart for possible food, rope, or anything else useful.

The first things I found were some large coarse-woven bags with shreds of dried lichen in them. Then there was a smaller bag containing–oh joy of joys–a coil of leather rope, two grapnels and a mallet. I guessed that the driver had delivered a load of dried lichen and was on the return trip when he ran into me.

I couldn't imagine what he or his friends had planned to do with the rope and grapnels–unless, perhaps, he or his friends intended to do some cave-climbing. I didn't know why he or they might want to do that, but the presence of those tools bothered me.

So did the construction of the cart itself, now that I looked at it. At first I'd thought it was made of some hard, fine-grained, pale wood bound together with leather thongs instead of nails. That puzzled me. The lack of nails couldn't mean lack of metal; the sword, and the axle, wheel-joints and tires of the cart were made of black iron.

Then I took a closer look at one of the slats, and realized that it wasn't made of wood at all. It was scraped, steam-shaped bone.

No wonder the cart was made without nails, I thought dully. Bone splits if you drive a nail through it. No wood, no trees, could grow down here, anyway: nothing but lichen and assorted animals. The crude iron was probably smelted and forged at those fire-pits. Limited materials, limited technology: these people didn't have much—except bad tempers. Who and what were they? I was too stupid with pain to think about it.

I found the last items in a bag under the seat: a dozen obvious long-range darts, bone-shafted, metal-tipped, with thin bone plates at the butt for feathering—slender throwing-darts, as long as my leg. They looked as if they'd been well used. I settled the darts where I could reach them easily, and sat back to study the land around me.

Ahead and to the right lay another fire-crater, much larger than the last one. It was also noisier: loud bubbling, a rumbling and scraping, a rhythmic pounding that came to sound like metal being hammered at a forge.

Considering that the natives were unfriendly and the crater seemed occupied, I chose to avoid it. I steered the lizards far around the fire-pit, hoping that none of the natives would come out and see the cart-lights as I drove past. In fact, they didn't.

Unfortunately, something else did.

My first warning was the lizards shying violently to one side, their hissing rising to whistling screams. I couldn't see what had scared them, but in another second I could smell it. *How can a* smell *be cold and greasy?* I wondered as I dropped the reins and picked up one of the darts. Torchlight glittered on something ahead and to my left. That was target enough; I threw the dart.

Something squalled like scraping rock, and there was a tangled thrashing at the edge of the torchlight. Something long and dark and reeking whipped close overhead, narrowly missing the near torch. I pulled out the sword and set it across my knees, hoping that the thing would see, take the hint and go away.

It didn't. A long glittery-black limb of something stretched out, raking at the cartwheel. I took up the sword, turned awkwardly and slashed down at it. There was a satisfying impact and screech, and an unpleasant splash as something spurted across my arm. The screeching and stink retreated fast into the darkness.

Whatever the fluid was, it burned. I dropped the sword into the wagon-bed, grabbed one of the sacks and wiped the burning liquid off my arm before it could do any serious damage. It left sore red spots, like a speckled sunburn. Where it had splashed my pants-leg it ate holes in the cloth. Where it had hit the wagon, it slowly stained the bones black. I took care to wipe it off the sword and the leather, hoping the cart wouldn't fall apart under me at some odd moment. My arm was throbbing again.

The lizards calmed down and slowed to a shuffle, and I turned them to face the wind again. As I glanced over the cart to check for remaining damage, I noticed something caught in the spokes of the off wheel. I reined the lizards to a halt and looked closer.

The object stuck between the bone spokes was clearly the tip of the arm/leg/ whatever of the thing that had attacked us, but it didn't look like part of any animal I knew. It resembled the tip of a cactus, and was about as big around as my lower leg. It was still dripping that blackish burning fluid. The wheel didn't show any damage beyond stains, but I didn't think it a good idea to leave the thing there. I pried it loose with the tip of the sword, dropped it on the ground and drove on. The smell of the burning blood lingered, greasy-cold and foul.

That, as it turned out, was lucky. As we went on through the dark I noted that the whisper-clickings approached often, but each time they'd come only so close and then pause, make a sound like suspicious sniffing, then turn around and go away. Apparently the weasel-shadow things liked the stench of cactus-beast even less than firelight. That was fine with me.

Meanwhile the pain gnawed its way through my attention, dulling everything else. There was no way to measure time. I began to doze off in fits and starts, and didn't snap back into full wakefulness until the two draft-lizards slugged determinedly off to the left. At first I tried to pull them back on course, but then I noticed what they'd heard: the faint gurgling of running water. I considered that the beasts probably needed it, and my canteen could use refilling too, so I let the lizards have their way.

In a few minutes we came to a small stream running through the lichen and stones. The lizards stopped at the stream-bank and put their heads down to drink. In the torchlight I could see nothing else but some small lizards that resembled gila monsters nesting in the lichens near the stream. I noticed the small lizards nibbling on the lichen, and guessed that if the creatures were herbivores they just might make good eating. I didn't know how long it would take me to get out of the cavern, and I was already hungry. I slipped off the wagon, slid out the dark iron sword and bashed three of the creatures before the others realized I was dangerous and skittered away.

As I was picking up my kills I noticed something moving overhead, high in the air on the far side of the stream, something round and pale. *Moon?* I thought stupidly, before I remembered where I was. At that point the thing came a little closer, and I got a good look at it.

It was the face of a giant lamprey.

I crouched there for a long moment, looking at the impossible thing, making certain that it wasn't just a pain-delirium vision. It was hanging about ten feet up in the air, and looked to be about two feet across. It was as flat as a dinner-plate, surrounded by a fringe of waving short tentacles, with a circular mouth that opened like an iris-lens and was full of pointed pale teeth. It was dirty-gray in color, and had no eyes that I could see. It seemed to be smelling its way toward the stream, swinging slowly through the air. I knew that behind that face there had to be a head of some sort, or at least a neck, but I couldn't see it yet. I had no idea what its body looked like, or how big it was. I didn't think those teeth belonged to a lichen-eater.

How can a lamprey live out of water? I wondered, watching the thing. Perhaps it was only thirsty. Perhaps it was just coming for the water, and if I stayed out of its way it would leave me alone. I tucked my kills into my sling and stepped away from the water. Good thing it was downwind, I thought, or its smell might panic the draft-lizards, and then where would I be?

But the thing changed direction, turning toward me. Its iris-mouth pulsed open and shut, sucking air. I realized that it didn't just want water; it smelled through that mouth-opening, or perhaps the tentacles. It had smelled the spilled blood of the dead lizards, and it wanted food.

All right, I grumbled silently, pulling out one of the lizards. *I can spare one.*

I tossed the lizard at the lamprey-face. It hit to one side and bounced, landing on the wrong side—my side—of the stream. The lamprey-face dived greedily after the carcass, dropped flat on top of it and began gulping up the body with a crunching/squelching noise. As the lamprey-face fed, I got a good look at its head—a featureless bulb—and its neck: round and gray, thin rings of what looked like cartilage joined by a semi-transparent gray membrane, about as thick around as my body. I didn't think the dull sword would cut through it, nor the Morning Star do it much damage, and I still couldn't see what the rest of its body looked like. I stepped back to the wagon and climbed in quietly.

Just as I lifted the reins the lamprey-face looked up again, wet teeth clacking, and started to bob and weave toward the cart. I didn't want the draft-lizards to see it; they might panic and run and overturn the cart– with me in it. *All right, you greedy worm!* I thought, growing sullenly peeved, as I pulled out the second lizard and threw it.

The carcass plopped on the ground a good way from the cart, and the lamprey- face plunged after it. It was a good thing the worm was blind, and hopefully deaf too, I considered as I pulled the draft-lizards' heads up and reined them back from the water. Though the lizards hadn't seen the thing yet, they must have caught a scent that worried them; flapping the reins on their rumps was enough to make them move quickly. They turned the cart neatly and began shambling away at a good quick shuffle. I didn't think the lamprey-face would catch up to us.

Then I heard a heavy splashing behind me.

I turned around and saw that, yes, sure enough, the damned thing was crossing the stream to come after us. I saw the blind face clearly, and got a dim glimpse of thick coils. There seemed to be no end to them. And the lamprey-face was moving much faster than I'd expected. Yes, it could overtake us. In fact, it would reach the cart in less than a minute at this rate.

I wasn't about to give that damned thing my last meal.

I dropped the third carcass under the cart-seat and reached for one of the darts. Then I turned again and crouched on the seat, hefting the dart, wondering where to hit the lamprey-face to best effect. Maybe piercing its neck would discourage it. I aimed a little below the fringed-platter face and threw the dart.

It struck well; I saw it hit and quiver. Unfortunately, all that seemed to do was annoy the worm. The lamprey-face gave a ridiculously thin whistle that sounded more peeved than hurt, and lurched after us with its teeth clacking like castanets and its coils grinding wetly on the stones.

Damn! Two meals and a good weapon wasted! was my first reaction. My broken arm twinged, and I began to actively hate that pestering worm. I pulled out the sword and waited, trying to think of where I could hit that thing that would hurt it.

The draft-lizards broke into a shambling trot, hissing nervously, as they finally guessed that something unpleasant was following them. They still didn't outpace the lamprey-face, which was grinding along like a slow freight-train behind us. It closed in on the cart, its blind head weaving down out of the air toward me. I lifted the sword and waited.

As it passed through the smoke of the off torch, the lamprey-face jerked back and irised its mouth as if it as if it had smelled something nasty.

That gave me an idea.

I tried to untie the torch-pole from the wagon, but the knots were too tight. I swore briefly and chopped the leather laces through just as the lamprey-face made another pass. The weight of the torch-pole hurt my bad arm as I put down the sword, and that put paid to any hesitance I still might have had. I took the torch-pole in my good hand, pulled back and waited until the blind head drew close. Smelling lizard blood, the circular mouth opened wide.

I reared up and jammed the torch straight into the gaping mouth, as far as it would go.

The effect on the worm was truly satisfying. The thing whistled in High C, yanked backward so hard and fast that it ripped the torch clean out of its pole-socket and almost pulled the pole itself out of my hand. The lamprey-face whipped backward, oily smoke and flames pouring out of its mouth, and went flopping and thrashing away in the dark. I could hear it rolling around long after I lost sight of it, and guessed that it might take that thing a good while to die. The draft-lizards were inclined to keep trotting, and I let them.

I had only the one pole-torch now, and it wasn't nearly as easy to see the ground ahead. I fitted my hand-torch into the empty pole-socket and tried to light it at the other torch, but couldn't manage the trick on the bouncing cart. I judged that we'd need to stop at the next fire-pit to renew the oil in the pole-torches anyway, and besides, I was painfully hungry and wanted to cook and eat my remaining lizard. I looked for a fire-pit ahead, saw a small but characteristic smudge of red light not too far off, and steered the team that way.

I was in luck; the fire-pit was small and its crater was, as I took care to make certain, unoccupied. There was barely enough room for the team, the cart and me between the oil-pool's edge and the crater wall, and I had a miserable time moving the team and cart safely into place. I fetched a heavy rock to pin the reins and keep the draft- lizards from straying, then also went and fetched some lichen and offered it to the beasts. They gulped it greedily, so I picked an armload of it and left them happily munching. I blew out the cart's remaining torch, cut one of the sacks into strips to re-tie the loose pole, pulled both torches out of their sockets and took them to the oil-pond to refill them.

Skinning, gutting and cleaning the lizard wasn't too difficult, given that I had no blade but the crude sword. Cooking it was a worse problem; I stuck the carcass on the end of the sword and held it over the fire to roast, but the sword's handle soon grew too hot to hold. I managed to wedge the sword in place with rocks, then leaned against the cart's near wheel and sat back to wait for my dinner to cook. It had to cook thoroughly, I reminded myself; there was no telling what parasites or plagues or poisons wild game might be carrying, especially down here.

Down here... Mean place, my mind wandered as I waited. I pulled out the Morning Star and studied the skull at its end. "'Alas, poor Yorick'," I muttered to it. "How long have you and yours been down here? Ten million years? More? Since before the other dinosaurs died? Is this lost Atlantis, or the source of the legends of Hell? How long did it take you folks to grow intelligence? And is this all you've done with it?"

The skull, of course, said nothing.

My throat felt sore, so I stuffed the Morning Star back in my belt and took out the canteen. The water had an unpleasant metallic taste; I wondered if it came from the battered canteen or from the stream flowing over mineral beds.

This was, I thought drowsily as I watched the lizard-carcass roast, a very mean place. I was bothered by the locals every time I turned around. Ugly things tried to hit me, snatch the cart or my team or my food… And all I was trying to do was get out of here. I didn't feel very good. My arm hurt like hell.

The lizard was actually overdone when I remembered to pull it off the fire, but I wasn't choosy. It tasted like oily leather. I ate it anyway, right down to the bones.

As I chewed the last of the bones I felt something slap my boot. I looked down to see a horned red snake, as long as my arm, striking determinedly at the sole of my heavy cave-climbing boot. Damn, but the local monsters wouldn't leave me in peace! I kicked the snake into the fire and watched it shrivel, then got up and went to the cart and crawled inside. The empty lichen-sacks sufficed for mattress, pillow and blankets. I fell asleep quickly, heavily, without dreams.

When I woke, everything was the same except that I felt worse. My arm throbbed like a bass drum. I was hot and feverish, and saw blisters coming up among the bruises and scratches on my skin. Apparently I'd picked up some sort of local rash, too. That was all I needed.

Time to get out of here. I lit and remounted the pole-torches, picked up the reins, whipped up the team and drove out of the crater, back into the wind.

I hadn't driven twenty yards before something landed hard on my back, and I heard teeth or claws scrabbling on the metal of the pack-frame. Without looking, I pulled out the Morning Star and swung it back over my shoulder like a Penitente's flail. One of the horns gave me a nasty poke, but it also took care of my unwelcome guest. I heard the thing squawk and fall with a leathery thump into the cart-bed, so I turned around to get a good look at it.

The thing was either a very scaly bat or a short-faced pterodactyl. It was woefully ugly, and it stank. It was a hell of a way to start the day.

I threw the thing out of the cart and drove on, letting the wind in my face wash away the stink. Between that smell and the residual odor of cactus-thing blood, the cart must have reeked amazingly to the local wildlife, for nothing else came to bother me.

Time passed, featureless, immeasurable. The darkness, monotony, fever and pain sent my mind wandering down curious pathways, remembering sunlight and open sky. I imagined walking up the path to my own front door in clean, soft air glowing with sunshine. I thought of a long hot bath melting away my assorted pains. I pictured the big double bed in the main bedroom…

And then I imagined Jan and Lee in it, celebrating their success. I imagined crushing both their skulls with a single blow of the Morning Star, then throwing their bodies out of the bed and lying down in it myself.

I don't know how many hours passed before I noticed a change that roused me from fever dreams. It was the wind, stronger and louder, closer to the source. I sat up and whipped the lizard-team to a shuffling trot, eager to be done with this place. Slowly but steadily, the wind grew to gale-force.

Now the land grew rougher, and the team could do no better than a walk. The ground sloped upward and the stones on it became bigger. The last of the fire-pits fell far behind, and the wind constantly threatened to put out the torches. Finally one of the torches did blow out, and a boulder too big to pass blocked the way. It was time to abandon the cart.

I halted the team and re-lit the torch, took out the climbing gear and canteen, the sword and the Morning Star. I turned the draft-lizards' heads around, tied up their reins and slapped them into a shambling trot back toward the dark plain below. I hoped they'd survive down there, that the torches and the assorted stinks the cart had accumulated would keep them safe, for they'd been good serviceable beasts. With luck, some troll or other would find them—and, I supposed, thank his troll gods for the windfall. There was no point taking a torch for myself, not against that wind. I waved a last farewell to the disappearing torches, turned toward the heart of the gale and climbed upward.

Nothing came to bother me in the roaring darkness, and in time I found the tunnel. It was another volcanic vent, but with far rougher sides than the one I'd come down. There were footholds and handholds in plenty, even ledges broad enough to rest on, and the ragged tunnel led upward at an easy enough angle that I could climb it one-handed in the dark.

It still took forever to climb. A day and a night, I think, it must have been; I remember sleeping on a broad ledge, waking to growing hunger and the eternal nagging pain, and finally thirst when the canteen went dry. Fever and pain distorted my time- sense, and I had to concentrate fiercely on each move. Twice I crossed patches of slick obsidian where the footing was treacherous. On one sharp rise I had to chop footholds and handholds with the sword, and the wretched thing broke before I was safely finished. I managed to climb it anyway, with a little help from the rope and grapnels. Once I came across a crack too wide for jumping, as a tossed stone told me, and I had to use the rope and grapnels with the wind fighting me at every throw.

That wind became a personal enemy, its constant roar blending with the low thunder of pain in my arm. In time it came to sound like a full orchestra playing some dark Impressionist symphony. A choir of impossibly high voices joined it, singing clever insults at me in every phrase, though I could never quite make out the words. Sometimes I sang and shouted back to them, but more often I saved my breath for climbing and only cursed the voices silently.

A dozen times I scraped my injured arm, and howled in pain while the wind- voices laughed. A dozen times I stopped to rest, and half of them fell asleep for uncounted hours. I crawled upward by slow and painful inches, feeling my way along until my good hand was raw. The sores on my skin itched like fire-ants, and more than once I dreamed that I was being eaten alive by tiny lizards. I slipped and almost fell a score of times. Twice I did fall, no more than a yard or two before I could catch myself, but hard enough to make my broken arm scream at me until I screamed back. As hunger and thirst added to the pain I remembered the lamprey-face, and wished that I'd burned the damned thing before giving it a single lizard. I wished I'd taken the troll driver's bottle, emptied it out and refilled it at the stream for a spare canteen. Above all, I wished I'd cut Jan's and Lee's rope before they cut mine.

I don't know how long the light had been visible before I finally noticed it among the shifting fever-lights in my eyes. What drew my attention was that it didn't shimmer and change; it was vague and distant and the pale blue of outside air, like sunbeam-shafts through a high cathedral window. I smiled benevolence at all the upper world—with two exceptions—and climbed toward it.

I came out through a shadowed gash in a cliff-face, into late afternoon sunlight, over-looking a barren and rocky valley. Steady wind poured through the valley and swept the cliff, pressing me almost lovingly against the rock as I worked my way down to the valley floor. I had no idea where I was, except that it was the true upper world, and not too far from the known location of Langspur Caverns. The sunlight felt wonderful; it seemed to bake the fuzziness out of my head, some of the hot throb out of my arm, and the miserable fire-ant itch out of my skin. The blisters burst and dried as I watched, leaving only glassy circular patches that looked like scales.

Lizard's scales...?

The thought bothered me, but I couldn't hold on to it in the pure joy of seeing the sky again, feeling the sun again, and walking on lighted ground again. I couldn't wait to find a familiar landmark and get myself back to civilization. I wanted a tall beer, a thick steak, a hot bath and a soft bed, in that order. I'd deal with Lee and Jan later; just now I was laughing-drunk on sunlight. I turned toward the sweet gold sun and walked westward out of the valley.

It was no more than a mile or so to the western ridge, and as I came over it I saw on the flats below–oh joy!–a two-lane blacktop highway. Roads meant traffic, people, a ride out of here. I hurried down to the shoulder of the road, looked up and down it, and waited.

In time I saw, off to my left, sunlight glinting off the grill of an oncoming truck. I remembered the last time I'd tried to hitch a ride, and grinned down at the trusty hand-made Morning Star in my belt. In daylight, the dangling three-horned skull looked even uglier. For that matter, I didn't look much better myself: dirt-stained, blood-streaked, bruised, ragged, still wearing my worn climbing-gear, skin studded with those scaly patches, with no idea what my face looked like by now. I'd have a great story to tell the driver. As the truck drew near, I raised my hand and stuck up my thumb in the time-honored signal.

The truck pulled up beside me and stopped. The driver hitched across the seat, opened the near door and leaned out to get a good look at me. I stepped forward to oblige.

As he looked at me, his jaw dropped. He gave a hoarse yell, turned around and tugged furiously at something tucked into his belt. I saw the handle of what looked like a dark iron bar.

No, there was no mistaking that action. Without thinking, I yanked the Morning Star out of my belt.

His weapon cleared first, and I got a good look at it as he swung it up to strike: a black steel crowbar.

I ducked forward and the bar came down flat across my back, clanging on the frame of my backpack. At that angle the blow was enough to stagger me, but not enough to knock me down. I came up swinging.

Damn, damn, damn, I thought wearily, as I smashed the Morning Star upward into his face, *Is it all to do over again?*

…I suppose I can manage to drive this truck, but I'd been hoping for an easier way home.

Cancel/Balance

Asher was manhandling the last crate onto the elevator, power-suit set on light, when the Kowtik Spaceport customs inspectors finally came down to the cargo bay. The righteous-faced one in the suit, of course, yapped and huffed because the cargo was already gone. The stone-faced one in the uniform simply walked up to the elevator and said, "Hold it."

Asher took her hands off the crate and stepped back. The Uniform took out his probe and poked it at all the crates in the elevator, one after the other. The Suit came trotting up, still yapping, waving his comm-pad around and generally getting in the way. The Uniform ignored The Suit, finished his inspection, turned to Asher and asked "Where's the rest?"

"Below, on the dock," said Asher, pointing. "You can ride down with this load."

"Alright," said the Uniform, reaching for the elevator button.

The Suit, still yapping, hastily jumped into the elevator before the doors could close in his face. He yapped the usual legal threats all the way down to the lower lock, all the way out onto the concrete dock where the rest of the cargo stood waiting, and all the way through The Uniform's inspection. He kept right on yapping while The Uniform took the pad, poked the keys, pulled off the printout, walked over to the Cargomaster—who was sitting on the transport cart, patiently slugging down a soda—handed the CM the printout and walked away. The Suit followed, still yapping, until they were out of sight and earshot.

"Why do they even bother sending the Suits?" Asher grumbled, hauling the last crate out of the elevator. "The Uniforms do all the work, anyway."

"To make jobs for bureaucrats, of course," said the CM. "Hey, just bring those green-tabbed crates straight over here. Don't even bother puttin' 'em in the pile."

It took another hour and a half to sort and tote and lock up the crates, by which time Asher was strongly in need of a good cold beer. She didn't bother going back to her quarters and changing clothes, but went straight to the locker, peeled out of the power-suit, hung it on the rack and walked off the dock. The guard at the service-gate didn't even look up as she slid her ID card through the slot and walked out. She could see the sign for the first bar less than fifty meters down the road, just beyond the ground car parking-lot. Asher was halfway past the parking-lot when an odd thought pulled her to a dead stop. The one thing the customs-inspection team hadn't checked was... Herself.

She'd been wearing the power-suit. A probe couldn't see through it. There was room enough in the power-suit to hide a liter of damn-near anything. Neither of the inspectors had thought to look in the power-suit.

Those decomp idiots! If I'd wanted to smuggle something...

Asher marveled over that all the way into the bar (standard set-up, low lighting), all the way to one of the small booths (standard plastic seats and table), and well into her first beer (likewise standard, but cold). She couldn't stop playing with the thought, but refused to think of the next step: that this little fact could maybe solve her ongoing financial problem.

No, she decided, she was definitely not going down that road. Taking a step over the line had gotten her into this mess in the first place, and another step could drop her out the airlock completely. No, she'd pay off the goddam debt the straight way, even if it kept her broke for another year. Close the door on that idea.

And of course that was when the big goon in the flash clothes slid into the booth across from her. "Hey, Asher?" he grinned, showing his big repro teeth. "Roan, baby, how you doin?"

Asher sighed, and grabbed for her beer. "Hello again, Muscleboy," she said, tired to death of this routine. "Don't you have anything better to do than follow me around the circuit?"

Muscleboy grinned wider. "Tigo wants his money," he said, as if she wouldn't know. "I'm his bill-collector."

Asher took a long swig of beer, too tired of this game to be afraid anymore. "If you guys know how to hunt me up in a nowhere port like Kowtik, then you know I haven't even gotten my landing-pay yet. All I got in my pocket right now is enough for two more beers. You want one?"

To his credit, Muscleboy shook his head. "What I want," he said, still grinning, "Is for you to go back to the *Heron II*, draw your pay, bring it all back here and hand it to me. And—"

Asher said the last words along with him: "'-don't keep me waiting, because I'm not a patient man'. Yeah, I know the drill." She finished her beer, enjoying his brief pole-axed look. "You also know that it'll be another three hours before the Paymaster clears the comp and gives us our bucks. You also know exactly how much I'm getting: $2400 and small change. You know how much that'll leave on the debt-"

"$9600," he said automatically.

"And how long it'll take me to work up the rest of it. You know it, I know it, and Tigo knows it. So there's nothing more to say, except that I'll see you here in about three and a half hours with the $2400."

In fact, now that she thought about it, Tigo knew she paid off reliably whenever she got money. She'd been paying him regular install-ments before Muscleboy ever showed up. What was the point of the bullying, then? Did the goon just do it for fun?

"You know what'll happen if-" he went into the standard routine.

"Yeah, yeah, I know. You threaten to break my arm, which is really dumb, because I can't work and earn the money if my arm's broken. We've all been there before. Don't bother." Asher finished her beer and slid out of the booth. "How about you give me a receipt when

I bring you the money?"

Muscleboy got that pole-axed look again, and Asher took advantage of his confusion to head for the door. She got out into the grease-flavored open air, thought for a moment, then ducked into the parking-lot and crouched down behind one of the cars. She raised her head just high enough to watch the street through the ground car's windows.

Sure enough, less than a minute later Muscleboy came out of the bar, scanned the street, swore when he didn't see her, then went stomping off toward the landing-field. Asher sighed, slid down the side of the ground car and sat on the tarmac. Three more hours with nothing to do but maybe drink two more beers, then go get the money. She'd be eating and sleeping on the ship again, pinching pennies, buying nothing, all this layover. It would be like this for another year, at least. She might as well have stayed home, gone on the dole, never gone to space. *Wouldn't have been any poorer, and at least wouldn't have to haul cargo-crates around or deal with the same old crap from Tigo's goon.*

"Hyumann?" a soft voice buzzed nearby.

Asher flinched, even as she looked.

It was a Kowtiki, sure enough. It looked like a furry coat-rack crowned with knobby lights and hung with scarves. It sounded like a bad intercom, and smelled of pepper. For all that they were carbon-based life-forms, the Kowtiki looked simply too alien to be called either ugly or beautiful. They were too fragile to be physically dangerous to humans, so only the real xenophobes could find them frightening. They were also receptive empaths, Asher remembered–and often liked to absorb the colorful emotions of humans.

Even so, they had standards of taste. Asher couldn't imagine even a sensation-hungry Kowtiki wanting to slurp up human glumness or depression, her own sour mood right now.

"Kowtiki," Asher acknowledged, pulling herself to her feet. "What do you want?"

"Money-trouble you have, yesss?" The furry coat-rack wriggled its long pegs suggestively.

"You guessed it," Asher admitted, peering at the knobby lights that were the creature's eyes. *An easy guess, seeing what I was feeling. But why ask me?* There was much commerce between Kowtiki and Humans, primarily traded goods. The services that Kowtiki occasionally wanted could venture into the bizarre. "Are you offering me a job?"

"Yesss," buzzed the Kowtiki. "But not here to speak. Come-sit-speak elsewhere."

"Not that bar," said Asher, glancing back at the door.

"No-no-no. Kowtiki place we come. I show.

Not far..." The Kowtik paused, its knobby eyes flickering. "No danger to Hyumann. Safe-safe."

Asher laughed. Kowtiki definitions of danger were much more elaborate than Human ones. 'Safe' was exactly what this place would be. *But don't eat or drink anything, just to be sure...* Asher realized that she was already halfway committed, that desperate for money. "All right," she agreed. "We go, we speak, I decide."

"You decide," the Kowtiki agreed, ambling toward the street. "Come-come."

I can always refuse, Asher told herself, as she followed.

The safe-safe place was across the street, around the corner, down the block and through an unobtrusive door, down a corrugated ramp and into a basement. It was definitely a Kowtiki meeting-place, bar, restaurant, whatever they called it. Visitors were obliged to remove their footgear before entering. The ceiling was dotted with tiny lights that gave the impression of stars, and hung with swags of cloth that occasionally dropped to form curtains. The floor and walls were padded with thick plush cloth that bulged into amorphous cushions of variable sizes, some large enough to form cozy niches. In the dim lighting it was impossible to tell how many Kowtiki were present, ambling here and there or lying sprawled amid the cushion-extrusions. Sounds were muffled further by the glassy tinkling of what passed for Kowtiki music. Asher's guide led her to one of the dim-lit nooks, where he/she/it promptly lay down and half-coiled itself around a squat toadstool of a cushion. Asher sat down, crossed her legs and waited.

"Eat? Drink? Other?" the guide asked, something in its tone or the set of its limbs suggesting that it didn't expect the offer to be taken seriously.

"No, thanks," Asher smiled. "Just talk. What's the job?"

"Smuggle," the guide said, very distinctly.

Asher stared at the Kowtiki for a long instant, then laughed. *Of course! It must have felt me playing with that idea as I went into the bar...*

She noticed that the Guide was rippling subtly all down its length, limbs twitching, knobby eyes blinking in sequence. Her laughter faded as she watched. The rippling stopped too.

Soaking up my laughter, she realized. *They enjoy the feel of our emotions, and don't mind triggering them.* She filed that thought away for future reference. "Yes, I can smuggle a little," she admitted, thinking hard of the limited space inside a power-suit. "Just what do you want smuggled, and where? How big is it, and who do I give it to? What's the pay, and how do I get it? I need details." *Am I really going to do this? Is it really worth the money?*

"Liter-size," buzzed the Guide, holding up one stubby limb. "Weight half-kilo. You can?"

"I can," Asher admitted. That was almost exactly the size and weight she'd been thinking about, visualizing, feeling, when she'd come into range of the bar. No wonder the Guide had picked her out.

"On ship you take. Off bring at next port. Raddanin."

Asher nodded, reminding herself to keep calm. The Kowtiki read feelings and sensations, not thoughts. "Yes, Raddanin is our next port." And she'd never seen a customs inspector look into a cargo-loader's power-suit there, either. "It can be done."

"There you meet Kowtiki dressed all in...you call green, think I." The Guide patted one of its scarves. "This color."

"Green, yes."

"That-one-with, you go. Parcel give, money get. Simple."

"Simple," Asher echoed. *Calm, calm, he/she/it can't read you if you're calm...* Raddanin, she remembered, was a crosspoint world: Humans, Kowtiki, four or five other intelligent races, owned chunks of it and mingled freely in the cosmopolitan cities. A Human meeting with a Kowtiki wouldn't be remarked upon. "How much?"

"Ten-thousand Hyumann-dolloh, in coin."

Asher twitched in something close to shock. That, plus her landing-pay, would clear the debt with Tigo and leave a little over. *I'll be free!*

She noticed that the Guide was rippling again.

Asher made herself calm down and think, remember that Kowtiki lapped up emotions, remember that they were also clever merchants, remember that they could lie as outrageously as any Human. It was remarkably convenient that one of them had come up with damn-near exactly the money she needed, at just the right time, at just the right place. *Think!* "That's...a lot of money for such a small package," she said, trying to raise up a feeling of nervousness, worry, to keep the Guide preoccupied. "What will I be carrying?"

The Guide rippled again, then sat up. All but three of its knobby eyes closed. "I explain," it said. "Law on Raddanin mostly Hyumann made, forbids many common goods of Kowtiki, much to annoy. See. Coffee it allows: harmless stimulant to Hyumann, poisonous to Kowtiki and Lerishanneth. Not-allows it harmless stimulant of Kowtiki, saying dangerous to

Hyumann. Most unfair."

"I can see that," Asher smiled humorlessly. Yes, she'd seen a lot of that.

"Kowtiki there this stimulant want, for themself, not to waste on Hyumann. Pay good price. You see?"

"I see..." *Not enough. Exactly what am I getting into?* "Exactly what is this stuff?"

The Guide flickered his eyes like a gunship's running-lights. "Kowtiki name *emishqualtig*."

It took two seconds for Asher to translate that. When she got it, she almost jumped to her feet. *Superflash!* "Superflash?!" she gasped. *God, no wonder the money's so good—*

The Guide rippled heavily, limbs intertwining, a soft purr buzzing from somewhere in its long body, licking up Asher's reaction.

Superflash... A 'harmless stimulant' to them? Like coffee to us? That might well be true, but the stuff's effect on Humans was legendary. It was a whopping hallucinogen that lasted for hours, or days, depending on the dosage. It also stimulated emotional responses like mad. Any emotion: sex, rage, fear, laughter, sorrow, ecstasy, love—anything, provoked by the environment or simply at random. There were stories that some Humans had successfully used it as an incredible aphrodisiac. There were other stories of Humans who had literally died laughing, or gone on murderous rampages, or scared themselves into catatonia. Its other names were Daredevil, Big Challenge, and Russian Roulette. It wasn't addictive, but that only added to its fearsome fascination.

No wonder it was illegal as hell on all Human-settled worlds, including Raddanin. It also commanded astounding prices.

The Guide writhed and purred louder. *If he were Human he'd be coming in his pants,* one corner of Asher's mind noted.

Right there, three facts clicked together.

Asher did her best to keep on feeling that wild mix of shock, fascination and yearning greed, and yes, the Guide kept on enjoying it—enjoying it too much to look at anything else, catch the subtleties of emotion and sensation that a cooler-minded empath could use to deduce specific thought. Keep that feeling coming, keep the Guide busy—and under that cover, think hard. Think fast. Don't look at the understanding that the Kowtiki on Raddanin sure-as-hell wanted Superflash for something more than the equivalent of their morning coffee.

Think.

I could buy my freedom with that money.

Think.

If I get caught, I'm dead.

Think.

The Guide and his cronies. Muscleboy and

Tigo. The law and my freedom.

And an image of acid and alkali canceling each other out. Perfect neutralization. Perfect balance. She had her answer.

Asher suppressed a smile, and let herself calm down.

The Guide's rippling faded away. It took a deep breath—which sounded like the faint whistling of panpipes—and sat up expectantly.

"Listen," said Asher, lowering her voice. "That's a big risk, really big trouble if I'm caught, and I only have the one trick to use. No, this is too big. I can't take the job..."

The Guide's limbs drooped, ever so slightly.

"...But I know someone who can." Asher let her hope rise slightly, and watched the Guide do the same. "In fact, I know someone who could smuggle in a lot more than just one liter..."

The Guide didn't move, only watched and listened.

"But he won't deal directly with you; he's too cautious. I can broker the deal, but it won't be easy. How much can you give me for making the arrangement?"

The Guide drooped slightly, eyes flickering, then rose a little. "Percentage," it buzzed. "Five percentage of any deal, can give."

"All right," Asher grinned, feeling—without effort—enough hope to make the Guide ripple.

"I'll go set it up as soon as I leave here. Where and when do I contact you?"

"Here, all day, night," said the Guide.

"All day?" Asher couldn't help asking. "What do you do for a living?"

"I work here." The Guide's limbs arched in something very like a Human shrug. "This club, my family owns."

"Ah," said Asher, keeping very calm, thoughts covered. "Okay, I'll go start on it right now." She rolled to her feet, watching the Guide. The Kowtiki did nothing to stop her, only waved one limb languidly in a sort of salute. Asher headed for the door.

As she paused at the bottom of the ramp to pull her boots back on, she heard, then saw, another Human coming down toward the club. It was a man, fairly young, wearing the swirling facial tattoo and half-shaved head of a fashionable Toughguy, and he looked uncoordinated enough to be halfway drunk already. Asher was already leaning against the wall, so she did no more than give him the ritual half-glower that meant Leave-Me-Alone-And-I'll-Leave-You-Alone. For obvious working stiffs like herself, that usually sufficed.

But Toughguy didn't seem to notice her at all. There was something fixed and glassy about his eyes, something obsessed, and he made his lumbering way straight for the clubroom door without a glance to either side, without pausing to take off his boots. The door opened for him, as if the door-watcher recognized him for a regular, or at least welcome, customer.

Asher stood gazing after the Toughguy for a long moment after the door had shut behind him, thoughts turning and clicking. Then she shoved her boots on, fast, and hurried up the ramp to the street.

The standard Human bar around the corner was just the same as it had been before, except that Muscleboy wasn't in evidence. Asher went straight to the bar, planked down a couple of dollar-coins and gestured for a beer. When the bartender came up with the glass of standard brew, Asher leaned close and asked: "Have you seen Mr. Muscles around since I left?" The barman narrowed his eyes, but shook his head. Asher thought about that, and smiled knowingly. She leaned closer, lowered her voice, and asked: "How do I get word to Mr. Tigo from here?"

The man's widened eyes told her all she needed to know, and he saw that she knew it. He shrugged. "Wait awhile, he'll call," he mumbled, moving away.

Asher smiled grimly, settled into her bar-seat and drank her beer with no particular haste. If she didn't get a contact within two hours, she'd simply go back to the ship and pick up her wages, then come back here and meet Muscleboy at the appointed time. In less than 20 minutes the bartender came back, holding a free-phone. He held it out to her without comment, but flicked his eyes imperiously toward the corner booth.

Nice and private, Asher understood. She got up and went to the booth before setting the phone to her ear. "Mr. Tigo?" she asked, as if there was any doubt. "Roan Asher here."

The familiar oily voice said the usual phrases about payment, but there was an edge of curiosity audible in it.

"I'll have the latest installment right here in two hours," she said, "But I came across something that I think you'd like to know about."

Of course, Tigo was interested. Asher briefly outlined the situation, noting Tigo's indrawn breath at the word Superflash, then got into the serious negotiations. "He didn't set any ceiling limit, nor say this was a one-time deal. So, if I broker the deal for you, will that clear my debt?"

Tigo, of course, wasn't about to commit to anything definite without more info.

Asher wound up taking the phone back

across the street to the club.

This time, she noticed when she came in, the number of curtains had increased–rendering visibility nil. Sound-baffles were now visible in the ceiling and upper sections of the walls, and the tinkling music was louder.

Still, Asher could hear the sounds of moaning and gasping, in a distinctly Human voice. *Your choice, Toughguy,* she shrugged, waiting for the Guide to come for her. *Anybody might dare it once, but you have to be really into it to go back for more._*

The deadline found Asher sitting on a barstool, her cashed pay in her pocket and the free-phone in her hand. Muscleboy showed up exactly on time, and grinned expansively as he saw her. Without a word, Asher got up and led him to the corner booth. Without a word, he followed. He'd no sooner sat down than he reached out one meaty paw for the money.

Instead, Asher slapped the open phone into his hand. "Mr. Tigo's on the other end," she said. "Talk to him first."

Wearing that slightly pole-axed look again, Muscleboy put the phone to his ear. Asher sipped her beer and watched his expressions run the gamut–surprise-joy-caution-joy-understanding–as he got his instructions. At the end, he closed the phone with a thoughtful look and almost absently held out his hand. Asher dropped the agreed-upon $1000 into it. "Don't forget to give me the receipt," she added.

Muscleboy frowned, but shoved the money in one pocket, took a notebook out of the other, scribbled briefly on the top page, tore it off and handed it to her. Asher read the simple note with a nod of satisfaction, put it in her breast-pocket and zipped the seal after it. She finished her beer and stood up. "Let's go," she said. "It's just across the street and around the corner."

"Yeah." Muscleboy lurched to his feet and lumbered after her, his toothy grin growing wider with every step. "Looks like I'm getting a promotion."

"Looks like," Asher admitted, as they moved out into the growing twilight.

"And you're off the hook for the other 11-K."

"That's the deal."

"A real win-win situation, y'know? Everybody's happy."

"That's how I like it."

"Anything else you like?" Muscleboy actually leered.

Can't you even be professional? "Here's the

door. Quiet, now." Asher led him down the ramp. The clubroom door remained shut, but she knocked on it: three-two-three. It opened briefly on loud tinkly music, and the Guide slipped out into the hallway.

"Yesss," it said, glancing at Asher, then looking Muscleboy up and down. "Yes! Hyumann-sir, this way please to come. Hyumann-mam, here please to wait."

Asher had to wait no longer than ten minutes before the Guide reappeared. It handed her a small pouch, which clinked. "$1000 fee here," it said, purring already. "Also map. At Raddanin, to marked place you come, wear green. Other half of fee get."

"Fair enough," Asher grinned. "Free, and with a little profit too."

The Guide shrugged again.

At Raddanin port, it was the same old story. Asher and the CM had the whole cargo out on the dock and sorted, and were cooling their heels over a couple of sodas, before the customs-inspection team showed up. It was another Suit and Uniform pair, The Suit yapping the usual threats and waving his comm-pad around while The Uniform silently and efficiently poked his probe at the crates and the big barrels. This time The Uniform unceremoniously grabbed the neck of Asher's power-suit and stuck his probe down her back under it. Asher yelled, in unfeigned outrage: "Decompress, you sucker! That thing's cold!" The Uniform said nothing, but only repeated the intrusion on the CM, who likewise grumbled. Again, it was The Uniform who poked the keys on the pad and handed the resulting sheet to the CM while the Suit yapped. The Uniform plodded silently away, The Suit trotted after him still yapping, the CM ignored them both and started hauling the cargo off to the assigned lockers.

Asher dutifully hauled her share, her back still itching where the probe had scraped it. *No, nothing down there, thank you.* The trick might work once, on Kowtik, but it wouldn't have worked here.

She wondered briefly how Muscleboy had gotten past inspection, if indeed he had. Probably he had; Tigo's operation had money and knowledge enough to pull that off.

She also wondered just how much—or how little—Superflash the Kowtiki had really wanted him to bring in. Not much, she guessed: just enough to make the story look convincing.

When the last crate and barrel were stowed, Asher hung up her suit in the locker, went back to her cabin, took a leisurely sonic-wash and changed into clean clothes—taking care to put on a vivid green shirt. She'd memorized the map on the trip out here, but took it with her anyway. The guard at the service-gate barely looked up as she slid her ID card through the slot.

The walk this time was a little longer, but Asher didn't mind. It was interesting to see how the six different resident races divided up the territory near the port. The Human zone took the right side of the street for a good three blocks, and the Lenisherrath paced it on the left. At the big intersection the Rrrem took over on the left and the Kowtiki began on the right. Asher checked her map, strolled up the right-hand side of the street, stopped at the next intersection, leaned on a utility-block and waited.

Soon enough, a green-draped Kowtiki ambled up, paused, looked her up and down, and tentatively buzzed: "Hyumann-mam Roan Asher?"

"That's me," Asher confirmed.

The Kowtiki nodded low, like a wind-bent fern. "Please, this way to come."

Asher got up and followed it.

Again, an unobtrusive door led to a ribbed downward ramp with a door at the bottom. Asher dutifully took off her boots and followed her new guide through the door. The decor and music inside were much the same as in the port-side club back on Kowtik, except that there were more and heavier curtains, dimmer lights, and more sound-baffles. The local guide led her through the hangings, around the cushions, away from the walls and toward the center of what had to be a really enormous room. Under the tinkling of the music, another sound grew steadily louder as they progressed. Asher recognized it for incoherent cries in a Human voice, and chewed her lip. Judging from the number of writhing, buzzing, oblivious Kowtiki bodies they passed, she guessed that business was jumping today. She had a fairly good idea what the central attraction was, and only wondered why her guide was taking her to see it. The last cur-tains parted, revealing a roughly circular area of low cushion-mounds, most of them filled–as was the floor between–by nearly convulsing Kowtiki. Her guide paused, trembling a little with the effort to retain control. It pulled a clinking pouch from its belt, handed it to Asher, then waved its limbs with a flourish at the big mound in the center of the room.

On the dais-like mound rested a large and sturdy containment-globe. The globe itself was transparent, but on the inside–probably from pinhead-projectors–were displayed constantly moving images of what appeared to be really gross porno, interspersed with splatter-scenes.

In the center of the globe, naked except for implements snugly attached to significant spots on his body, thrashing and howling mindlessly, was Muscleboy. His eyes were rolling aimlessly, mouth loose and wailing, arms flailing like a drunken windmill. It was hard to see under the attached gear, but Asher was fairly sure he sported a straining erection. His face bore the mottled, bloodshot look characteristic of Superflash.

"This-one strong and healthy maintains," the guide explained. "Very long time he will last."

"Is that why your... relative preferred him?" Asher guessed.

"Also emotings strong, uncontrolled, used to unfettered indulgence. Easily stimulated."

"Not like me," Asher grinned.

"Clever-clever Hyumann-mam," buzzed the guide, dipping its limbs in appreciation. "Clever, our purpose to guess."

"I knew it wasn't just about the drugs. Does Tigo realize that what you really paid him for was... his goon's 'service contract'?"

"Not said, but surely he guesses. Price we paid much too high for small amount of drugs smuggled. Also, for assignment of his Hyumann-sir specifically we did ask."

Asher looked at the blindly writhing Muscleboy, and almost felt a moment's pity for him. Almost. "Did he object to taking the

Superflash himself?"

"Not. But confess, we did somewhat manipulate. 'Test of guts' called it. Also test of product. He then did not refuse."

Asher chuckled, remembering. "So everybody's happy... except maybe the law-boys."

"They know not. No reason have they. None of drug to common sale goes; we ourselves for our... performers keep." The Kowtiki bowed its limbs toward her. "Happy you also. This one to-you did intimidate, threaten, oppress. Your vengeance now enjoy."

Asher laughed as she sank down on the remaining untenanted cushion-mound. Yes, this was revenge, and it was sweet. *So much for breaking my arms, Muscleboy!* She noticed several of the club patrons beginning to ripple and roll in her direction, and realized what else the guide/manager had paid her for.

Asher laughed again, and didn't mind a bit.

WIHQSH
(THE END)

Other Work by

Leslie Fish

FOR LOVE OF GLORY

OBLIVIOUS

OF ELVEN BLOOD

REVOCARE

A DIRGE FOR SABIS
(WITH C. J. CHERRYH),
COLLECTED IN THE SWORD OF
KNOWLEDGE TRILOGY